BRIGHT SKY PRESS

2365 Rice Blvd., Suite 202 Houston, Texas 77005
Box 416, Albany, Texas 76430

Text copyright ©2008 Andrea White
"The Lessons of Classroom 506," *The New York Times.* September 12, 2004 ©Lisa Belkin

10   9   8   7   6   5   4   3   2   1

Library of Congress Cataloging-in Publication Data

White, Andrea, 1953-
Window boy / by Andrea White.
p. cm.
Summary: After his mother finally convinces the principal of Greenfield Junior High to admit him, twelve-year-old Sam arrives for his first day of school, along with his imaginary friend Winston Churchill, who encourages him to persevere with his cerebral palsy.
ISBN 978-1-9339779-14-4 (jacketed hardcover: alk. paper)
1. Churchill, Winston, Sir, 1874-1965–Juvenile fiction. [1. Churchill, Winston, Sir, 1874-1965–Fiction.
2. Cerebral palsy–Fiction. 3. People with disabilities–Fiction. 4. Imaginary playmates–Fiction.
5. First day of school–Fiction.] I. Title.

PZ7.W58177Wi 2008
[Fic] – dc22

2008000492

Book and cover design by Cregan Design,
Ellen Peeples Cregan and Marla Garcia
Edited by Lucy Herring Chambers and Nora Krisch Shire

Printed in China through Asia Pacific Offset

Window Boy

Andrea White

b

BRIGHT SKY PRESS

HOUSTON, TEXAS ~ ALBANY, TEXAS

To my friend, Maconda, on the occasion of her birthday,

With special appreciation to
Franci Crane, Elena Marks, Sis Johnson and Michael Zilkha,

And with gratitude to Lisa Belkin for her inspirational article.

"We're all worms, but I do believe I am a glowworm."

-Winston Churchill

Chapter 1

As always, Sam Davis, age 12, is staring out his window. It's a double-sided picture window, shaped like a basketball court: rectangular, with a line down the middle. The blue drapes are pushed to one side, leaving him a clear view of Stirling Junior High.

If it weren't for the rutted field between them, Stirling Junior High would be in Sam's backyard. The school, a flat building, stands adjacent to a concrete playground with a metal roof and an outdoor basketball court. In his eagerness to get as close as he can to the court—and to basketball, the best game in the whole world—Sam is resting his forehead against the glass.

When he sneezes, Sam's head rears back. His wheelchair slips forward, and he bangs his head against the glass.

"Sam, don't lean on the window."

His caretaker's footsteps sound behind him, and Miss Perkins takes his hand. She claims that she's an "older young woman," and when Sam looks at her, he thinks: it's true. Her gray hair and white nurse's shoes are old, while her clear eyes, strong body and unlined skin are young.

Sam and Miss Perkins are alone again tonight. Sam's mother is eating at her favorite Italian restaurant: Fred's. Although Sam would like to go, he's never been to Fred's. Too many stairs. He has to content himself with the long skinny breadsticks that his mother brings home.

"Are you ready for bed, Sam?" Miss Perkins asks.

Sam could speak if he weren't feeling lazy. Instead, he looks down with his eyes. This means no.

"O.K.," Miss Perkins says. "Do you want me to read to you?"

Sam looks up: yes.

"I got a new book from the library about Dwight D. Eisenhower. Do you want to try it or keep reading about Winnie?" Miss Perkins asks.

"WWWWiinnnie," Sam says. Winnie is their nickname for Winston Leonard Spencer Churchill.

Miss Perkins' tread is light as she walks away. When she returns, Sam knows she will be carrying a medium-sized, blue book: *My Early Life* by Winston Churchill.

When Miss Perkins first started reading about Winston Churchill, Sam felt resentful. Sam thought he was just an old man with baby-pink skin who liked cigars. The Prime Minister of England, the man who fought Hitler during World War II—what did Winston Churchill have to do with him? But as his caretaker read about the boy Winston Churchill, Sam began to listen.

Young Winston Churchill was inventive; he built elaborate forts. He was brave; once Winston jumped off a bridge and fell thirty feet. He was also mischievous. At school, angry at being scolded, Winston kicked, stomped and tore his headmaster's straw hat into pieces. Sam doesn't know what a bad fall feels like, but he understands how it feels to be angry. And he used to have temper tantrums all the time. There is just so much other people don't understand.

One night, as Miss Perkins' soft English voice was rolling over him, putting him to bed, her words took on a quality almost as if Winston himself were calling him through time—speaking directly to Sam.

When Miss Perkins put down the book, Sam thought about the fact that Winston Churchill, a great orator, had stuttered as a boy. Since Sam didn't talk well either, he was curious. In his mind, he asked: *How?*

To Sam's surprise, Winston Churchill answered, *I practiced, old chap.*

That's when Sam learned something very important. Although the voice was in his own head, he didn't know what the voice was going to say next. The voice was like a friend.

As Sam waits for Miss Perkins to return with the book, he keeps his eyes fixed on the basketball court, hoping. Just past the circle of light thrown out by the crooked lamp post, there in the shadows, he spots movement. Often, a boy named Mickey— Mickey Kotov— comes out on the court at night, always alone.

Suddenly, Mickey dribbles the ball into the light. Mickey is small. Maybe as small as Sam, although Sam looks smaller, crumpled in his wheelchair. Watching Mickey run around the court so fast, Sam wishes again that when his brain got damaged as he was being born, his legs hadn't become useless sticks. It's O.K. that talking is difficult for him. But basketball players need to run.

Sam has a secret. He dreams of playing basketball exactly like Mickey. But he wouldn't want Mickey's life. Sitting at the open window this past summer, he's learned more about Mickey than his name. Mickey has a father who screams at him.

"Mickey, stop hiding. Come hooome."

"Mickey Kotov, yoour'e the vorst boy that God ever made."

"Mickey, I need your help with the plumving."

Mickey jumps, and a ball arcs against the dark sky. The window is shut tonight, but it doesn't matter. In his mind, Sam hears the whoosh of the basket. He wants to yell for Mickey. To cheer, "Yeah.

Good basket." But Miss Perkins settles into the chair next to him and interrupts his daydream.

"Anywhere?" Miss Perkins asks.

"Surre," Sam says.

When Miss Perkins opens the book and begins with the story of Winnie failing another exam at school, her voice is confident and strong, but Sam is too excited to listen.

Tomorrow, Sam thinks. Tomorrow is my first day of school. Why I might even meet Mickey!

*　　　　*　　　　*

On the bus heading home to her apartment, Miss Perkins sits down next to a man wearing an army shirt and camouflage pants. A patch covers one of his eyes, making the other appear especially dark and fierce. The *Stirling Sun* newspaper rests on his lap, with the date facing her: October 3, 1968.

Miss Perkins was born in 1918. It's hard for her to believe it's already 1968. "I'm only 50, but I've seen so much in my life," she muses out loud.

The soldier says, "I know what you mean."

"I was born in England. But I came to America after the Second War. Lived here for almost twenty years. I work for a woman who has a crippled child," Miss Perkins tells the soldier.

The soldier nods.

"Sam's got cerebral palsy," Miss Perkins continues. "He's stuck in the wheelchair all day long. But he's a beautiful boy." She sighs, thinking of Sam tonight, lying in bed, his dark hair against the white pillow and a crooked grin on his face

"I'm sure," the soldier says.

"His mum loves him. I know she does. Her husband left her

when she refused to give up the boy. She won a lot of money from the lawsuit. Enough to pay me all these years, yet she seems to have run through most of it. My grocery budget is half of what it used to be."

"Lots of people got their troubles, but they don't talk about them," the man says.

"I've taught Sam to say about two hundred and fifty words. He's learned to write, too… Well, really I write, Sam just points at letters. But he can read. That's why I insisted that he has to go to school. His mum argued with me. She said, 'Miss Perkins, I'm afraid that a tough kid, one of those neighborhood boys, will hurt Sam.'"

In the midst of her musings, Miss Perkins' gaze falls on the black patch covering the man's eye. She wonders if he's in pain. "So how were you injured?"

"Vietnam," the soldier answers gruffly.

"I was a Londoner during World War II," Miss Perkins tells him. "I saw a lot that I don't want to remember. We used to sit in the kitchen next to our old wooden wireless. In those days, we never knew when a bomb was going to fall. Our wireless made Churchill's voice sound sort of scratchy, but he got his message across. He never gave up, and neither did we."

"Please," the soldier interrupts. "I would like…"

But Miss Perkins is wound up. "I'm no coward." She straightens her shoulders. "We British know how to fight. I don't understand these kids who are protesting the Vietnam War."

"Ma'am, excuse me." The soldier signals towards the aisle. "Long day." He mumbles something about a headache.

Miss Perkins angles her knees to allow the soldier room to hurry out. He dares to plop down in an empty seat in front of her.

She stares at the back of the soldier's head. Despite all this talk in the '60s about peace and love, people used to be friendlier, Miss

Perkins thinks.

The bus stops at Chestnut Street and 14th, and the door opens. Several long-haired hippies wearing ragged T-shirts jump on. The last person to enter is a woman holding a baby.

Miss Perkins moves to the window to leave an aisle seat open. As she had hoped, the woman sits down next to her. Her tiny mouth completes the triangle of her high cheekbones. She holds an infant who is wearing an adorable smocked pink dress.

"How do you do?" Miss Perkins asks hopefully.

Chapter Two

The next morning, Sam finds himself facing the narrow field. He barely notices the tin cans rusting in the sun, or the newspaper pages lying half-embedded in the dirt. On the other side lies his dream: Stirling Junior High.

Miss Perkins stands behind him, gripping his wheelchair. Even though his chair is good and steady, Miss Perkins and Sam have never crossed a field like this before. Sometimes, even sidewalks are hard for them—like the patch of rotten concrete in front of the barber's shop. Although the field's grassy edges and dirt center look treacherous, this is their only route. By road, Stirling has to be almost a mile away.

"We can do this," Miss Perkins mutters to herself.

Sam keeps his eyes fixed on the school's green, wooden double doors. Most public buildings have stairs that bar his entrance. But the doors of this one-storied school appear to welcome him.

"Let's go," Miss Perkins mutters as she starts across the grass.

Sam begins bouncing up and down. His insides feel like he's swallowed one of those Mexican jumping beans that a man on the corner of Third Avenue and Elm Street sells along with spicy peanuts.

Sam tries to distract himself from the creeping nausea. He thinks of Winnie. *Stiff upper lip, old chap.* Sam hears Winnie's cheerful voice in his mind. *You don't want to get sick on your first day of school.*

Winnie's words remind Sam of the purpose of this choppy ride. Sam is going to have a teacher, Mrs. Martin. And be with other kids. Not just kids on television, real kids who play basketball, chew gum and eat ice cream cones. He is going to have schoolbooks.

At this moment, Miss Perkins hits a big bump. Sam's wheelchair rears, and his teeth chomp down on his tongue. He won't say "Ouch," because Miss Perkins might stop. He doesn't want to be late for his first day of school. Tears spring to his eyes, and his mouth tastes faintly metallic, and sweet at the same time. He puzzles over the taste, and then he realizes that it's blood. He's never swallowed his own blood before and finds the act alarming.

You can't spend all your life wishing for the experiences that other kids have and then complaining when you have them, Winnie says. Sam imagines his friend's voice often as a lecture.

My tongue doesn't work that well as it is, Sam tells Winnie.

Well, you didn't bite it off, did you? Winnie retorts.

Before Sam can answer, the wheelchair jolts again, and Sam looks up. To his surprise, he notices that while he's been arguing with Winnie, they've made progress.

We've almost reached the dirt, Winnie points out. His tone is one of proud accomplishment, as if he himself is responsible.

Sam reminds himself that although Winnie can be a pest, he can also be a good friend.

When the wheelchair clears the grass, something wonderful happens. The journey becomes easier. Not as smooth as carpet, but the baked dirt is less bumpy than Sam's least favorite surface: rotten concrete.

"I told you we could do it," Miss Perkins says, after she catches her breath, and Sam knows that she has been worried, too. "Now, if only school will go as well. I wonder if you're on the sixth grade level."

Sam can't wait to find out either. Miss Perkins has been teaching him since he was three, and Sam's afraid that he is hopelessly behind.

"Your mother promised Principal Cullen that I would stay with you," Miss Perkins continues.

Public schools aren't required to accept kids in wheelchairs. Sam's mother had to meet with the principal many times before he agreed that Sam could attend. This is why school has already begun.

"I couldn't bear to be apart from you anyway. So Abigail Perkins is going back to school, too!"

Miss Perkins has told Sam all this and more several times already. He knows that talking is just her way of comforting herself. He guesses that, like him, she has an uneasy stomach and sweaty palms.

"Maybe, you shouldn't talk that much at first. Give the kids a chance to get used to you." Miss Perkins laughs. "Come to think of it, I should button my lips, too."

Sam smiles at the idea of a quiet Miss Perkins.

Sam doesn't wear a watch, but the swarm of kids on the school grounds lets him know that the opening bell has not yet rung. His cousins from California have warned him about the bells, and he is prepared for a sharp sound to pierce the air at exactly 8:00 a.m.

The school is built on top of a small rise, and Miss Perkins groans from the effort of pushing him uphill. Sam feels for his caretaker and wants to help her, but he can't concentrate on Miss Perkins' predicament. Soon, they will reach the concrete sidewalk that winds past the basketball court. He longs to see the bent basketball rim and the crooked light post up close.

Yet when Miss Perkins reaches the top, he barely notices the geography of the playground. As if a television and radio were blaring at the same time, Sam is met by a jumble of laughter, conversation, footsteps, shouts and cries. This noisy confusion is the vibrant life that he has always imagined happening outside his apartment. Almost as exciting as the State Fair that he and his mother visited once with its cotton candy and clowns.

Kids in all sizes and shapes and with different hair colors race around him. They smell of sweat, hair oil, tennis shoes and gum. Except for the rare occasions when his San Diego cousins visit, Sam is seldom in the presence of other kids. Now he is surrounded by them and enthralled by their perfect strides.

Like Sam, a few of the boys sport white T-shirts under their button-down cotton shirts. Yet, while many of the boys are dressed in blue jeans and tennis shoes, Sam is wearing khakis and loafers. Most boys' hair touches their collars.

I've got to let my hair grow, Sam thinks. What for? He asks himself. To fit in, I'll need more than long hair.

A girl passes so close to Sam's wheelchair that he could reach out and touch her. Sam is afraid that this girl is taller than he'll ever be, even when he grows up. Her long blonde hair is pulled back with a red bandanna. He winces when he notices the silver braces railroading her teeth. Miss Perkins says that he's lucky that he has perfect teeth because braces hurt.

As the girl rushes confidently past him, he remembers another one of Miss Perkins' favorite sayings: "You were meant to be exactly like you are."

Sam tries to make himself believe.

"Stirling has never admitted a handicapped student before," Miss Perkins is saying. "Sam, you are the very first. We're both going to have to be patient."

The double green doors. Sam is almost within spitting distance of Stirling Junior High, and he is no longer listening to Miss Perkins. In his imagination, he feels like the doors are magic. Once he passes through them he will become a different boy, with a more active life.

But you won't find a better friend than you already have, Winnie says.

Hush, Sam thinks, scolding him. *I don't want to listen to your bragging.*

A student with reddish-brown hair opens one of the doors for Miss Perkins. Sam recognizes him from the playground as a fanatical basketball player. Sam envies the boy's freckles—his mother tells him that freckles are caused by too much sun— and the boy's long arms and big hands, so useful in basketball.

Miss Perkins smiles at him. "Why, thank you, young man."

Instead of answering, the boy continues to stare at Miss Perkins.

Sam takes in Miss Perkins' frizzy gray hair and white nurse's shoes. For the first time, it occurs to Sam that having Miss Perkins as a companion is going to make it harder for him to make friends, and he is embarrassed by her.

Then, he remembers a scene from *My Early Life.* Once Winnie's housekeeper had gone to visit him at boarding school. Winnie kissed her on the cheek in front of all the boys. One of Winnie's classmates called it the "bravest act" he had ever seen.

As Sam and Miss Perkins pass into the halls of Stirling Junior High, Sam promises himself, I won't let the boys' opinion of Miss Perkins bother me. I'll be brave like Winnie.

Chapter Three

Room 114. Sam reads the big numbers above the wooden door.

A woman wearing a nubby blue skirt that falls above her knees and a tailored white shirt is standing near the entrance. She is petite like his mother but the resemblance stops with size. Although the woman's brown hair is shiny, her dark eyes don't sparkle. Sam decides that the woman's face looks strict.

"May I help you?" she greets them.

This must be his new teacher, Mrs. Martin. He's sorry to hear that her voice matches her eyes.

"This is Sam Davis, and I'm Abigail Perkins," Miss Perkins answers cheerfully.

The woman's thin eyebrows rise above her horn-rimmed glasses. She grasps Miss Perkins' arm and leads her a few steps away.

"He's my new student?" Mrs. Martin's voice is not so soft that Sam can't hear.

Sam reminds himself that Winnie often created a bad first impression. How often had Miss Perkins read that, *"The first time you meet Winston, you see all his faults, and the rest of your life you spend in discovering his virtues"*

"Yes, ma'am," Miss Perkins says.

Sam tries to hold his neck straight.

"I was told that the boy had cerebral palsy, but he looks like he needs special instruction. I have thirty kids in this class," Mrs.

Martin protests.

As he has in the past, Sam wonders if his keen ears are really a blessing.

"I understand. I'll stay with Sam," Miss Perkins answers his teacher firmly.

"This is a 6th grade class. Are you sure he's on grade level?" Mrs. Martin asks.

"Well, you see," Miss Perkins confides, "he can't be tested properly."

His mother has told Sam that Mrs. Ellsworth, the school's vice-principal who performs student testing, is on maternity leave.

"So until Mrs. Ellsworth returns," Miss Perkins continues, "Principal Cullen agreed that Sam could be with boys and girls his own age. And since speech is difficult for Sam, we're not sure what level he's on."

Mrs. Martin gives a little sigh and approaches Sam. Her crestfallen expression reminds him of his mother's when she has to wash the dishes.

"Hello." Mrs. Martin bends down and introduces herself to Sam.

Sam does his best to smile at her. Her glasses and her stern expression had fooled him. Up close, he realizes that his new teacher is young. He doesn't know any college students, but he guesses that she looks like one.

Inside the classroom, a boy shouts, "Give me my pencil. You stole my pencil."

Mrs. Martin rushes away, yelling, "That's enough. Enough!"

Miss Perkins grips the handles of his wheelchair and pushes him forward. It's only then that Sam notices that the classroom door is narrow. Suddenly, he's afraid that his wheelchair isn't going to fit. To his relief, he barely edges through.

He's terrified when he feels all the kids' eyes on him. About thirty kids are sitting behind wooden desks all in rows. He scans their faces. Some eyes are filled with curiosity, many with pity, a few with fear. He searches the whole room without finding any that hold just basic friendliness.

To work up his courage, Sam takes a deep breath, but before he can say hello, Mrs. Martin nods at Sam. "Class, this is Sam Davis. Since Sam is unable to talk, Miss Perkins, his nurse, will be attending with him."

I can talk, Sam wants to protest, but he doesn't dare shock the kids with his voice. Not yet. He remembers Miss Perkins' advice. Best to let the other students get to know him gradually.

"Why don't you push him over there?" Mrs. Martin points at a table labeled "Science table," crowded with a small forest of potted plants, two avocado seeds in water, a jar of magnets, a scale and a few stray erasers.

Miss Perkins must have decided not to argue with Mrs. Martin either. She obediently wheels him over to the table and settles herself in a small chair next to him. As she pats his leg, she whispers, "That's my boy, Sam. Stay calm. Let's count potatoes."

Sam feels insulted. Miss Perkins is acting as if he might stage a tantrum inside the classroom.

"One potato, two potato..." Softly, Miss Perkins encourages him, and out of habit, Sam begins counting in his head. During World War II, Miss Perkins' family had recited this rhyme in their basement while they waited for the bombs to stop falling. When Sam gets upset, his body becomes as rigid and lifeless as a board. As he follows along now, his body grows softer until he is aware that he is breathing again.

Finally, after the sixth potato, Sam has calmed down enough to admit to himself that, maybe, Miss Perkins' concern wasn't entirely foolish. His teacher's remark did make him angry, and perhaps, when he was younger, he might have howled.

Sam is noticing the posters on the wall—a map of the world with the State of Massachusetts marked in red, a reading chart alongside pictures of Zeus, Hera and the other Greek gods, and a picture of the solar system with red, blue and green planets—when the bell rings. It's louder than Sam expected, but by holding onto the armrest, he manages not to jump in surprise.

And the next thing he knows, Mickey Kotov slips through the door. In the harsh light of the classroom, Sam is able to see Mickey clearly for the first time. He's a dark-headed boy with perfect features, an uneven part to his hair and specks of mud on his black slip-on tennis shoes. By his rounded shoulders and downcast eyes, Sam knows that the boy feels like he's done something wrong. But he's only a minute or so late.

Although his version of whistling is wet, Sam longs to whistle. The only boy whose name Sam knows in the whole school is in his class!

Mickey ignores Sam's smile, but when Sam's gaze shifts, he sees that the girl next to Mickey is watching Sam. Her white-blonde hair frames a sharp nose and close-set blue eyes. She's wearing a red and white plaid dress with a black sash.

"Mickey, this is the third time this week that you've been late," Mrs. Martin says. "After the pledge, go straight to the principal's office."

Mickey's blank expression doesn't change.

"This is Principal Cullen," a loud voice announces over the intercom. "Good morning, students. It's another great day at Stirling Junior High. Please stand for the pledge."

Papers rustle. Knees knock against desks. Feet shuffle as the kids stand and put their hands over their hearts.

Sam glances at Miss Perkins. His seat belt is easy for Miss Perkins to unbuckle, but she doesn't like for him to stand or walk more than necessary. She and his mother are both scared of injuries. Since she makes no move to remove his belt, Sam can't stand. Instead, he squeezes his arm muscles until his hand grazes his shirt. Once he's in proper position, he turns his attention to the class. Instead of looking at the flag, he finds that all of the students are staring at Mickey.

Mickey is the only kid who is not reciting the pledge. His lips are stubbornly pressed together. His long arms dangle at his sides. His eyes are downcast.

"He speaks Russian," one boy says softly.

"He's a spy," another says.

A few of the kids snicker. "We're fighting the Russians in Vietnam."

"I'm fighting Mickey," another says.

Mickey must be from the Soviet Union, Sam decides. That would explain his father's heavy accent. But Sam is surprised, because Mickey plays basketball better than most Americans.

Chapter Four

For the next thirty minutes, Mrs. Martin reviews old tests and collects homework. When the business of the class is concluded, she says, "Get out your math notebooks." Pencils drop on the floor. Books thud.

Miss Perkins removes her notebook from her large, black purse. Sam's wheelchair has a foldaway tray, and she pulls it out. She tears a piece of paper from the notebook, writes Sam Davis on it in her big rolling hand and lays it on the tray.

"Could I borrow your eraser?" someone hisses.

"You were supposed to bring your own," a girl's voice answers.

Mrs. Martin begins writing a list of problems on the board:

$1{,}258 \div 93 \quad 20{,}957 \div 11 \quad 19{,}899 \div 15 \dots$

"You have fifteen minutes to work these problems to the nearest decimal," Mrs. Martin says briskly. "Turn them in when you're through."

$1{,}258/93$. Sam easily computes a partial answer in his head: 13. But he's surprised that the numbers left over are too small to be divided by 93. He has no idea what to do with these extras. Out of the corner of his eye, he sees Miss Perkins tapping her pencil on the page.

Miss Perkins has taught him addition, subtraction, multiplication and division. Usually, she writes the problem on a piece of paper, and he shows her the answers by touching the numbers on a special pad. But he has never attempted a problem that has leftovers before. Miss Perkins is always saying that she has taught him all she knows. For the first time, Sam realizes maybe this is true.

"Sam," Miss Perkins whispers. "Let's see if we can figure out the math at home."

Speaking their private language, Sam looks up at the ceiling. He wishes that he were a whiz at math. And he begins fantasizing that Mrs. Martin has asked the question: Who knows what to do with these leftover numbers? He would say, "I do." Yet, since he doesn't know the answers to the real questions, not a single one of them, he begins to feel dumb.

I never liked math, Winnie says. *The figures were tied into all sorts of tangles and did things to one another which were extremely difficult.*[2†]

Hearing Winnie's voice makes Sam long for his safe spot by the apartment window. Even though Sam's spent thousands of hours at his window dreaming about school, all of a sudden, he's homesick.

After all, his wheelchair separates him from the other kids. Not only do the rest of the kids have desks, they're all grouped together in the middle of the room. He's parked next to the potted plants. He can't complete the first assignment of the day. No one looks at him, not even the teacher. Miss Perkins is occupied copying down the problems. He feels like he's not attending school so much as watching it—from a closer place to be sure, but still like television.

At least, I don't see a birch here, Winnie adds.

Sam knows that the teachers at Winnie's school used to punish students with a stick.

I was thrashed often, Winnie remembers.

Be quiet, Winnie, thinks Sam. *You're making me nervous. Besides, I can talk to you anytime. While the kids are busy, I want to study them.*

At first, the class had seemed to be one multicolored animal with many heads, arms, and legs, but now that Sam's been here awhile, each kid is starting to look different.

His gaze drifts over again to the second row, third desk, and to the blonde girl sitting there. Although the girl doesn't smile, she doesn't look away. Her blue eyes are filled with…not friendliness, but interest. Could this girl be a possible friend?

Next to him, Miss Perkins sighs over the math problems.

Sam feels sure that he and Miss Perkins will be better at English. Although it's hard for Sam's eyes to focus on small lettering, he can see large print. To teach him to read and write, Miss Perkins created a big alphabet on poster board. Then, she set out an easy book on his tray and held a magnifying glass over the pages. After six months, they had worked up to *My Early Life*. Whenever he had finished a page, he nodded. At the same time that he was learning how to read, Miss Perkins taught him how to write. To select his first letter from the alphabet, he used his right pointer finger: *P*. Then Miss Perkins wrote the letter down on a piece of paper. His first word was *Perkins*. Next, with his caretaker's help, he dictated short sentences, like, *I am Sam*. Then paragraphs. For the last several years, he finished whole essays, mostly about Winnie.

Mrs. Martin's voice interrupts Sam's thoughts. "Time to turn in your papers, please."

A few kids sigh. Several file past Sam and Miss Perkins. One by one, each member of the class drops his paper in a box on the teacher's desk.

Miss Perkins fidgets next to him.

"Is that everybody?" Mrs. Martin looks at Sam.

Sam's chair is suddenly so uncomfortable that he can barely stand it.

Miss Perkins smiles. "Sam and I are going to work on our problems tonight."

A couple of kids snicker.

"I would have liked to see a sample of Sam's work," Mrs. Martin says.

It's the first day of class, and Sam has already disappointed his teacher. He almost doesn't hear the next part of Mrs. Martin's comment.

"But, of course, tomorrow will be fine," Mrs. Martin adds before turning away. She instructs the class, "Now take out your vocabulary notebook and write down the words on the blackboard."

Sam looks at the blackboard. Miss Perkins starts whispering the vocabulary words to him, but Mrs. Martin's handwriting is so big that even he can read the list:

Definition

Forbidden

Extraordinary

Despair

Perverse

Sam can't concentrate. He's too upset.

You are such a good boy, Sam, Winnie says, *that you don't even know what it means to be bad. A teacher of mine once said that she thought that I was the naughtiest small boy in the world.*[3]

Sam doesn't answer. One of the many things that Sam finds annoying about Winnie is that Winnie talks about Sam and himself in the same breath. Winnie's a world leader. He's just a boy in a wheelchair.

But don't you see, Sam? I was just a boy once, too. A boy nobody believed in.

Remind me, Sam pleads.

Remember that list that you wrote for Miss Perkins about all the things that I did wrong in school? Winnie asks.

I remember. Winnie's headmaster wrote to his mother that he was "very bad" and a "constant trouble to everybody." He was flogged often. Once Winnie had even tried to blow up a school building.

I promise, Winnie boasts. *None of my teachers or fellow students would ever believe that someday I'd be the greatest man in the world.*

Mickey appears in the doorway, with his shirt untucked. Although he sits down at his desk, the boy doesn't bother to take out his notebook or pencil. Instead, he squirms around on the hard seat as if struggling to get comfortable.

Mickey notices Sam's gaze, and his small features scrunch up into a frown.

Sam feels confused and wants to explain: *It's me, the boy who is always watching you from the window. You're a great basketball player. Come talk to me.* But since he can't say any of these things, to be friendly, he winks at Mickey.

Unexpectedly, Mickey's dark eyes flash with anger.

"All right, class," Mrs. Martin says. "Put up your vocabulary notebooks. You may go to recess."

Recess. What is Sam going to do during recess? Who will talk to him? He nervously shifts in his chair.

Mrs. Martin turns and begins cleaning the blackboard.

Each kid who races out of the classroom takes a bit of the excitement with him. Finally, only Mickey remains seated. Sam is startled to find that the boy is still looking at him. He licks his lips nervously. Could Mickey be a tough kid? One of those hoods in a leather jacket that his mother always worries about. He knows that if a bad kid wanted to, he could toss Sam out of his wheelchair and jump on his stomach. And what would Sam be able to do to stop him? Nothing.

"I'm going to the restroom, Sam," Miss Perkins says. "You don't need to go, do you?"

"Nooo," Sam says. The restroom arrangements that have been made for Sam are complicated. He's not looking forward to his first trip.

"I'll be right back," she calls over her shoulder as she leaves the room.

Mickey stands up, and Sam is shocked when, instead of heading out the door, Mickey veers toward him.

Mickey squats down next to Sam. He's so close that Sam can smell the bacon on his breath. He can see a faded purple bruise on the side of his head. Scarier still, he can see the hate in Mickey's eyes.

"Stop steering at me. Ve're not friends," Mickey whispers urgently.

Before Sam has a chance to answer, Mickey runs off.

One day, when Sam was five years old, he and his mother were watching the Boston Celtics play the Philadelphia 76ers on television. Since Stirling is only two hundred miles from Boston, like most people in town, Sam and his mother are diehard Celtics fans. At the time, Sam was trying to puzzle out how people, just ordinary people, could walk, run, dance. How did the right leg know to come down when the left leg lifted? It seemed remarkable to Sam that the teenagers he watched on Dick Clark's *Bandstand*, a dance show, could move their two arms, two legs and ten fingers at the same time. But the Celtics were in a different league, almost superhuman.

Not only did the individual players know how to walk, run and shoot—acts that required control over at least 14 separate digits—they seemed to move as a single organism. With the Philadelphia 76ers committed to stopping them, the entire Celtics team—five pairs of legs, arms, feet, fingers, toes, hands—were united together in a single goal, the basket.

Sam will never forget seeing Bill Russell jump off the ground holding the basketball in one hand. Wilt Chamberlain, even taller than Russell, bounced up as though he had springs in his shoes and tried to block him. But Bill Russell looped the ball over Chamberlain's head.

Beating long odds, Bill Russell's basket dropped in.

That's when Sam became a basketball fan.

Now that Sam is older, he is no longer in awe of basic skills like running, shooting and jumping, but he is still amazed by the greatest players. How can Bill Russell pivot after a rebound and, in one motion, make a perfect overhead pass to start the fast break? How could that great point guard, Bob Cousey, accurately make a pass behind his back without looking at the target, running in a parallel lane?

After Mickey has left, Sam sits in the empty classroom, looking at the thirty desks lined up in uneven rows. He has always wanted to find someone—besides his mother—to talk to about basketball. It won't be Mickey, he thinks regretfully.

Chapter Five

Although Miss Perkins is walking down the hallway of Stirling Junior High, her thoughts are far away. The bell for recess—its jarring cry— had reminded her of one particular afternoon. It was the fall of 1940. The Battle of Britain was raging. She had been passing a primary school—breathing in the familiar smell of coal dust and cabbage—when the alert had sounded. Air raid sirens were spaced every fifteen blocks or more. The one she heard was to the south but was shortly followed by another one, even closer. Not all of London's children had evacuated, and peering through the windows of the school, she could see students streaming down the stairs into the basement. Their innocent, excited faces. Their navy blue and white uniforms. She can remember marveling: this could be a normal scene. Students rushing to recess. To play football. To swing. Only it's not. The students are hurrying to a shelter. By hiding, these kids hope to get what everyone wants: a chance to live a good life.

How many of those kids had died during the war, she wonders?

Miss Perkins reaches into her large bag and takes out a tissue. She blows her nose. The sight of Room 114 shakes her out of her mood. A girl with blonde hair is peeking inside the classroom. Miss Perkins reminds herself. I'm in America. The war is over, and I have a job to do. A boy whom I love.

The blonde's dress is a little too fancy for school, something an old-fashioned mother would pick out. Miss Perkins can't say why,

32

but she thinks the girl seems lonely.

Miss Perkins taps her on the back. "Hello. I'm Miss Perkins."

The girl turns around. "I'm Ann Riley," she says.

"Why aren't you outside for recess?" Miss Perkins asks.

Ann shrugs. "My best friend is sick."

"Well, maybe you can help us, because I have a problem," Miss Perkins says.

Ann looks down the hallway as if she wants to run away.

Miss Perkins has seen this look before, and she does what she always does—she starts talking faster. "Sam is a good boy. It's his first day at school. You seem like a very nice girl. It would mean a lot to both of us if you introduced yourself to him. I don't want to go into the classroom with you because I want him to think your visit is your idea. Could you do us this favor and make a sweet boy's day?"

Ann keeps her eyes fixed on her clean white Keds.

Miss Perkins nods at Room 114. "Go ahead. I'll join you in a few minutes."

Slowly, the girl turns the corner into the classroom.

*   *   *

The girl with the blonde hair enters through the door. At first, Sam thinks that she's returned because she's forgotten something. But instead of her desk, she heads straight for him.

Before Sam can even try to stiffen his neck muscles, she's standing next to him.

"I'm Ann."

Sam is amazed. While his body is bent; his smile, crooked; and his brown hair, wavy; everything about Ann is straight, including her hair, which falls like a sheet to her shoulders, and her even lips. *You're beautiful,* he thinks.

"When my grandmother was in a wheelchair, I got to push her around. I'd like to push him," Ann says, as if to herself.

To say yes, Sam starts to look up until he remembers that she won't understand. He takes a deep breath. He dreads speaking for the first time to anyone, much less to a girl his own age, but Miss Perkins is nowhere in sight. He makes an "O" with his lips and pushes air out so he won't be so loud. "YYes," he says.

His voice is softer than it usually is. Still, she jumps back.

"You can talk?" she asks.

Sam likes her very much and thinks she is a brave girl for speaking to him, but he can't help feeling resentful when she acts so surprised. "YYess, I can," he says firmly.

He's proud of this 'yes I can.' He thinks it's one of the most perfect 'yes I can's that he has ever uttered. Out of sheer joy, he's getting ready to repeat the phrase when Miss Perkins strolls into the room.

"He talked to me," Ann tells Miss Perkins excitedly.

Miss Perkins smiles at Ann. "Mrs. Martin misunderstood me. Sam doesn't like to talk, but he can when he has to."

Ann nods her head. "May I push his wheelchair?"

"That's a jolly good idea." Miss Perkins smiles. "Don't you think so, Sam?"

Sam looks up.

"Sam is so happy," Miss Perkins says. "He would love to have you push him. I promised his mum I would keep him buckled up at school. Let me just check his seat belt. We have enough problems without a broken leg." She pulls Sam's seat belt tight.

Ann studies the controls. "So how do you get the chair out of park?"

In the hallway, some metal lockers are hanging off their hinges, the yellow tiled floor is littered with paper, and the only trashcan is

34

overflowing. But with its dark wood paneling and high ceilings, the school still manages to look distinguished. A tattered bulletin board announces in large print. "Parents' Club Meeting Tonight. Help raise money for our Sports Teams."

"These are the sixth grade lockers," Ann says. On her tour, she is pushing Sam behind two tall boys from Mrs. Martin's class. When Sam recognizes them from the basketball court, he feels as if he has just finished a layup, his heart is pounding so hard with excitement.

Ann points at the boy with reddish-brown hair who had opened the door for them earlier. "That's Charlie Simmons. He's the captain of our basketball team. His father is a pilot in Vietnam." She nods towards the stockier boy. "The other boy is Bobby Sur. He's always chewing gum, even though the teachers tell him not to."

"III wattcch them." Sam tries to explain his habit of viewing the team from his apartment window.

"What did he say?" Ann asks Miss Perkins.

Without looking, Sam knows that Ann's face is twisted in confusion. He dislikes talking to strangers, but every once in a while he will say 'hello' to the grocer, the mailman or a neighbor. When this happens, the person will stare at Sam as if he were speaking a foreign language, maybe Vietnamese—like the Viet Cong Sam sees on the news.

"I can't hear him," Miss Perkins says. "This hallway is too noisy."

Sam has noticed that when Miss Perkins can't understand him, she often blames the noise. Sometimes, he resents her attempts to protect his feelings. Now, he wants to point out that although the players are a few feet away from him, he can hear their conversation perfectly. But this thought is complicated to communicate, and he gives up before he begins.

"Have you signed up any new players?" Bobby asks Charlie. His tone is confidential, and Sam feels privileged to overhear him.

I know a lot about your team, Sam wants to tell them. *I see things that even you may not notice. Because you're playing, and I'm just watching.*

Charlie frowns and shakes his head. "No."

"We're a tall team. I don't understand why we can't score," Bobby complains.

You need a good point guard, Sam thinks. Of all positions, Sam likes point the best. Although usually the shortest player on the team, not only does the point guard need to be able to dribble, he needs to stay confident and make things happen.

"I don't understand why we can't score either," Charlie says.

Your team has all the elements, Sam imagines himself telling them. *You should be scoring. But you're too slow. No one is driving the ball.*

The basketball players duck into the restroom.

Ann stops at the end of the hall, "This is the cafeteria."

Sam peeks inside and sees a large room with a green linoleum floor and lots of brown formica tables. A woman with a mop is cleaning.

"We're going to eat in the classroom," Miss Perkins tells Ann.

Thinking about his messy eating style, Sam tenses. He's not always able to keep food in his mouth, and sometimes he coughs it up. He feels certain that Miss Perkins is about to repeat one of her frequent observations: No offense, Sam dear. You are not your most attractive when you eat.

"The cafeteria makes good fish sticks. That's too bad," Ann says.

As Ann pushes him away from the cafeteria, Sam is amazed and grateful that Miss Perkins has managed to stay mum about his eating habits. Her uncharacteristic silence gives him hope that she won't share with the other kids the details of his diagnosis or of his mother's lawsuit against the doctor who delivered him.

They face the clock on the wall. It's 10:28. "The bell is about to ring," Ann points out.

"Thank you so much, Ann, for this tour," Miss Perkins says.

"Sure." Ann begins pushing Sam back toward the classroom. "My mother is a nurse."

"Is that what you want to be when you grow up?," Miss Perkins asks.

"Maybe a doctor," Ann says shyly.

"GGGood ddoctor," Sam agrees. He knows many doctors, and he can't imagine Dr. Adams—when he was younger—spending his recess pushing around a strange boy in a wheelchair. Maybe if Ann becomes a doctor, the shots that she gives won't hurt as much.

"What did he say?" Ann asks.

"Sam, what did you say?" Miss Perkins leans toward him.

Sam repeats his compliment.

"He's saying that he thinks you'll be a great doctor," Miss Perkins explains.

"Thanks," Ann says.

"WWWelcome," Sam says. He would like to ask her to push him again, but her giggle stops the question from forming inside his throat. His tongue feels like a useless wet blob.

Ann giggles again.

Sam feels himself grow hot with embarrassment. He decides that Miss Perkins may be right. It's probably better if he stays quiet. And yet...

Chapter Six

Elm Street Apartments is a dark six-story building. "Crumbling Georgian," his mother likes to say. The windows are large, but the back, like the front, has no awnings. Off to the side, a drained pool, which is dry even in the summer, has begun cracking. When his parents moved into the apartments, they had been new, but according to his mother, the apartments have been going downhill even faster than the neighborhood. After detouring around a patch of uneven concrete, Miss Perkins pushes Sam up to the back entranceway.

Sam smells the apartment building even before he enters it. One couple from China cooks spicy food. Six kids live in an apartment on the first floor, and their mother keeps a pot of hot dogs on the stove all day and night. Wood is rotting in the corners of the window frames, and mildew freckles the halls.

Miss Perkins leans on the elevator button, and moments later, she angles his chair into the small metal space. They can hear the elevator creak and groan as it travels upward.

The elevator door opens onto the second floor. As Miss Perkins pushes him down the hallway, Sam realizes that he feels as worn out as the frayed carpet. He's smiled more than he ever has in his life. His face muscles—from smiling—and neck muscles—from trying to hold his head upright—feel like Jello.

Apartment 207. Home. Paint peels off their brown door.

As usual, it takes Miss Perkins too long to find the key in her purse. It is so large. Sam jokingly thinks of it as "The Suitcase." He hears the English mug that she carries everywhere bang against the jar of ointment for her rheumatism attacks. Sam wants to tell her to hurry up, but he reminds himself that either way, he'll still be sitting in his chair. This thought—not much is going to change—gives him the patience that he needs to control himself.

"Now tell me, how am I going to make dinner and iron your mother's frilly shirts exactly like she likes them?" Miss Perkins glances at her watch. "In two hours?" She looks around at the small but neat kitchen and living area, as if she expects the apartment to answer. It's decorated in blue and green, his mother's favorite colors. In a burst of energy one weekend, she had tie-dyed the pillows herself. To allow Sam to maneuver better, the linoleum floor is without carpet, and all of the furniture—a television, couch and card table—is pushed against one wall or the other.

Miss Perkins takes Sam's schoolbooks out of The Suitcase and drops them on the counter.

Sam knows that setting books down is a normal act in so many households, yet the sight of the stack makes him sit straighter in his chair. *I went to school!*

"Do you mind if we don't work on math tonight?" she asks.

Sam looks down.

Miss Perkins stares at him. "I have to confess. I don't know how to solve those problems."

"MMe either," Sam says, but he's disappointed. How can Miss Perkins teach him how to do the problems if she doesn't know her-self? It's only the first day, but he has a hunch that Mrs. Martin is going to be too busy to spend much time with him.

"Well, your mother told me that we don't have to take tests until Mrs. Ellsworth returns and you're properly placed, so I don't think we should worry about a little homework. Besides, I've got a lot of ironing to do. I don't want to fall behind and upset your mother. I better get busy. Where do you want to be?"

"Wwwwindow."

Miss Perkins pushes him to his favorite spot in front of the window.

Below Sam, the whole Tomcats basketball team is positioned on the court. After years of watching different teams, Sam's excited to finally know a team by name, even the gym teacher. Mr. Fitzpatrick who Sam met in the halls today is standing on the sidelines. He is wearing gray knit shorts and a T-shirt and holds a whistle in his mouth.

Charlie Simmons, the red-headed captain, is tall—maybe about 5' 10". But he's slow. Bobby Sur, the pimple-faced center is taller—maybe 6 feet—and even slower. In class, Mrs. Martin had called on some of the other boys. A.J. Douglas, a blubbery kid with big hands, is always tripping over his huge feet. He can palm the ball but he can't dribble it. Larry Veselka, a pale boy with blonde hair, runs as if he is moving underwater.

Suddenly, Sam has a great idea. The Tomcats could use a fast boy like Mickey. He wonders, why isn't Mickey on the team? Maybe the fact that Mickey is Russian has something to do with it. He remembers Mickey's almost spooky accent today as he hissed at him. "Stop steering at me. Ve're not friends."

Or maybe, Mickey's not on the team because he's so mean. He might have even fought some of the kids. Sam reminds himself not to look at Mickey in class tomorrow. But what about here at the window?

Don't worry. Sam tries to reassure himself: if Mickey looks up at the apartment, all he will see is a dark window. But not knowing, Sam shudders.

The lock clicks.

Sam's neck won't let him turn, but he doesn't need to see his mother to know that her dark hair crowns pale skin and flashing gray eyes. He hears a familiar sound, his mother singing. A Beatles song. "Yellow Submarine. Yellow Submarine." One of Sam's favorites. "We all live in a yellow submarine."

My wheelchair, Sam thinks, is my yellow submarine.

"Aren't you happy tonight, ma'am?" Miss Perkins says.

"Hello, Miss Perkins."

Sam is disappointed when instead of rushing towards him, his mother lingers in the entranceway. He strains and turns his neck as far as it will go. Because his chair is slightly angled, he can just glimpse his mother standing in the doorway with her blue coat still on. She is holding a small sack from Corner Market. Miss Perkins towers over her.

"I know that this will mean a late, late night for you, but a friend asked me to go dancing tomorrow night."

Dancing? Sam is all for his mother having fun, but he doesn't like thinking about his mother dancing. Mothers aren't supposed to dance, are they?

"Could you? I mean, would you?" his mother continues.

"Sure. Sam and I will have a great time," Miss Perkins agrees. Although her voice is hearty, Sam knows she's not smiling.

His neck hurts too much, and Sam has to turn his head away from the scene at the door.

"Thank you," his mother says. "Oh, how was school?"

"Lovely," Miss Perkins answers.

"Good," his mother says. "Did Sam make some friends?"

"Yes, ma'am," Miss Perkins says. "A nice girl named Ann."

"Do you like his teacher?" his mother asks.

"She's brand-new and very nervous, but not a bad sort," Miss Perkins agrees. "Not really."

"SSSchool!" Sam bursts out enthusiastically.

The sharp points of his mother's high heels announce her approach. Sam has never understood why his mother wears shoes that make walking harder than it already is. She is leaning over him now, and he longs to reach out and hug her. He doesn't want to let her go until he has told her every detail of his day at school.

"I'm glad to hear you liked school," his mother says softly into his ear.

Just once, Sam wishes that his mother would ask him a question. But tonight, she does the next best thing. She looks out his window.

"You're always watching that basketball court." His mother squeezes his shoulder too hard. He knows that she means it as a sign of affection, but this hurts. "Sometimes, I wonder what goes on in that head of yours."

Her shoes tap, slide and glide as she heads toward her bedroom. Sam tries to decipher the unfamiliar pattern. Finally, he understands. His mother isn't walking. She's dancing.

"Time for dinner," Miss Perkins says. She waves a plate of mashed potatoes and pureed green beans before his nose.

Sam hates green beans, but it's hard not to eat them when Miss Perkins controls the spoon. As he swallows the disgusting green mash, he listens to his mother talk on the phone. She is pacing their small apartment, and her voice cuts in and out. "I've been really busy, lately, Celeste. The law firm has a new client, Mr. Jordache..."

Sam has only met Celeste McGregor once. She is a mousy woman who brought his mother a stack of movie magazines when she came to visit. His mother's many friends come and go from his life like shadows.

"He's promised to take me dancing...," his mother says into the phone. "You're always saying that I'm too young to give up on my life. Well, I'm starting to agree with you."

While Sam keeps a watchful eye on the court, he pays attention to the rise and fall of his mother's voice rather than to her words. He's waiting for Mickey.

Maybe it's because Sam saw Mickey up close today, but for the first time he imagines Mickey away from the basketball court. He imagines Mickey living in an apartment about the size of Sam's. But Sam's apartment is generally quiet. What would it feel like to live with an adult who shouted all the time? Nowhere to go. Nowhere to hide. Sort of like being chained to a wheelchair.

Sam's disappointed. The court stays empty. Mickey doesn't come out tonight.

Chapter Seven

At nine p.m. that night, Sam is lying on his bed which is low to the floor. His body feels heavy like it always does when he is settled for the night and doesn't need to make the effort to move for another eight hours. Higher than his bed, his table and chair are the only other pieces of furniture. Sam likes rooms which are nearly empty. It's easier to get around in his chair.

The shuffle of house shoes stops, and Sam's heart flip-flops when the light floods through the open door.

Although his mother is a small woman, the end of his bed sinks with her weight. Her dark hair, not yet rolled onto orange juice cans, falls to her shoulders in waves. His own curly hair and long dark eyelashes are the reason that people say, "You look just like your beautiful mother."

"Hi, MMom," Sam greets her.

"Hi, Sam," she answers softly. She has her hand behind her back. "I just wanted to tell you that I am so happy that you had a good day at school."

"GGGood," Sam says, meaning: yes, today was a good day.

"I'm proud of you, more proud than you'll ever know."

Sam feels his chest expand.

"When I came home from school on my first day, my father gave me a pony," his mother says.

This is a familiar story. As Sam repeats the pony's name in his head: *Peter,* he experiences the sadness that he always does when he thinks of his grandparents who he rarely sees and hardly knows.

"Peter," his mother says. "My mother braided Peter's tail with a green ribbon. For a joke, my father put a Teddy bear on Peter's back."

Along with his mother, Sam laughs at this memory. Since he thinks that his laugh sounds like a dog's bark, he refuses to let loose around anyone besides family.

"So," his mother says slowly. "Even though we don't have room for a pony…" her voice trails off.

Sam knows that his mother misses her childhood home in the country. His grandparents' farm is far away, and he and his mother don't have the money to visit.

"I still had to buy you something."

She holds out a small, clay pot. The cactus is the size of his tongue, with prickles all over it.

"You always say you want a plant." His mother smiles. "This one isn't much trouble."

"Thannksssssss," Sam says. He tries to get his mouth around the three syllables, *For the cactus,* but he is tired, and his mouth is stupid tonight.

His mother places the cactus on his bedside table and kisses his forehead. It is true that Sam has asked for a plant before. He likes being outdoors, and he had wanted some greenery in his room. But a cactus? Where did she get this idea?

She squeezes his shoulder more gently this time and starts for the door.

From experience, Sam knows that the spot where her fingers touched will stay warm for a long time.

His mother pauses with her hand on the light switch. Her skin looks even softer than the white silk of her robe. "Good night," she calls.

Sam remembers Winnie's description of his mother: *She shone…
like the Evening Star. I loved her but at a distance.*[4][†]

It's an experience that Sam has had over and over again. Winnie
always expresses Sam's thoughts better than he can himself.

His mother flips the switch.

To put himself to sleep, Sam presses his face against the wall and
listens to his mother. Through the thin walls, he hears her singing.
"Yellow Submarine. Yellow Submarine."

I wish I knew what was going on in that head of yours, he tells her.

Chapter Eight

Saturday morning, Miss Perkins pushes Sam towards the barber shop. The day is beautiful, and Sam smiles at all the vendors: Mrs. Chang, who sells newspapers and magazines at the corner kiosk; Don, the aged man who shines shoes; the toothless woman who sells roasted chestnuts—"Chestnuts. Get your hot roasted chestnuts here." Sam has lived on Elm Street for twelve years and, as always, memories flood out of the doors and the windows as he rolls by. In the distance, he sees the bench in front of Baskin-Robbins. As they pass the store, he watches the boy with the ponytail scoop a dip of chocolate ice cream.

One Saturday, two years after the divorce, his father picked Sam up at the apartment and pushed him down Elm Street. Although Sam's memory of his father's face is shadowy, he has a clear recollection of his father's back. Standing in line to buy Sam a cup of chocolate ice cream, his father looked tall, much taller than anyone else in Baskin-Robbins. His dark hair was cut in a perfect straight line above his blue oxford shirt. Not knowing that Sam needed help eating, his father set the cup down on the plastic tray attached to his wheelchair. Sam wanted to please his father. If he was no trouble, maybe his father would come back for another visit. So he didn't ask his father to spoon the ice cream into his mouth. On the way back to the apartment, the ice cream turned to milk.

His father never came back anyway.

Although Miss Perkins and he have already passed Baskin-Robbins, Sam keeps thinking about it. Once his cousins, three boys from California, took him there. Sam was 8 and his oldest cousin, Josh, was 12. Josh had quickly gotten lost. Sam had kept his finger pointed in the right direction until Josh had trusted Sam enough to follow his lead. His relationship with the three boys changed after that day. His cousins play baseball, not basketball, but Sam likes them anyway. He looks forward to their visits.

Helpful Dry Cleaners is the corner store with the blue and red awnings.

A few years ago, Gently-Used Books was torn down to make room for Helpful Dry Cleaners. But Sam can never pass the site of the old bookstore without hearing Mr. Vincent's booming voice. "Come in. Come in. The only two Churchill fans on Elm Street."

"Any more books about Churchill?" Miss Perkins had asked Mr. Vincent after they had devoured *My Early Life.*

"Well, of course, there's Winston Churchill's book *Heroes of History.*" Through his bifocal glasses, Mr. Vincent had looked down at Sam with a doubtful expression on his face.

"We'll take it," Miss Perkins had said.

That purchase had started Mr. Vincent's habit of quizzing Sam when he entered the shop. "Hitler was diabolical," he would say. "What does that mean?"

Sam would struggle as hard as he could to pronounce a one-word definition, like "DDevilish."

But no matter how simple Sam's answer, Mr. Vincent would always say, "Sam, my boy, you are amazing."

Miss Perkins passes a young mother pushing a stroller, and suddenly in front of Sam are three boys dressed in blue jeans. He recognizes them from the halls of Stirling Junior High. They are big: maybe eighth graders. All of them wear their hair below their ears;

one has hair almost to his shoulders.

"Let's go to the record store," the boy with the longest hair says. His shirt has a black guitar on it. Sam guesses that the arrow-shaped object in his hand is a guitar pick.

"I can't believe that girls like Paul," the shortest boy says.

"Yeah," the third says. "I like Ringo." He is carrying drumsticks.

Sam is sorry when Miss Perkins stops to gaze in Corner Market, and he loses sight of the boys. A few pumpkins are already filling the store window—a hint of the holiday to come. Then, he sees the row of prickly cacti. Excess Inventory Sale. 50 cents. The mystery of his mother's recent gift is solved. She loves sales.

"I'll come back," Miss Perkins mutters to herself as she starts pushing Sam again. Normally, Sam likes to go to the barber shop, but not this morning. He tries once more to communicate with Miss Perkins. "No MMMister John," he says.

"For years, I've put up with your complaints about going to Dr. Adams," Miss Perkins says.

Of course, Sam hates to go to Dr. Adams. He has to go often. Sometimes even every week or so. Dr. Adams has a great aquarium in his waiting room with lots of goldfish, but who likes to be prodded, stuck, twisted, given shots?

"Don't tell me you're going to start on Mister John," Miss Perkins scolds him. "Mister John has been cutting your hair since you were born. Goodness knows, I was angry, too, when he made us wait for a whole hour. I could have used the time on my chores. Still, we don't have a reason to boycott him."

Sam doesn't have a problem with Mister John. He doesn't even remember the hour wait. Why should he? Sometimes he feels like his whole life is one long wait.

Elm Street Barbers. Next to the red and white pole, a man sits on a bench. He jumps up and holds open the door for Miss Perkins.

The bell tinkles as they enter.

"Noooo cut," Sam tries again.

*   *   *

Miss Perkins pretends that she doesn't hear Sam and pushes him through.

Of the three green barber chairs in the shop, only one is in use. Mister John smiles at Sam and calls, "Hey, Sammy boy. How's it going today?" Mister John is a thin man with a small waist. His face is shaped like his hour-glass body—long with a curve below the wide cheekbones and full again at the jaw. His hair is oily and his mustache waxy. He has five grown sons and their photograph as small boys, faded now, is tucked into a crack in the mirror. A cream-filled shaving brush is lying on the counter next to a razor.

Miss Perkins waves.

The man sitting in the barber's chair has a rounded stomach. A blue bib tucked under his double chin falls to the floor. His skin is clean and slightly pink; he's just been shaved. As he turns towards Sam, his eyes bulge—as if a boy in a wheelchair is as strange as a flying teacup and biscuit. Miss Perkins has never gotten used to the rudeness of strangers. Hurriedly, she pushes Sam over to the far wall so Sam won't catch the man's gaze.

As she turns the wheelchair towards the small television mounted in the corner, Sam's reflection appears in the paneled mirror behind the line of green barbers' chairs. True. Sam's body is twisted, and his neck is floppy. His smile is crooked and a tiny bit wet—although drool isn't nearly as much of a problem for Sam as it was when he was a young child. Then, he was less in control of his body. Less able to communicate. More prone to rage. Now, except for minor details, Sam looks like any other boy his age should look.

Why, he's handsomer than most.

The fat man has no business staring at her Sam!

The television's sound is turned off but on the screen, a group of long-haired hippies is sitting in front of a college building. They appear to be singing and chanting. A few are strumming guitars. A girl wears a lei around her neck. A small fire is burning in front of them.

One boy with hair down his back carelessly tosses a bundle into the fire.

The camera zooms closer, and Miss Perkins identifies a familiar red, white and blue pattern. Why, these kids have thrown a flag into the fire! An American flag, the symbol of her adopted country.

A commercial for Kodak cameras, advertising Instant Photos, comes on the screen, but Miss Perkins can't shake off her anger towards these students. Don't they understand that sometimes countries need to fight to stay safe?

She was twenty-two that horrible summer after France was defeated. When Hitler had started bombing London, she was only ten years older than Sam. America hadn't entered World War II yet. Everyone thought that Hitler was going to invade and conquer England.

But the Royal Air Force had held Hitler off. They had bombed Hitler's planes. Made it too costly for him to continue. She will never forget the night that she and her parents had listened to the wireless. Tears were streaming down her father's face when Winston spoke of the brave pilots, *"Never…was so much owed by so many to so few."* [5]

And it was true. After she finished her shift at the hospital as an aide, she volunteered until late into the night, cutting up sheets, rolling up bandages. She would have done anything for those pilots. After all, England won!

The view on the screen shifts back to the students strumming

51

their guitars.

Instead of protesting and keeping the country safe, these college students should get down on their knees and thank the United States military, Miss Perkins thinks.

Mister John sweeps the bib off the man.

The customer presses a few bills into the barber's hands. "See you again next week," the man says. He trudges out but not without shooting one last curious glance at Sam, Miss Perkins notices bitterly.

Mister John turns to Sam and says, "Now for my favorite customer."

Miss Perkins is horrified when she glances at Sam. Sam is usually full of smiles. But today his lips are pressed together, and he is staring stonily ahead. As a customer, Sam is more trouble than most, and she counts on his sunny personality to win over the vendors whom she frequents. "Mister John, I don't know what's wrong with Sam today," she apologizes.

"Nooo cut," Sam says loudly, rudely.

Miss Perkins' mouth drops open. What has happened to her obedient boy?

But when she looks at Mister John, she's surprised to find that the barber is grinning at her. "Didn't you tell me that Sam was starting school?"

"Yes," Miss Perkins says. "But he's only been there a few days—not long enough to learn such bad manners."

Mister John smiles. "None of the kids want haircuts these days. Their attitude is bad for my business." He shrugs. "But what can I do? You've got to change with the times."

On the screen, the police are dragging the protesters away and throwing them in a paddy wagon.

"Well, my goodness," Miss Perkins says. "I never thought...."

"If you don't mind me saying so, Abigail, you can't have it both

52

ways. You can't put Sam into the world and ask him not to try to fit in it."

Sam looks at her. His grin is more crooked than usual. "PPPlease..."

Slowly, Miss Perkins nods her head. "I suppose we can wait another week," she says slowly.

Mister John holds the door for them. "I hate to say this, Abigail. But don't come back too soon."

Chapter Nine

It's Monday, Sam's second week of school. Although a few kids have smiled at him, besides Ann, no one has talked to him. Ann hasn't spoken to him since last Wednesday when she had a conversation with Miss Perkins. "My mother's in charge of the bake sale. She's the president of the PTA. They're trying to raise money for coaches. Even uniforms." Afterwards, she had mumbled a few words to Sam along the lines of, "We got the meanest teacher in the Sixth Grade. I wish I had Mrs. Smith."

The recess bell rings.

Ann shoves her books in her desk and wanders near Sam. She is standing with her hands at her side as if she wants to start a conversation but is too shy, which is funny because he has heard the boys call Ann "bossy."

Sam feels his feet and fingers tingle with excitement.

"Ann," Miss Perkins calls. "Do you mind watching Sam while I go to the restroom?"

"Sure," Ann answers. She hurries over to the science table and sits down in Miss Perkins' chair. She turns and looks eagerly at him. Sam has seen this same expression many times before, sort of curious and a little malicious. When Sam's cousins came for their first visit, Josh, the oldest one, had looked at him like this, too. When Miss Perkins left them alone, Josh had begun firing questions at him. At first, Sam didn't understand why. Then, he realized that Josh was trying to figure out if he was retarded.

"How many potted plants do we have?" Ann asks.

Of course, eleven potted plants sit on the table next to Sam. It's easier to sign numbers than to try to get his tongue wrapped around them, and Sam is often lazy in the morning. After a good night's sleep, it takes him a while to get used to the limitations of his body again. As Sam slaps one finger then another on his tray, he feels like he's a trained dog.

"Are you saying eleven?" Ann asks.

Sam looks up.

"So you can count?" Ann asks.

He looks up again.

Ann places her finger on the side of her cheek. "Let me think of a harder question. How many desks are there in the room?"

Sam says "thirty," and for extra measure, he holds up three fingers and then makes the best zero that he can. Ann points to each desk, counting.

"You're right," she murmurs.

Sam's glad that she seems to have run out of questions. To try to put an end to the game, he breaks the silence, "WWhenn's your bbirthday?"

"In May," Ann says.

"MMMee too," Sam says. "MMMine is May 10th."

"Mine is May 17th," Ann says.

Sam points at himself. "LLLLike sharing May bbbbirthdays."

Ann giggles.

Miss Perkins ambles back in the room.

"I'm starting to understand him a little better. He said that we were both born in the same month," Ann announces.

Sam hates when people talk about him as if he weren't in the room. If his mother or Miss Perkins commits this offense, he puckers his lips just right and tries to form spit bubbles. When they are nice and juicy, he lets them loose on his lips. But since he's new at school, he decides to let Ann's crime pass unpunished.

Marigold Green pokes her head into the room. Like Ann, she has blonde hair, but she wears hers in a ponytail. She's shaped like a torpedo, and her blue corduroy dress is tight around the waist. "Ann?" she calls out. Since Sam senses that Marigold is afraid of him, he doesn't like her.

"Come on in," Ann calls to her.

Marigold shakes her head before disappearing.

"Why won't your friend come in?" Miss Perkins asks. "We don't bite."

"She's shy," Ann explains. "Miss Perkins, I need to go to recess with Marigold. We're practicing a dance routine."

"I understand, Ann," Miss Perkins says.

"But tell Sam," Ann says to her as if Sam weren't in the room.

You already told me, Sam thinks.

"That I'll come again soon." Ann pauses. "Maybe not tomorrow." She shakes her head. "But sometime."

"That will be nice," Miss Perkins says.

"I'll think up some more questions for him," Ann says.

Like what's two plus two? Sam can't help but feel grouchy.

"That will be wonderful, dear," Miss Perkins says.

Ann runs out the room.

I had a hard time with girls, also, Winnie admits.

Girls didn't ask you baby questions to find out if you were retarded, Sam points out.

True, Winnie answers. *But once a lady told me that she hated my mustache and my politics. I told her that there was absolutely no reason that she should touch either.*[6]

56

I just wish that the inside of me was outside so everyone could know me, Sam says.

We all do, Sam.

Chapter Ten

For Miss Perkins' day off—Sunday—Sam and his mother have a routine. If it's not raining, they go to Paul Revere park and sit outside while his mother reads her newspaper. Sam enjoys the sun on his face and the smell of fresh grass while he listens to his mother comment on the news.

"This Vietnam War is horrible, Sam. Over 500 men died this month. Not just kids. But men as old as me. And no halt to the bombings." After she tells him the latest news, she always pauses, contemplating. "That's why I can't meet any nice men. They're all dying in Vietnam."

If it's raining, they watch cartoons on television. His mother enjoys Bugs Bunny more than he does. Or they listen to music on the radio. His mother's favorite Beatle is Paul McCartney. She likes him because of his soft eyes. She sings along with all their songs, but her favorite is "All You Need Is Love."

Sam and his mother have their own secret which they keep from Miss Perkins: jelly donuts. Miss Perkins scolds his mother. "Jelly donuts aren't nutritious. Just fix the boy a bowl of cereal."

But this Sunday morning feels a little different. His mother wets his hair and combs it for the second or third time. She buttons the top button on his shirt and insists that he wear his blue jacket even though it is small and uncomfortable.

His mother steps back and takes a hard look at him. "Ready," she says finally.

I was ready a long time ago, Sam thinks resentfully as she pushes him out the door onto Elm Street. They are headed for the Corner Market where she buys her paper.

Neither of them are morning people, and usually they enjoy the Sunday quiet. But this morning his mother is talking, and her constant stream of advice is giving him a headache. "People, especially men, like polite boys, Sam. I hope that you will always do your best to be polite…"

The spire of their church appears in the distance. It's the tallest building on the block with a stained glass window of the disciple Paul. His mother chose this church because it's the only one in their neighborhood with an entrance ramp.

"We should go back to Sunday school. How long has it been since we've been there? Two months?" his mother continues.

Sam isn't sorry that his mother hasn't taken him to church lately. Too many old ladies like to pat his cheek and call him a "brave boy."

She pushes him through the front door of Corner Market.

A man standing at the magazine rack whips around when they enter. Like Sam's father, he is tall. But while his father had an athletic build, this man is stocky. A crop of dark hair sits on top of his head. His cheeks are the color of strawberries; his eyes, stern and his mouth, unsmiling. But what catches Sam's interest are the rings on his fingers. Two of them. One has a big diamond in it.

"Why, Mr. Jordache!" his mother exclaims. Her lovely eyes are wide. "What are you doing here?"

"Hello, Mrs. Davis." Mr. Jordache makes a half-bow but keeps his eyes fixed on her. "Just buying a paper," he says. The man's voice is low and gravelly.

"This is my son, Sam," his mother says quietly, and for a reason that Sam doesn't understand, he senses that she is afraid. "Sam, Mr.

Jordache is a new client at the law firm."

For an instant, Sam wonders if his mother planned to meet Mr. Jordache this morning. She never makes him wear his blue coat to the park. But then he realizes that this can't be true. His mother had acted surprised to see Mr. Jordache, hadn't she? Still, Sam understands that Mr. Jordache is important to his mother in a way that he can't interpret. "HHello," he says in as friendly a tone as he can muster.

"Hello, young man," Mr. Jordache says. "Your mother has told me quite a bit about you. She's very proud of you."

"TThanks," Sam says.

There's a long pause while Mr. Jordache and his mother stare at each other.

"Well," his mother says. "I hope to see you next week, Mr. Jordache."

"Perhaps, Mrs. Davis. Perhaps…" Mr. Jordache says.

"Oh," his mother says in a small voice.

"Nice to meet you, Sam," Mr. Jordache says. When he walks out the door, Sam notices that he has forgotten to buy his paper.

His mother turns towards the counter.

"What can I get you?" the Indian grocer says in his lilting voice.

His mother doesn't seem to hear him.

Both his mother and Mr. Jordache appear to have forgotten their purchases. "PPaper," Sam says, trying to be helpful. But he is thinking hard.

"What's that?" the grocer says.

"PPaper," Sam repeats.

His mother seems to wake up. "We'll take a newspaper," she says. She turns to Sam. "And how about some jelly donuts?"

To say yes, Sam looks up, but he's not fooled by her bright smile. His blue coat. The extra care she took to wash off his face. Her endless lecture about politeness. When Mr. Jordache left the store without buying anything, Sam had decided that his hunch must be correct. His mother and Mr. Jordache had planned to meet at Corner Market. But why? He worries that Mr. Jordache may be the man that his mother's been going dancing with. He hopes not. He doesn't like to think about that man's fat fingers with their big rings holding his mother's hands.

Sam hates secrets. Of course, he keeps a lot of them himself, but with his uncoordinated tongue, he doesn't have any choice. As his mother sets the bag of jelly donuts on his tray, he thinks: *You shouldn't keep secrets from your son. Not a single one.*

Chapter Eleven

On Wednesday night, Sam is sitting at the window when he sees his mother's old station wagon cross the parking lot. Although she's gone out every night this week, tonight, she's promised to stay home. He'll watch *Bonanza* or *Bewitched* with her, whichever one she wants. Or if she'd rather, they'll play Hangman or Tic-Tac-Toe. His mother refuses to play checkers with him anymore. She claims that Sam's too good.

He sees her lock her car like she always does and then stare up at the dark sky. Why is she moving so slowly? She's already late. She ought to be hurrying to join him.

He hears his mother's key in the lock. Again, the sound is a grudging noise, without excitement or joy.

The door opens. Instead of rushing towards him, she lingers at the entranceway to talk to Miss Perkins. Monday and Tuesday night, she went out with her friends. Is one of her friends Mr. Jordache?

This evening is his turn. The delay is not fair!

"Are you ready to watch a little television with Sam?" Miss Perkins is saying. "He's been waiting for you."

"I'm sorry that I'm late, Miss Perkins," his mother says. "And I'm afraid that I need another favor."

Sam's head droops.

"Is something wrong?" Miss Perkins asks.

"Could you stay late one more night?" his mother pleads. "It would mean so much."

Sam can't hear Miss Perkin's answer, only his mother's heels finally rushing toward him. They sound like a Morse code signaling all that is wrong with Sam.

She is standing a few feet away from him. She has on a simple blue skirt and a red silk shirt. Her hands are pressed together almost as if she were praying for his forgiveness. "I promise, Sam. I'll watch television with you tomorrow night. It's just that tonight's important…" His mother's voice trails off in a mute plea for his forgiveness.

Sam drops his head back as far as he can—which is not far enough to allow a view of the ceiling. He lets it fall like a hammer on the tray. *I don't want to wait one more day. Not one more minute. Not one more second.*

Sensing his mood, his mother says, "Sammy, you need to be a good boy while Miss Perkins gets you dinner. O.K.?"

"TTTonight," Sam barks defiantly.

"Don't be angry with me." His mother rumples his hair. "You know I love you. I'm trying to make a life for both of us. Not just me."

"Noowww," Sam demands.

"One day won't make any difference," his mother says. She kisses him on the forehead and hurries off to her bedroom.

"A day can seem like a long time to a child," Miss Perkins chides her.

Good old Miss Perkins. At least she understands, Sam thinks as he readies himself to make his views known. He can feel the familiar stiffness in his legs. His back begins to arch.

"Of course, it's not my place to tell you how to run your life," Miss Perkins says. In a friendlier voice, she adds. "Do you want a bite of dinner before you go out, Mrs. Davis?"

"My friends are waiting for me. I don't have time," his mother says.

When Sam was younger he couldn't control the next stage, but now, he opens his mouth on purpose. The scream pours out of him. "NNNNooo!"

He slumps and slouches until he is able to flop out of his chair. His back lands on the floor with a loud thud. His legs are akimbo from his body. He opens his mouth so the spit will pour out. He knows that he makes a disgusting sight. But he doesn't care. He shifts his weight and orders his legs to stomp. They decide to obey.

Thump. Thump. It sounds as if he is kicking loose the pipes in the apartment walls.

He feels his mother and Miss Perkins rushing toward him.

A baby wails, and he hears a series of thuds coming from the apartment above. Probably, an upstairs neighbor is pounding on the floor with a broomstick.

He experiences a vague sense of unease when he realizes that, once again, he has bothered the other tenants. But nothing really matters except that his mother promised that she would stay home tonight. "NNoo!" he yells.

"Stop him," Sam hears his mother cry. "I can't stand it. He's too old to act this way."

"Shut up down there!" a muffled voice shouts from upstairs.

Miss Perkins kneels next to him. "Oh, Sam," she whispers in his ear. "Please...please...be quiet. I understand why you're upset, but we don't want Mr. Crowe to get angry with us again."

The mention of their landlord actually makes Sam pause. But it's too late. The phone has already started ringing. Unfortunately, Mr. Crowe's elderly mother lives next door.

"Mr. Crowe's calling. We're going to get kicked out of our apartment. We're going to be beggars like Ronald predicted," his mother cries.

"It's all right, Mrs. Davis," Miss Perkins says. She kneels and grabs his ankles. She presses his feet to the floor.

"Hush," Miss Perkins whispers. "We've spoiled you…Hush… You're going to get us in serious trouble."

From the apartment above, the baby's wail grows louder. The phone rings and rings. It sounds like someone is calling to report an emergency like a fire.

"Please, Miss Perkins, make him stop," his mother begs. She is wringing her hands.

The phone stops ringing, and Sam hears his mother's anxious voice.

"Yes, sir. Yes, sir. No, it won't happen again. Yes, sir. But, sir, I promise…."

Lying on the ground, Sam's hands and feet feel cold. He is moaning and rocking from side to side. Miss Perkins starts massaging his neck. Her fingers are warm and strong, and he feels the cold stiffness of his body start to melt.

With her hands on her hips, his mother stands over them. Sam tries not to care that a few months ago, he had overheard Mr. Crowe threaten his mother. "If you cause any more trouble," he had warned, "you'll have to move.."

"Is Mr. Crowe O.K.?" Miss Perkins asks his mother.

Sam doesn't like hearing the anxiety in Miss Perkins' voice. Or seeing the panic in his mother's gray eyes. He stops squirming.

"I did my best," his mother answers her. "If I wasn't afraid that Sam would make another scene, I would tell him how angry I am …"

"He's better, ma'am," Miss Perkins says. "You can talk to him now."

His mother leans over him. "Sam. Oh, Sam. Why do you make my life harder than it is?"

His mother's hair falls down on his chest. She is so close to him that he can smell her breath. So sweet, like flowers. Her gray eyes are turned on him, giving him her full attention. "MMMom," he cries affectionately.

His mother shakes her beautiful dark curls. "What am I going to do with you?"

Give me what I want. Stay home with me tonight, he thinks. "HHome," he says.

As she often does when Sam tries to start a conversation, his mother frowns.

"If you'll take his right side, Mrs. Davis," Miss Perkins says. "I'll take his left."

Miss Perkins and his mother help him climb back into the wheelchair. As soon as Sam is settled again next to the television, his mother hurries away. The screen of the television is blank, which is how Sam feels. Drained. Exhausted.

Miss Perkins bends down and begins whispering in his ear. "I wish you hadn't made a scene. You're too old for those, and Mr. Crowe is too cross. Promise me, my dear boy, that you won't have another one." She stares into Sam's eyes.

Sam looks up. He doesn't like to remember how many times he's given her this same promise. By his count, twenty-two.

"That's my good boy," Miss Perkins smiles at him. "We'll have lots of fun tonight. Just you and me. Tomorrow night, your mum will stay home. I'm sure of it." She wheels him over to the kitchen and bends towards him until their noses are inches apart. Her blue eyes bore into his. "Are you thirsty? Do you want some water?"

"No," Sam says.

"I'm going to finish dinner. Please, dear boy, remember your promise."

Sam looks up.

A few minutes later, his mother comes out of her bedroom.

"Another new dress, Mrs. Davis," Miss Perkins remarks.

Since Miss Perkins hasn't asked a question, Sam's eyes fly to his mother's face. Often, she gets angry when Miss Perkins scolds her.

"Now, now, Miss Perkins," his mother retorts. "A girl's entitled to a new dress every once in a while."

Sam's relieved when he hears his mother's joking tone.

In the small entranceway, his mother whirls around, causing her dress to glitter and sparkle. It's the color and texture of moonlight with tiny black straps crossing her thin shoulders. She carries a gold purse in one hand. Her spiked high heel shoes are what make him feel sure that she's going dancing. They are so high and glittering, that he can only imagine them floating across a dance floor.

"I'll be back in a few hours, Miss Perkins," his mother calls.

When the door slams, Miss Perkins hurries to his side. "Now that I have the pot pies in the oven, can I read to you about Winnie?" she asks.

Instead of answering, he clenches his teeth. He's not going to say a single word tonight. *I'm never going to talk to you again*, he thinks.

"The silent treatment, huh?" Miss Perkins says. "That doesn't work with me." She leaves, returning with *My Early Life*. She sits down on the blue and green couch. "Anywhere?" she asks, as usual.

Sam looks down to signify 'no.'

Miss Perkins ignores him. *I went for a row with another boy a little younger than myself,*[7†] she reads. "Oops." She stops. "Let me find a cheerier chapter."

"NNNo," Sam says.

"But Winnie almost drowns. You don't want to hear about that, do you?" Miss Perkins says.

Sam looks up.

"I'm trying to *improve* your mood," Miss Perkins objects.

Sam doesn't answer.

† Reprinted with permission of Scribner, an imprint of Simon & Schuster Adult Publishing Group, from MY EARLY LIFE: A ROVING COMMISSION by Winston Churchill. Copyright© 1930 by Charles Scribner's Sons; copyright renewed© 1958 by Winston Churchill. All rights reserved.

"O.K., then," Miss Perkins says, giving in to his mood. *When we were more than a mile from the shore, we decided to have a swim, pulled off our clothes, jumped into the water and swam about in great delight.*[8†]

Sam understands this story about drowning. When he was no older than two or three, his mother was giving him a bath. She turned to go answer the telephone. The water was pouring out of the faucet, and the tub was filling.

"Mmmom," he called when the water was to his chin. But in speaking, he had accidentally inhaled some water and choked. He struggled to keep his head up, but he slipped. When he tried to breathe, he sucked in water instead. Everything had grown dark, and then he felt her hand in his hair, yanking him up.

"Sam, why did you do that?" his mother scolded him. She was drenched from head to toe. "Tell me you're all right."

Sam had vomited water. When he finally managed, "Mmmama," she hugged him harder than she had in his life. Nearly drowning was almost worth it.

A few weeks later, his mother had hired Miss Perkins. His mother had never bathed him again.

The flow of Miss Perkins' familiar voice begins working over Sam like a massage. After a while, he is able to listen to Winnie's story.

When we had had enough, the boat was perhaps 100 yards away. A breeze had begun to stir the waters. As we swam towards the boat, it drifted farther off.

Sam imagines Winnie and his friend playing and laughing as the boat floated away.

Up to this point no idea of danger had crossed my mind. The sun played upon the sparkling blue waters; ...the gay hotels and villas still smiled.

† Reprinted with permission of Scribner, an imprint of Simon & Schuster Adult Publishing Group, from MY EARLY LIFE: A ROVING COMMISSION by Winston Churchill. Copyright © 1930 by Charles Scribner's Sons; copyright renewed © 1958 by Winston Churchill. All rights reserved.

Before Miss Perkins reads the next words, a chill tickles Sam's back.

"But I now saw Death as near as I believe I have ever seen Him."[9†]

Just like Sam had felt when he almost drowned, grayness expands to fill every corner of his mind.

"Death was swimming in the water at our side, whispering from time to time in the rising wind which continued to carry the boat away from us at about the same speed we could swim."

"No help was near. I was not only an easy, but a fast swimmer, having represented my House at Harrow, when our team defeated all comers. I now swam for life."

Sam believes that the Allies won World War II because of Winnie's leadership. That's why every time that Miss Perkins reads this part of Winnie's story, Sam thinks about how much history would have been different if the breeze had been just a little stronger. Or if Winnie hadn't been on a swim team.

The hundreds of speeches that Winnie wouldn't have written. Without Winnie, England would have probably surrendered to the Nazis. The Nazis would have killed every decent person on the whole island. Or so Sam believes. Sooner or later, the United States would have ended up fighting Hitler and Japan without its major ally.

"Twice I reached within a yard of the boat and each time a gust carried it just beyond my reach; but by a supreme effort I caught hold of its side in the nick of time..."

"I scrambled in, and rowed back for my companion who... had not apparently realized the dull yellow glare of mortal peril that had so suddenly played around us."

As a teenager, Winnie had already felt the dull yellow glare of mortal peril. Sam's twelve, and he's never felt it. Slipping in the tub doesn't count. That's one of the things that he hates most about life in a wheelchair. Winnie took risks. Sam will never face strong currents, land mines or enemy soldiers. Not even a rival basketball team.

I understand, Sam, Winnie interrupts. *You just want the right to be brave.*

*   *   *

On the bus home, Miss Perkins is hunting through her purse for a Kleenex when she spies a crumpled piece of paper. Her hands close on it, and she pulls it out. Imagine that. Her purse is so messy that she hasn't seen this precious piece of paper for many months. It's one of the first essays that Sam wrote. She was afraid that she had lost it. Unlike his later ones, it is unsigned and untitled, but she has named it. She calls it the *Sam, I Am* essay.

She opens it and begins reading the hurried letters that she copied down that day as Sam pointed to them.

MISS PERKINS SAYS THAT I AM A BOY OF MANY GIFTS AND THAT IT IS A GOOD THING THAT I HAVE CP OR OTHERWISE I'D BE VAIN AND PROUD.

SHE SAYS THAT I WAS MEANT TO HAVE CP. WHICH IS GOOD BECAUSE SAM IS ALL I AM.

Miss Perkins kisses the paper, coffee-stained and dirty at the edges. She hunts up her old brown wallet, unzips the slot for change and carefully folds it inside.

Chapter Twelve

This second week, school has slipped into a routine. Sam and Miss Perkins arrive on time each day. With Miss Perkins in a chair at his side, Sam sits in his spot next to the Science table.

Before turning her attention to the other kids, Mrs. Martin greets Sam pleasantly. Although Miss Perkins has tried to tell Mrs. Martin about Sam's skills, they've always been interrupted. Mrs. Martin has promised that she will find a time to meet with them one afternoon after school.

The bell rings. Sam notices that as usual, Mickey is not in his seat. During class, Sam has been trying not to stare at Mickey. This is easy in the mornings, since Mickey is always late.

After the pledge, Mrs. Martin writes on the blackboard, 'National History Essay Contest.'

For a reason that Sam doesn't understand, he senses more excitement than usual today in the classroom.

Bodies are squirming in chairs. Necks are craning. Students are whispering. Bobby passes Charlie a note.

As if Mrs. Martin has eyes in her back, she whirls around.

Sam guesses that the unlucky kid is going to be Bobby but instead, Mrs. Martin swoops down on Charlie. Mrs. Martin crumples the note and angrily tosses it into the trashcan.

Under his teacher's hostile stare, Charlie's freckled face grows redder over his white button-down shirt.

"They're good kids," Miss Perkins mutters.

Although both Sam and Miss Perkins have stayed quiet in class, that hasn't stopped Miss Perkins from giving Mrs. Martin plenty of advice under her breath.

"What are you doing?" Mrs. Martin demands.

"We're just trying to work out the lineup for the game," Charlie explains.

"Don't ever let me catch you passing a note again, all right?" Mrs. Martin says.

"Yes, ma'am," Charlie says. He is so tall that he barely fits behind his desk. Sam has overheard Charlie say that he is already thirteen.

Mrs. Martin returns to the front of the class and clears her throat. "Boys, Mr. Fitzpatrick told me that there is a Tomcats game this afternoon."

The boys cheer.

Sam wants to join in, but he's too self-conscious about his voice.

Mrs. Martin scowls at them. "But if I catch anyone else not paying attention, the whole class will have to stay inside during recess."

Bobby groans. Charlie presses his lips together as if to prevent a sound escaping from them.

"Now, take out your notebooks," Mrs. Martin orders. "In preparation for a national essay contest, we're going to start a short unit on World War II."

Sam loves studying World War II. Even better, after school, he's looking forward to watching the Tomcats play.

Mrs. Martin writes on the blackboard: "Pearl Harbor." She begins talking. "World War II started when Japan bombed the United States on December 7, 1941."

Sam can't believe his ears.

He knows that the United States entered the war on December 7, 1941. But he also knows that World War II began long before that. On September 1, 1939, Hitler invaded Poland. Soon afterwards, Churchill became the prime minister of England. After France was defeated, England, led by Churchill, battled the Nazis alone. *What about the Battle of Britain, Mrs. Martin?* Sam wants to cry. *You're leaving out many important events.*

"Churchill, Roosevelt, and Stalin were known during the war as the Big Three," Sam hears Mrs. Martin continue. "All of these men were great leaders, but Roosevelt was the most powerful and important."

Roosevelt? Sam likes Roosevelt. After all, Roosevelt used a wheelchair. But his teacher's statement totally overlooks Winnie's heroism as Britain fought on alone, waiting, hoping, and praying for the U.S. to enter the war. Sam wants to remind Mrs. Martin of the great speech Winnie made when England was so unprepared and under-equipped to fight Hitler. He hears Winnie's gravelly voice: *"I have nothing to offer but blood, toil, tears and sweat."*[10]

How can Mrs. Martin be saying these things? When Sam has choked down enough outrage to be able to listen, he hears Mrs. Martin say, "Eisenhower chose June 6, 1944, as D-Day. D-Day took the Germans by surprise."

What about Winnie, Mrs. Martin? Sam thinks.

Mrs. Martin picks up a piece of chalk and begins writing.

"So now write down the names and dates on the blackboard:"

December 7, 1941

June 6, 1944

September 2, 1945

Franklin D. Roosevelt

Dwight D. Eisenhower

Pearl Harbor

In her ten-minute lecture, Mrs. Martin has managed to completely overlook Winnie. Sam must defend his hero. But what to say? He considers the words that he has practiced speaking out loud most often: Mother, window, school, food, fan, hello, sad...

Then, some random words that Miss Perkins and he had worked on pronouncing: dictator, trapped, ocean, potato, Peter...None of the words fit. Mrs. Martin goes on to explain the Pacific theatre of the war.

In the middle of her description of Hiroshima, Sam finally opens his mouth. He doesn't even try to speak softly. He bursts forth with the only word that he has mastered that has even a slight application to her lecture:

"NNNNo." It sounds harsh, guttural, even to his own ears.

Mrs. Martin jumps. The kids all stare at him, their eyes bugged in horror. Yet, he's so intent on righting the wrong that he doesn't even feel ashamed.

Mrs. Martin puts her hands on her hips and turns toward Sam. "What did you say?"

"NNNo," Sam repeats.

"I told you guys that he talks a lot," Ann says. "But you wouldn't believe me."

"He sounds Russian," Sam overhears A.J. Douglas say. "Maybe he's a Communist, too."

"Sam's really seven years old. That's why he talks so bad," Bobby Sur announces.

Such crazy stuff makes Sam want to both laugh and cry.

When Mrs. Martin hurries over to Miss Perkins, the sight of his teacher's raised eyebrows drives his classmates' nonsense out of his mind. Miss Martin's narrowed eyes target him before they shift to Miss Perkins.

"I thought you said Sam couldn't talk," his teacher says to Miss Perkins.

"He doesn't like to talk very much," Miss Perkins explains. She has a patient smile on her face.

"I've told you that I have my hands full with thirty kids," Mrs. Martin interrupts. She sounds as if she is close to tears. "Why is Sam disrupting my class?"

"Beg your pardon, ma'am. Sam wasn't trying to be noisy." Miss Perkins stares thoughtfully into space. Sam can almost feel her thoughts probing his mind. "You see, we both are very fond of Winston Churchill," she continues. "Me being from England and all. I think he was telling you something about Churchill, weren't you, Sam?"

Sam looks up.

A.J. Douglas who is sitting next to Bobby reaches over and cuffs him.

"Cut it out!" Bobby cries as A.J. laughs loudly.

Mrs. Martin scolds the class. "Behave yourselves!" She turns back towards Sam. "As you can see, I can't drop my guard for a minute," she says.

"They're just kids excited about a basketball game," Miss Perkins says softly.

Mrs. Martin jerks away and returns to the front of the classroom. Her serious face quiets the uproar. She wipes her chalky hands on her dark plaid skirt, but then to Sam's surprise, she stares blankly at the blackboard as if she's forgotten all she knows. Finally, she says, "You have all been so unruly that I should cancel recess."

The class groans just as the bell rings.

"But if you can prove to me for once that you can keep completely quiet," Mrs. Martin says, "I'll let you go."

Abruptly, the shuffling, rustling, tapping, creaking, sneezing and whispering stop. All Sam can hear is the sound of his own breathing. The silence continues for so long that he feels like it's a wet glass that any minute is going to slip out of the kids' hands and crash on the floor.

Sitting alone in a wheelchair, Sam has learned to play games with time. By daydreaming, he can transform hours into minutes and minutes into seconds. But every once in a while, his magical formula for shortening time fails, and he becomes like a kid with a normal body.

Sam notices Charlie squirming in his seat, and he feels sorry for him. Sam has sat for hours in his chair with an itch on the back of his neck that he can't possibly scratch or a fly buzzing around his ear that he could never catch. Or a thirst that a single glass of water completely failed to quench. And he knows what it's like to have a second last for a whole year.

Mrs. Martin looks up at the clock. It's three minutes *past* ten. "Good job." She smiles. "Dismissed."

Charlie hoots. "Tomcats, let's meet on the court."

Take me with you, Charlie, Sam thinks.

The boys and girls hurry out of the classroom. As Mrs. Martin picks up the eraser and begins wiping the blackboard, Miss Perkins calls out to his teacher, "Mrs. Martin, please don't be angry with Sam."

Mrs. Martin turns and takes a few steps toward them. She moves almost as slowly as Miss Perkins at the end of a hard day, and Sam guesses that she's tired.

"Sam just wanted you to know that we think Sir Winston is a great man," Miss Perkins says.

Sam looks up.

Miss Perkins searches Sam's eyes for more. "Sam also wanted to tell you that World War II began before the United States started fighting."

You knew she was wrong too, Sam thinks. *Why didn't you say some-*

thing, Miss Perkins?

Mrs. Martin sighs. "The United States declared war on December 7, 1941. Is that better?"

"Yes, ma'am. We like that better, don't we, Sam?" Miss Perkins says.

Sam moves his chin upward in agreement.

He's sorry when the creak of a door interrupts them.

The school secretary heads toward them. Her heels are even thinner than Sam's mother's. Although Sam has never been to a circus, he believes that balancing on such sharp little points ought to be a circus act.

The secretary hands Mrs. Martin a piece of paper. "From Principal Cullen," she says. Her voice is nasal, grating.

"Thank you, Miss Rawles," Mrs. Martin calls as the secretary exits the room.

When his teacher unfolds the principal's note and begins reading it, Sam can feel her attention leaving them and traveling down the hall to Principal Cullen's office.

"You see, in our spare time at night, we read about Winston Churchill. We've finished every book about him that there is…." Miss Perkins continues.

Sam feels sorry for Miss Perkins. She never seems to know when to stop talking.

"It's a bond that Sam and I have…."

Mrs. Martin slips the note into her pocket, and Sam notices that his teacher's hands are trembling. Just like he fears being a bad student, he guesses that Mrs. Martin is afraid of being a bad teacher. His teacher's gaze shifts to the door.

Sam must speak to her before she leaves. He takes a deep breath. "Ssssorry." The word comes out too loud. He knows that it's wrong to shout and it's worse to shout an apology. He feels his face start to grow red.

Mrs. Martin looks at him, puzzled. "Did you say, 'sorry'?"

"SSorry," Sam repeats his apology. This time he has more control over his volume, and his 'sorry' sounds only a little drawn out, more like sorrrrry.

Mrs. Martin comes closer. Next to him, he senses Miss Perkins clenching her hands. He knows that she is thinking, "She better not be rude to my Sam."

A faint smile appears on Mrs. Martin's thin lips. "That's O.K., Sam," she says to him. "I understand that you were just trying to defend Churchill."

Sam tries to grin back at his teacher.

Mrs. Martin leans so close that Sam can see the smudge on her glasses. As they gaze at each other, suddenly, her eyes flash with decision. "I've been meaning to ask you.... Can you stay after school this Wednesday? We can get to know each other a little better," she says.

"Yess," Sam says.

"That would be great," Miss Perkins says. "We would..."

Mrs. Martin straightens up. "Now, you'll have to excuse me," she interrupts. "Principal Cullen wants to see me." As if to herself, she adds, "I hope my class wasn't too loud." She turns and walks briskly out the door.

Sam confronts the empty desks. He hates being the only kid in the whole classroom. It's one of the loneliest feelings in the whole world. He feels much lonelier in the empty, quiet classroom than he ever does in his spot at the window.

He worries that by speaking out in class, he has scared Ann away. Just when Sam is about to give up on her, Ann wanders in. Although some of the girls wear pants, Ann always has on a dress. Today hers is blue— the color of her eyes.

"Hhhi, Ann," Sam says.

"Hi!" Ann said. "You're sure talking a lot today."

Miss Perkins blows her nose in her handkerchief. She finishes by dabbing it with quick little pats. "He's just shy. Now that he knows you, he'll start talking all the time."

"Nnnot all," Sam says happily.

Ann laughs. She takes the brake off the wheelchair. "Let's go."

*　　　*　　　*

After school, Miss Perkins pushes Sam down the aisle of baked goods in the cafeteria— the PTA's bake sale. Flat and layered chocolate cakes. Lemon cookies dusted with white sugar. Thick packages of brownies. "I want to buy some brownies for us," she says to Sam. "Besides, this bake sale will be a good opportunity for us to meet people. Ironing will just have to wait."

In the room crowded with students and parents, Miss Perkins spots Marigold and Ann, but she doesn't see any boys from Mrs. Martin's class. She looks around at the clusters of chatting mothers. They seem to be a nice working-class group. She guesses that she'll find some friends. She always does. But she knows from experience that she needs to approach them in stages. Let them get used to us first, she thinks. Then, we'll introduce ourselves.

Miss Perkins begins examining the brownies. She wants to find some without nuts.

"Excuse me," Miss Perkins hears someone say. When she looks up, she finds a woman with faded blonde hair and blue eyes standing behind the counter. She has a strong jaw, wide shoulders and thick arms. Miss Perkins smiles at the woman, but she doesn't smile back.

"I'm Kathy Riley, president of Stirling's PTA."

So this is Ann's mother, Miss Perkins thinks.

Mrs. Riley nods her knobby chin in Sam's direction. "That can't be the boy in Mrs. Martin's class."

Miss Perkins corrects Mrs. Riley and introduces Sam and herself. Although she instinctively doesn't like the woman, she decides to give her a break because of Ann. "Ann has been so kind to Sam. She's such a sweet girl," she says.

"Ann mentioned…," Mrs. Riley sputters.

Mrs. Riley holds herself as if life hasn't gone exactly as she'd planned. As if she's had to fight for what's hers. "I had no idea…," the woman continues. "Why, there are thirty kids in that class."

"I'm sorry," Miss Perkins says. "I don't understand what you mean." But she knows exactly what Mrs. Riley means, and she feels worried.

"May I help you?" Mrs. Riley asks quickly.

Miss Perkins points at a pack of brownies. She pulls out her wallet—for once, she finds it right away. When she unzips it, she sees Sam's essay. She has the impulse to wave the *Sam, I Am* essay in the self-satisfied woman's face. To say, you don't have any idea what my boy is capable of thinking or feeling. But she merely plucks out a few quarters and puts them on the counter.

As Mrs. Riley turns to make change, Miss Perkins glances over her shoulder in time to see Mrs. Martin come through the cafeteria door. She is holding the hands of a girl and a boy. Twins. Probably no older than two.

The girl has short brown hair and the boy, black. The boy is clutching a Teddy bear; a long stream of snot is running down the girl's nose.

"Here's your change," Mrs. Riley says.

"Thank you," Miss Perkins says. She notices the direction of Mrs. Riley's gaze.

Unlike the man in the barber shop, she's not staring at Sam as though he's a curiosity. Her eyebrows are knit together and her lips are pursed in anger, as if Sam were a threat. "If you don't mind me asking," Mrs. Riley says. "Who admitted Sam? Mrs. Ellsworth is out. Did Principal Cullen talk to him?"

Miss Perkins pretends not to hear Mrs. Riley. "Enough socializing for today, Sam. We better get home so I can do the ironing." She pushes Sam as fast as she can towards the door.

On her way out, Miss Perkins waves at Mrs. Martin but the teacher doesn't see her. Both the twins are crying. At the door, she turns. Mrs. Martin is bent over, trying to comfort one, then the other crying child without success.

Miss Perkins knows just how she feels. Not enough hands. Not enough arms. Not even endless love is enough.

Chapter Thirteen

Around 6 p.m., Sam is sitting at the window when he hears the door burst open.

"Miss Perkins, there are some rat droppings by the coatrack," his mother complains a few moments later.

Once, Miss Perkins set a rattrap by the trashcan in the kitchen. When they returned home from an errand, Sam spotted an animal caught in the metal wire trap. The poor rat's body was twisted. Just as he had had to turn away from the sight, now he tries to shut out the sad memory.

"Oh, my goodness," Miss Perkins says. "I'll sweep up after dinner."

"Hey, Sam," his mother calls.

"I thought you were going out tonight, Mrs. Davis?" Miss Perkins says.

"My plans got canceled," Mrs. Davis explains.

"Well, that's great news for Sam," Miss Perkins says.

His mother sighs.

To cheer her up, Sam calls out, "BBBasketbball." The Tomcats are playing on the school court. Because the game was scheduled after the Bake Sale, many of the parents are watching from the sidelines tonight.

His mother's footsteps pause at the coatrack. Then, he's happy to hear her pattering towards him. As she kisses him, he notices that her cheeks are flushed—with the cold weather or pink makeup, he can never tell. Together, he and his mother look out the window. Sam doesn't know the exact score, but the Tomcats are losing badly.

He wants to tell his mother, *These are the Tomcats. I'd give anything to be able to help my Sixth Grade team.* But sometimes, his enthusiasm drives her away.

In the silence between them, Sam thinks about how hard his mother's life is.

How badly she feels that the money that she won from the lawsuit is already gone. How difficult it is to type and take dictation long hours every day. How much her back hurts and her feet ache. How she misses her parents and her childhood on a farm, riding horses. How she'd like to be able to buy a new dress every week. How much he loves her when she laughs.

His mother takes a deep breath.

Sam waits for her to speak, but she doesn't.

He thinks about one of the best conversations he ever had with his mother. She told him that his father had gone to college on a basketball scholarship. During one game, his father claimed, he had picked out his mother in the stand. She was wearing a green dress. Later, a friend introduced them. After a brief courtship, Sam was born. Although the story has a lot of holes, Sam has never been able to get his mother to tell him more.

His mother points at the court. "Look at that boy."

Sam has no idea which boy his mother is talking about.

As if his mother can read Sam's mind, she describes him: "The one with the sandy hair and freckles. The tall guy. He's wide open."

Charlie Simmons is holding up his hands.

Almost as soon his mother stops speaking, Larry Veselka passes Charlie the ball. Charlie catches it in front of his chest.

"There he goes!"

Despite dribbling the ball on his foot, Charlie darts inside for a perfect layup.

"That boy got a break," his mother says dreamily. "I can imagine what it must feel like. All of sudden, nothing matters except that the player can shoot."

Yes, Sam longs to say, *I think so, too*. Trapped by all those sharp elbows and stretched arms, a clear shot must feel almost as good as being able to run with twisted legs.

"Of course, basketball's just a game," his mother says softly. "In real life, you don't get breaks."

Are you sure? A few months ago, everything had seemed weighted against Sam, but now that he's attending school, he is starting to feel like he has a chance.

The phone rings, and his mother hurries away to answer it.

Sam's gaze remains fixed on Charlie Simmons. Does Charlie still feel the wonder of that basket inside himself? The glory of that ball arcing and finding its way to the one spot where it is supposed to be. Sam would give anything to know. Already, Charlie's holding his arms out, asking Bobby Sur to pass him another ball.

Sam listens with one ear while his mother chats on the phone to Celeste. "Joe—Mr. Jordache—had to go out of town. It was going so well." Her voice peters out.

As far as Sam is concerned, Mr. Jordache can stay out of town.

Mr. Fitzgerald blows his whistle, and the two teams line up in one wavy line. Then, the line breaks in two, and the players start passing by each other rapidly and shaking hands.

The Tomcats trudge off the court. Although Sam's team has more height and talent, they have still managed to lose the game.

Chapter Fourteen

At recess the next day, Sam waits for Ann to unlock the brake on his chair.

"Can I push him outside today? I really want to," Ann says to Miss Perkins.

Usually Ann just pushes him down the hall and around the cafeteria and back. Sam can't believe his good luck.

"I don't see why not," Miss Perkins answers.

Does Sam dare ask Ann to take him to watch basketball? Can he convey the question with one word, basketball? He's never tried the word with anyone but his family before. Still, it's worth the risk. The closest that he has ever been to a basketball is his view from his window.

What does one feel like?

Sam would love to be so close to the court that he could see the expression on Charlie's face as he makes a basket. As he blocks a shot.

From a courtside seat, he'd love to hear the team's feet as the boys race up and down, and the thump of the ball when it bounces off the metal backboard. He can't think of anything except the word 'basketball.' He breaks the word "basket" down into three sounds and practices them over and over in his head. BBas Kit Bol.

As Ann pushes him down the hall, he makes up his mind that he won't let an opportunity pass him by. If Ann gets close to the court, he will point and shout, "BBas...Kit ...Bol."

If Ann doesn't understand him, Miss Perkins will translate.

Sam is determined to get near that court.

The sun is shining as they travel down the concrete path to the playground. Ann pushes Sam faster than Miss Perkins does. Normally, his safety belt is annoying, but today he's grateful that it's strapped tightly around his waist.

On the field, some girls and boys are playing kickball. Mickey is alone on the tetherball court. Mickey hits the ball so hard that Sam can't count all the times that it wraps the pole.

Ann and Sam stop near Marigold and the other girls, who are practicing dance steps. Twenty yards away, the whole basketball team is stationed on the court.

When Marigold notices Sam, her shoulders slump, and her face falls. "Are you going to play with that cripple again, instead of me?" she shouts.

"I'll be right there," Ann calls.

Lots of people have called Sam a cripple or a spaz. Miss Perkins tells him that they don't mean anything by it. Marigold just doesn't know any better, Sam reminds himself.

But still he feels sorry that Marigold doesn't like him.

"What should I do with you?" Ann asks herself. Then as if she has had a brand-new idea, she says. "Is there something you want to do, Sam?"

Sam lifts his finger and points at the basketball court. The word that has been waiting on his tongue for so long pops out. "BBas…Kit …Bol."

"Did you say, basketball?" Ann asks.

"YYYes," Sam says eagerly.

"Of course," Ann says. "You're like my little brother. You like sports." She starts pushing him over to the court.

When Ann had driven him in the halls, she had been cautious, but today hurrying to return to Marigold, she begins pushing him even faster. With his belt tight across his waist, Sam likes her speed.

As they come within range of the court, A.J. Douglas misses a pass, and the basketball whizzes toward Sam. If Sam doesn't act quickly, he's going to touch a basketball for the very first time—with his head. He doesn't want to get hurt, but worse, he doesn't want to be embarrassed. He decides to do one of the things that he does best and slumps down in his seat.

Ann turns Sam away from the path of the speeding ball, and it bounces harmlessly against the side of the chair.

"Watch out!" Ann shouts at the basketball players.

Charlie runs over and collects the ball.

With her hands on her hips, Ann does not seem the least bit intimidated by Charlie—despite his height. She seems to think that not only does she have a right to be courtside, but Sam does, too.

"You're not our boss," Charlie says. "What are you doing so close to the court anyway?"

"Sam wanted to watch," Ann tells him.

One of the things that Sam hates about his wheelchair is that people have to look down at him. At least, Charlie meets his eyes when he asks, "You like basketball?" He bounces the ball.

Ever since Sam began watching the court from his window, he has been waiting for this moment. "YYYYes," he bursts out.

Charlie's grin widens. He tries a fancy dribble behind his back but misses. The ball rolls away.

"YYYes, I dddo," Sam repeats himself.

Charlie points at a spot about five feet away next to the crooked light post. "Wheel him there so he won't get bopped," he orders Ann before he runs after the ball. Obediently, Ann pushes Sam over to the spot. She leans close to Sam, and her blue eyes intently search his. "I've got to go, O.K.? Marigold will be angry with me unless we work on our dance routine today."

Sam looks up. His heart is so full that the word spills out: "TTThanks."

"O.K.," Ann says.

As Ann rushes away, Sam is sure that she has no idea how happy she has made him. For once, he can't blame his inability to tell her on his stubborn tongue. Even if he could talk easily, he wouldn't know what to say. How could he describe the thousands of hours that he has spent with his eyes fixed on the court and dreaming?

I'm the only one to whom you tell your dreams, Winnie boasts.

Hush, Sam tells him.

Miss Perkins joins him. "I leave you alone for five minutes, and you decide to join the basketball team, Sam. What am I going to do with you?"

He knows Miss Perkins isn't really scolding him.

"Ann told me that I needed to come quickly because you almost got hit in the head."

With the thump of the basketball sounding nearby, Sam is barely listening to Miss Perkins. At last, he's graduated from his window. His wheelchair is resting on dirt. He almost got hit by a ball. He's part of the action.

Sam goes over what he knows about the Tomcats. His team has some strengths. Charlie, A.J., Larry, Bobby and the others are big guys and decent shooters, but they are all clumsy dribblers. None of them is what the television announcers would call "a good ball handler."

Charlie is not a bad shot, but he's such a poor dribbler that he has to keep his eyes on the ball when he should be watching the court. A basketball game presents all players with chances to score. Some are planned, but many are random. A few are easy. Most are nearly impossible. A point guard has to analyze possibilities and feed the ball to the player who is—or will be—in the most likely position to score, sometimes before that player even understands his opportunity himself. Without that key player, the Tomcats are a car without an engine. An army without a general.

If only Charlie would come talk to him again. Sam could tell him about Mickey. With Mickey as point guard, Sam is convinced that the Tomcats could be a winning team.

Chapter Fifteen

It's Wednesday afternoon, and Mrs. Martin has promised to stay after class to work with Sam.

For the last hour, Sam has listened with interest while different members of the class read stories from Greek mythology. He has always liked tales of escape—after all, what is basketball except a game about freeing oneself to shoot? And he had really enjoyed the story of Theseus trying to get out of the labyrinth. But now, Sam's neck feels weak from trying to keep his head from nodding forward.

Mrs. Martin is collecting the Mythology books and piling them on her desk. "We'll finish tomorrow."

The final bell rings.

"I heard that Mrs. Ellsworth, the vice-principal, is about to return from maternity leave," Miss Perkins whispers to him. "By the time she gets back, we've got to have Mrs. Martin on our side. Otherwise, Mrs. Ellsworth could make us attend a younger grade or even go to a different school." She squeezes his arm. "So that's a good boy. Do your best now, O.K.?"

This is Sam's classroom. His school. Mrs. Martin is his teacher. The thought of leaving and starting all over again is frightening.

"OOO.K.," Sam says. Even though he is so tired today, he is happy when he sees Ann heading over to him.

"Ann, have I ever showed you that Sam can read?" Miss Perkins says quickly. Her gaze is fixed on Mrs. Martin. "He can't read small lettering," she explains. "But I made this special alphabet for him." From a side pocket in his wheelchair, she unfolds a cardboard sheet. The alphabet is written in large, black letters. She unfolds the plastic tray across his wheelchair and places the alphabet on it. "Think of a question."

"What's my name?" Ann asks.

Another silly question, Sam thinks as he points to the letters that spell 'Ann.' He decides to keep going. Even though he is bored with Ann's questions, he is grateful to her for spending so much time with him.

Miss Perkins is jotting down the letters.

Sam points to: "Ann is nice." But he would love to say: *Take me to the basketball court every day, and I'll be your friend forever.*

"Does Sam like to read and write?" Ann asks Miss Perkins.

Before Miss Perkins can answer, Mrs. Martin joins them.

Sam wills his neck to stiffen. Miss Perkins is counting on him to impress his teacher.

Ann turns to leave.

Mrs. Martin stops her. "Ann, why don't you stay a minute? I could use your help with Sam."

"O.K.," Ann says. As if Sam were her student, she moves closer to him. Sam feels the golden hairs of her arm brush against him.

Mrs. Martin shakes her head. "Sam," she says. "Thank you for staying after school. It's hard to talk during class. May Ann and I ask you a few questions?"

Sam starts to answer 'yes,' but Miss Perkins interrupts. "I think he could go to college, Mrs. Martin, if he had the chance. I never graduated from high school myself, but my boy could do anything that he wants to do."

Ann holds up a sheet with the alphabet written on it in big letters. "I could ask him his favorite color, Mrs. Martin."

"Sam, tell Mrs. Martin your favorite color," Miss Perkins directs.

Obediently, Sam lifts his right finger and points at the 'G' on his alphabet chart, but he longs to say, *Ask me something hard.*

"He likes green, ma'am," Miss Perkins explains. "I think it's because he doesn't get to go outside that much. Green is the color of the great outdoors. He likes the grass, the trees."

"Would you mind?" Mrs. Martin interrupts. "Could Ann and I question the boy?"

Miss Perkins' sweet face falls. Sam knows that her feelings are hurt.

"Please, ma'am. Go ahead," she answers in her most dignified voice.

"You like Churchill?" Mrs. Martin asks.

"He knows everything there is to know about Sir Winnie, why he could..." Miss Perkins starts to detail his encyclopedic knowledge of Winnie, but Mrs. Martin touches Miss Perkins' arm.

"Where was Churchill born, Sam?" Mrs. Martin asks. "Ann, write down his answer."

Quickly so that Mrs. Martin won't change her mind, Sam points to the letters for "Blenheim Palace."

"How does he know that?" Ann asks no one.

"Sam's correct, ma'am," Miss Perkins breaks in.

"Shhh," Mrs. Martin says. Behind her horn-rimmed glasses, his teacher's eyes are sparkling. "Sam," she begins cautiously, "When I asked you the question, 'Where was Churchill born?' and you answered, which of these did you hear in your head?

"Number one: Blenheim Palace, or Number two: Churchill was born in Blenheim Palace." Mrs. Martin looks at Ann. "Ann, hold up the poster board so that Sam can choose."

This is an unusual question. Sam starts to feel excited, too. He points at number two.

Mrs. Martin turns to Miss Perkins. "He hears sentences in his head," she says. "Does he hear paragraphs, too?"

"YYes," Sam says to Mrs. Martin. He wants to shout, *At last, someone at this school understands.*

Ann stares quizzically at him, as if he is a Math problem she can't solve.

"I'm sure that he has a whole book in his head. Why..." Miss Perkins begins to brag about Sam.

"Has this boy's I.Q. ever been tested?" Mrs. Martin interrupts.

"I don't know that we need to, ma'am," Miss Perkins disagrees. "Sam's smart. I tell him something once; he remembers. He knows so much. He just doesn't know how to communicate all that he knows."

Mrs. Martin takes a deep breath. "Miss Perkins, I can see that I need to spend a little time with Sam after school each day. I'll ask my babysitter if she can stay later."

"That's a jolly good idea," Miss Perkins says. "He'd like that. It would mean a lot to both of us, ma'am."

"Will you talk to me again after school tomorrow?" Mrs. Martin asks.

Sam eagerly looks up. He would love to.

"He's saying yes," Miss Perkins interprets.

"I know what he's saying," Mrs. Martin says brusquely. "Ann, you may go now. Thank you for your help."

Before Ann can leave, Sam begins pointing at some letters on his alphabet.

Sam's finger moves so fast that Ann has to borrow Miss Perkins' pencil again. Ann looks down and reads her notes, "Same time. Same place." She smiles at Sam. "You're funny!"

"You, Ann, are beginning to appreciate my dear Sam." Miss Perkins directs her words to Ann, but she keeps her gaze fixed on

Mrs. Martin.

"You've made your point, Miss Perkins," Mrs. Martin says quietly. "I'm excited. I think Sam's going to be a good student."

Somehow, Sam finds the energy to grin at his teacher.

Chapter Sixteen

Sam and Miss Perkins roll home after another day of school. The bumps and jolts of the field which had seemed dangerous at first have become easy, leaving Sam's mind free to review the day. He had a good conversation with Mrs. Martin. He got to spend recess parked next to the basketball court. Ann promised him that she would push him outside tomorrow. Although the air is crisp, the sun is shining. The leaves are starting to turn red and gold; and the wind is rushing through Sam's hair.

Until he sees Mr. Crowe, Sam's thinking that October 14, 1968, is one of the greatest days of his life.

When their landlord wants to talk to them, his mother is either behind in her rent or Sam has been too noisy. The sight of Mr. Crowe waiting for them is always bad news. Today, as Mr. Crowe watches their progress across the field, he shades his eyes from the sun. He is a skinny man with a face pocked like a moon. He wears a black suit, with a dark tie and a white shirt with a crumpled collar.

Miss Perkins reaches him. "Hello, Mr. Crowe. Beautiful day, isn't it?" she says.

Sam is not fooled by her forced cheerfulness.

Mr. Crowe wags his long finger at them. "I've gone to your apartment several times. Where have you been?"

"Sam is going to school," Miss Perkins brags. "He's in the sixth grade."

Sam's grin bursts out, but his landlord ignores him.

"I have a letter for Mrs. Davis," Mr. Crowe says.

"What is it, Mr. Crowe? A love note?" Although Miss Perkins laughs, Mr. Crowe's disapproving expression doesn't change.

The stern expression on the man's face tells Sam that Mr. Crowe is aware of every spit bubble that Sam has ever blown in his whole life. Every tantrum that he has thrown. Every mean thought that he has had.

So Sam is not surprised when the white envelope that Mr. Crowe pulls out of his pocket has 'Davis' written on it in block letters.

The letter is about me, he thinks.

Although Miss Perkins' hands are always helpful, Sam notices that they don't reach for the note.

"This is a legal matter," Mr. Crowe warns.

Reluctantly, Miss Perkins accepts the envelope. "I'll give it to Mrs. Davis."

Mr. Crowe nods and starts heading to his car. It's the dark Oldsmobile parked in the almost empty parking lot.

In jumbled order, Sam remembers his last noisy tantrum, the shouts of his neighbors, and his mother's new silver dress. He remembers his mother's expression and imagines her thinking, "You are going to ruin me!"

His stomach feels as though he just took a big swig of sour milk.

They start to cross the parking lot. "Let's just hope that your mother paid her rent on time this month. If not..." Sam's worry blocks out the meaning but not the rhythm of Miss Perkins' words.

As they wait for the elevator, Miss Perkins grows quiet. Finally, in her normal cheerful tone, she adds, " Well, we won't think about Mr. Crowe. Another good day at school. We did it, Sam. Mrs. Martin likes you."

Inside the apartment, Miss Perkins sets the envelope on the

kitchen counter where his mother can't miss it.

"Window or T.V.?" Miss Perkins asks.

Now that Sam has watched a basketball practice from the sidelines, he is even more impatient than usual for Charlie and the team to appear on the court.

"WWindow," Sam chooses.

Miss Perkins parks Sam at the window.

Since Sam can't turn his neck, he always has the nagging feeling that something important lies just beyond the range of his vision. Even if a letter from his cousins lay on the kitchen counter, he couldn't swivel around to see it. Tonight, he's glad that the kitchen counter is as inaccessible to him as China.

Miss Perkins kisses him on the head and then hurries off.

As soon as she leaves, Sam remembers that since the Tomcats have a game at another school, they're unlikely to practice. So on a day when Sam really needs to be distracted, the court remains just a gray stretch of lined concrete.

Although he has no right to hope, his heart jumps when Charlie and Bobby approach the court. They set their schoolbooks down under the light post and start shooting. Bobby stands underneath the basket, and Charlie passes him the ball. Bobby shoots a layup. Sam tries not to grow too excited. They're probably just warming up before the game.

Sure enough, a few minutes later, A.J. yells to the boys, "Let's go!" Although Bobby stoops and picks up his books, Charlie doesn't. They both run after A.J.

Sam is worried for Charlie. Did he forget his books on the court? If they're still there in the morning, Sam will tell Miss Perkins.

Another older team wanders out and begins practicing. Sadly, Sam realizes that watching nameless kids is no longer satisfying. But what can he do? He doesn't want to listen to the radio or watch television. After the excitement of the last few weeks, his old routine is beginning to bore him.

For homework, Sam repeats a list of prepositions. Mrs. Martin wants the class to memorize them in an exact order. 'To From Under Down.' *Is 'Under' supposed to be before or after 'Down'?* he had wanted to ask. *Why does the order matter? For that matter, why is grammar important?* Mrs. Martin must have explained these mysteries to the class in September before Sam started school.

Oh, no, school is often pointless, Winnie pipes up. Now that Sam goes to school, Winnie usually waits until nighttime to speak. *I remember my first disastrous Latin lesson too well. My teacher wanted me to memorize the Latin word for 'O, table.'*

Although Sam isn't in the mood for this story, he lets Winnie drone on.

'What does 'O table' mean?' [11†] *I asked.*

'O table,' my teacher explained. You would use that in addressing a table. And then seeing that he was not carrying me with him, he added: you would use that in speaking to a table. But I never do, I blurted out in honest amazement.

If you are impertinent, you will be punished severely, my teacher said.

I don't care about your awful teachers, Winnie, Sam interrupts. *I like my school.* In order to drown Winnie out, he repeats to himself the list of prepositions: *to, from, down, under..."*

You are a better student than I was, Winnie says. *Where my reason, imagination or interest were not engaged, I would not or I could not learn.* [12†]

Despite himself, Sam is touched. He is a better student than one of the greatest men who's ever lived. *Thanks, Winnie.*

It's true, Sam. In all the twelve years I was at school no one succeeded in making me write a Latin verse or learn any Greek except the alphabet.

Sam doesn't want to admit his lack of enthusiasm to Winnie. But

† Reprinted with permission of Scribner, an imprint of Simon & Schuster Adult Publishing Group, from MY EARLY LIFE: A ROVING COMMISSION by Winston Churchill. Copyright© 1930 by Charles Scribner's Sons; copyright renewed© 1958 by Winston Churchill. All rights reserved.

the truth is that he is tiring of his grammar lessons. To keep his mind occupied, he plays Tic-Tac-Toe in his head. Then, he plays another game with himself. He thinks of an important moment in Winnie's life and recites a speech or a remark that goes with it. When he was thirty-two and couldn't find a wife, Winnie was trying to impress a lady, and he said, *We're all worms, but I do believe I am a glowworm.*[13] When the war was still going badly for England, Winnie said: *This is the lesson: never give in. Never, never, never, never...*[14] Sam thinks about how much he hates Adolf Hitler. About the millions of people who the dictator trapped and killed. And how glad he is that the Allies won. He thinks about anything that takes his attention away from Mr. Crowe's envelope.

The last rays of twilight have disappeared, and the crooked lamp lights an empty circle around the basketball hoop. When the smell of meatloaf fills the apartment, he hears a key in the lock.

His mother walks straight to Sam and kisses him on the top of his head. "Good to see you, son. I bet you had another good day at school." When she starts towards her bedroom, Miss Perkins says, "Mr. Crowe wrote you a letter."

"Please, no problems," his mother mumbles. "I've had a rough week."

"Yes, ma'am," Miss Perkins says.

Yet, her high heels hesitate for only an instant before they tap their way directly to the kitchen counter.

The paper rips as she tears the envelope. Sam tries to decipher the letter's contents from the rhythm of his mother's walk, but her sharp steps to the bedroom aren't fast or slow, soft or loud. They're ordinary. Later, when his mother sinks onto the couch, he uses his keenest hearing, but his mother doesn't ask Miss Perkins about their day. Miss Perkins doesn't tell his mother about Mrs. Martin's class. His mother doesn't say, "I'm tired."

It's as if none of the three of them can talk.

"I have dinner ready," Miss Perkins says, breaking the silence.

"I'm not hungry," his mother answers.

"Oh, Mrs. Davis," Miss Perkins pleads. "Things can't be so bad that you can't eat."

What things are you talking about? Sam wants to ask them. *Do the things have to do with Mr. Crowe?* Miss Perkins and Mrs. Martin don't feel the need to share their adult lives with him. It's frustrating to catch only bits and pieces of meaning from overheard conversations. To stare out of a window at an empty basketball court.

Miss Perkins sets his mother's plate on the table. "Let me know when you've tried the meatloaf, Mrs. Davis," she calls to her. "I cooked my mother's recipe."

Eventually, his mother wanders over to the table. Her chair scrapes the floor as she pushes it back. "It looks delicious," she says.

Sam waits but he doesn't hear the ice tinkling in her glass or the silverware clanking against her plate. Against this background of unnatural quiet, Miss Perkins arrives with dinner. As she feeds Sam ground-up meatloaf, mashed carrots and milk-soaked bread, he counts the stars.

"Good," Sam says. He means the meatloaf is good. Miss Perkins is good. Everything would be good, if Mr. Crowe's threat weren't playing over and over in his head like a broken record. *A legal matter.*

Sam's counted 147 stars when Miss Perkins asks: "Are you ready to go to your room?"

Sam starts to look up to say 'yes,' but he notices a moving shadow on the court. At first, he thinks it's a big dog, but when the figure steps nearer the light, he sees that the hopping, weaving and jumping shape is Mickey. "OOpen wwindow?" he asks.

"It may be a little cool," Miss Perkins comments. But she cranks the window open and lets Sam keep watching.

Mickey Kotov is alone. He balances the ball on his right hand and steadies it with his left. Unlike in the classroom, Mickey looks at home on the court.

When Mickey shoots, Sam listens to the sweet sound of the ball slicing cleanly through the hoop and thumping on the concrete. One. Two. Three hoops.

Unexpectedly, another shadow bobs and weaves onto the court. The next moment, Sam makes out the tall captain of Stirling's basketball team. He's standing underneath the crooked light post. Charlie Simmons is never on the court this late at night. Then, Sam remembers Charlie's forgotten books. He must have come back for them.

Although Sam has never seen Charlie try to trip Mickey or heard Charlie call Mickey a 'foreigner,' he's not surprised when Mickey ignores Charlie and keeps playing basketball alone.

Sam scoots to the edge of the wheelchair. Now, Charlie will see for himself that Mickey is a great basketball player. For a few minutes, Mickey hits baskets as if he were a scoring machine. Five. Six. Seven. Eight. *Yeah, Mickey*, Sam cheers him on.

Charlie approaches, and soon Charlie and Mickey are standing together underneath the basket. One figure is tall; the other short and slight. Sam can see their mouths moving, but until they begin raising their voices, he can't make out their words.

"I didn't mean it that way," Charlie calls out.

Mickey backs away. "Oh, yeah, well, you have a terrivle team!" he shouts.

"Well, we wouldn't let you play anyway," Charlie answers. He picks up his books.

"Vecause I'm Russian, right? Vecause I have an accent. And vecause on the first day of skool, I didn't know to put me hand over me heart for your stupid pledge."

"You said those things. I didn't," Charlie shouts before turning his back on Mickey.

No. Don't go, Charlie, Sam wants to cry out. *Mickey's just the player you need.* But Sam's dreams can't stop Charlie from fading away into the darkness.

Mickey tries for a few more baskets. Unusual for him, every single one pings the bent rim. He bangs the ball down hard on the court before he runs away.

Chapter Seventeen

After Miss Perkins has tucked Sam into bed, through the thin walls, he hears voices.

His mother moans. "Crowe has evicted us from the apartment."

What? Mr. Crowe can't kick them out. Apartment 207 is Sam's home. But deep down Sam understands that Mr. Crowe can. It's just that the threat has hung over his head for so long that it has stopped seeming real.

"Mrs. Davis, I told you that you needed to start paying your rent on time," Miss Perkins scolds her. "Still, Mr. Crowe has no business kicking a boy like Sam out of his home. Tomorrow, I'll give that fellow a piece of my mind."

"It's no use. He's never sent me an official letter before," his mother's voice sounds hopeless. "We're going to end up living on the street just like Ronald predicted."

Sam's heart fills with dread as though he's in a hole in the ground and earth is tumbling in on top of him. How can he live without a home? Without his spot by the window?

"Now, now, Mrs. Davis. Don't worry."

If Sam weren't feeling so low, he would smile. Miss Perkins is trying to soothe his mother just like she calms Sam.

"Mr. Crowe's letter says that if we move out by the end of next week, he won't sue me for all the back rent that I owe," his mother says.

"We'll figure something out. We always do," Miss Perkins says.

"Just when I was beginning to hope that I might be able to start a new life," his mother cries.

"There. There," Miss Perkins says.

"It's not you who'll have to live on the street with a handicapped child!" his mother snaps.

Their voices are softer now and not even Sam's great ears can make out the words.

A few minutes later, the front door closes. He can hear his mother's footsteps heading towards her bedroom. He longs to feel his mother's soft touch, but remembering how upset she sounded, he has little hope that she will tell him goodnight.

Sam's fear grows to fill the silence. Because of his endless hours spent lying on his back, he has identified a world on his bedroom ceiling: three continents, fourteen rivers and twenty-two islands. He has memorized every detail of the view from his window: the number of doors leading to Stirling Junior High, the shapes of the oak trees on the lot, the exact bend in the crooked light post. The Tomcats, his special team—he knows every player's name—practice on the court below.

Apartment 207 is the only home that he has ever known.

Sam thinks of someone else who was afraid that she was going to lose her home. Miss Perkins. He wishes that she were with him now.

In her lecture, if Mrs. Martin hadn't skipped over the Battle of Britain, she would have told the class that during the winter of 1940, Hitler had relentlessly bombed London and other parts of England. About forty-five thousand civilians died, including some people who Miss Perkins knew. Although Miss Perkins refuses to name these people or even talk about them, Sam feels their presence with him tonight. He's imagining the loneliness and terror of Winnie and Miss Perkins, the survivors. Night after night, they lay in their beds wondering when the next bomb was going to explode. Would their house be a target? Would they be alive in the morning?

The Battle of Britain is the occasion for one of Sam's favorite speeches. He has asked Miss Perkins to read it to him again and again. Just hearing Winnie's words makes him feel brave.

In his head, Sam starts reciting the speech, *We shall fight on the beaches, we shall fight on the landing grounds, we shall fight in the fields and in the streets, we shall fight in the hills; we shall never surrender.*[15]

When the old ladies at church call Sam a 'brave boy,' their flattery makes him angry. He has never respected the sitting-in-the-wheelchair type of bravery. He admires the World War II type of bravery: firing guns, dodging bombs, making great speeches, standing up to an evil man like Hitler. Yet, tonight, he decides that even though he's just lying in bed, bravery is what he needs most.

What will the world feel like without his home? A trap that is cold, dark, and lonely. Like that winter in London.

I won't leave. I don't want to go, Sam thinks. The shadow from his bureau falls onto his bed, and Sam pretends that it's Mr. Crowe. *Take that.* He punches Mr. Crowe with loose fists. The bed sheets are twisted, and his blue blanket has fallen onto the floor. Lying there without covers, his hands and feet are freezing but he reminds himself: during the Battle of Britain, Winnie and Miss Perkins slept despite the bombs exploding and the shells whistling in the night.

Sam wraps their bravery around him like a blanket so that he, too, can sleep now.

We shall fight on the beaches, we shall fight...

*   *   *

After leaving the apartment, Miss Perkins hurries down the aisle at Corner Market. She eats most of her meals at Mrs. Davis', but she likes to keep tea, biscuits, cream, and a few other items in her cupboard. She looks forward to her late-night snacks. A cup of tea takes the ache right out of her feet. It's her miracle drug.

She is selecting a box of biscuits from the shelf when a snippet of conversation startles her.

"Can you imagine? A disabled student at Stirling?" a woman's shrill voice says.

"We pay taxes. That's not fair to the rest of the kids," a man's voice answers.

"That's what our P.T.A. president says," the woman replies.

Miss Perkins drops the box of biscuits into her basket and hurries to catch a glimpse of these obnoxious people.

At nine o'clock, Corner Market has only one clerk, and the checkout line has backed up into the aisle. She nearly bumps into a man with a limp. His Asian wife is selecting a jar of pickles. Nearby, a man with a gray mustache is smoking a pipe. The woman next to him is flipping through a knitting magazine. Miss Perkins isn't sure which of the couples were guilty of the offensive conversation. So she glares at each of them.

Imagine the nerve, Miss Perkins thinks as she trudges home with her grocery sack in her arms. The nerve of Mrs. Riley. The nerve of whoever it was in the grocery store. She suspects the woman with the knitting magazine and her mustached husband.

And on top of everything else, Mr. Crowe. Their heartless landlord is evicting the Davises. It's as if the whole world is turning against Sam. Except for me, Miss Perkins sighs wearily.

How fast will Mr. Crowe act, Miss Perkins wonders? Could Mrs. Davis really have to move as soon as next week? Sam loves his apartment. He loves his window. What are we going to do? Miss Perkins thinks as panic rises in her throat. Despite the cold night, her anger makes her feel hot.

But as she waits at the corner for the light to change, Miss Perkins remembers a sign that she used to pass on her way to work during the war. A golden crown drawn on top represented the King. The text was simple but powerful:

"Stay calm and carry on."

That's what she did during the war. That's what real Londoners do. Muddle through. By the time the light has changed, her breathing has slowed. A nice cup of tea. With a biscuit. She'll feel better after she's drunk her cup of tea.

Chapter Eighteen

The next morning when the bell sounds for recess, Ann rushes to Sam. She helps him unfold his plastic tray and sets some note cards on it.

"I made these for you," she offers and starts turning them over.

"Charlie, Bobby, Jonathan, Ben, Daisy, Betty, Nancy, A.J., Tom, Celia, Larry, Jan, Kent, Hanna, Marigold, Jack, Katy…" she reads, her words tripping over each other in excitement. "I made one for Mickey, too, even though no one ever talks to him."

"Thhanks," is all Sam says, but he wants to tell Ann, *People don't talk about Mickey because they don't know him. If they knew him, they would be saying what a good basketball player he is.*

Ann turns over a "hello," "what's your favorite song?" and "a thank you" card. She grins at him.

"Thhanks," Sam says.

The next card reads, "Tomcats Score!"

"Thhanks." Sam smiles. He can't wait to show this card to Charlie Simmons.

"These are lovely, lovely cards, Ann," Miss Perkins says.

Ann turns over the last card. It says, "Goodbye." Underneath in smaller letters, she has written, "I will miss you."

Miss Perkins looks at her, puzzled. "We're not going anywhere, Ann."

"My mother said…" Ann begins, and her face grows as red as her favorite dress.

"Hum," Miss Perkins says. She picks up the goodbye card.

Sam is barely listening. The two of them need to stop talking. They are wasting his recess time. Impatiently, he points at the card that says, "Tomcats Score!"

"Sam wants to go to the playground," Ann says.

"What?" Miss Perkins seems lost in thought.

Ann repeats herself.

"Well, what are we waiting for?"

Sam points at the "thank you" card but he can't help wishing that Ann had made more cards. He'd love to have one that said, "Hurry up!" Or "It's about time." Or for use when Miss Perkins is particularly long-winded: "SHUT UP."

Ann slips on her coat. It's blue with white buttons.

"I'm ready," she says.

Thoughtfully, Miss Perkins places the goodbye card onto the tray.

Chapter Nineteen

The stars are out tonight, Sam thinks as he stares out his small bedroom window.

"Did your mother tell you that she was going to be late?" Miss Perkins puts her arms around his waist and helps him scoot to the edge of his chair. She pulls at his pants, and he wiggles out of them. It sounds complicated, but it's like a basketball play. Miss Perkins knows her part, and he knows his. One hip at a time. He focuses on his right side. Then his left side. Then he does it again.

"NNNo," Sam says.

Miss Perkins pops a nightshirt over Sam's head. Sam holds his arms sideways for only a few seconds before they begin trembling. "Sometimes, your mother overreacts to life's problems. I wonder what she's planning? But why am I thinking out loud? I guess it's because like my dear late mother used to say, my brains are in my mouth. But you shouldn't worry. No matter what. Everything will be all right."

Sam slides out of the wheelchair.

As she always does, Miss Perkins grabs his elbow. "Be careful now. You have enough problems without a broken leg."

Sam walks/hops the step and a half to the bed. It is covered in a blue blanket. He leans his back against the mattress.

Miss Perkins takes a deep breath. She wraps her strong arms

around his legs.

Sam helps her by scooting his trunk as far as he can onto the bed. His legs bounce when she drops them.

"There you go, sweetie." She pulls the sheet and blanket up to his chin. "Now, goodnight. If I'm here late again, I might as well get a little extra work done."

Sam's eyes turn in the direction of the well-worn book on the bedside table, but Miss Perkins doesn't reach for it.

"Sam, hon, I'm sorry. Your mother has been going out so much lately that I have piles of laundry. Besides, you know all the stories. Why don't you tell yourself the one about Winston's escape from prison in South Africa?"

Sam looks up. He understands. He doesn't want his mother to get angry at Miss Perkins for getting behind in her chores.

"And be sure to say your prayers. We've got plenty to be thankful for," Miss Perkins finishes.

"NNight,"

"Goodnight, luv," she answers as she turns off the light. "I'll be in the apartment until your mother gets home."

Sam prays his standard prayer, always something along the lines of "If I am to be as I am, if that's your plan, please make me all I can be." Afterwards, he is content to listen to the lullaby of apartment sounds: Old Mrs. Crowe's television next door, a dog barking in the parking lot, the traffic on Elm Street. Soon, the swoosh and hiss of the iron begin.

Like Miss Perkins, Sam wonders where his mother is tonight.

Finally, he reaches the point where he decides, what else do I have to do but to take Miss Perkins' suggestion and tell myself a story?

Miss Perkins had mentioned the prison story, one of Sam's favorites. Why not? Sam thinks. Even though it's a true story, he begins, Once upon a time….

Long before World War II, even before World War I, England fought a war against a group of Dutch farmers called the Boers. Both groups hoped to control South Africa.

During the War, the Boers captured Winnie and imprisoned him. Although Winnie managed to escape, he was still in great danger. Unless Winnie made it back to British territory, he would be hanged. To accomplish this feat, he had to cross three hundred unfriendly miles without getting recaptured by the enemy.

Pursuit would be immediate, Winnie reminds Sam. *Yet all exits were barred. The town was picketed. The country was patrolled, the trains were searched, and the line was guarded. Worst of all, I could not speak a word of Dutch or Kaffir, and how was I to get food or direction?*[16†]

You hitched a train, Sam reminds him. The future Prime Minister of England spent the night buried under a stack of empty coal bags. At daybreak, Winnie jumped off.

I was sprawling in the ditch considerably shaken, but unhurt, Winnie says. *I had one consolation: no one in the world knew where I was, I did not know myself.*

Sam can't remember the name of the village that Winnie stumbled upon. He just knows that Winnie picked a random house and knocked.

A man holding a revolver opened the door. "What do you want?" he asked in a foreign language.

I'm Winston Churchill, Winnie said. *I'm making my way to the frontier. Will you help me?"*

For a long time, the man didn't answer. Eventually, the man motioned Winnie inside and closed the door behind them. Then, he thrust out his hand to Winnie and blurted: *"Thank God you have come here! It is the only house for 20 miles where you would not have been handed over. But we are all British here and will see you through."*

"I wonder where Mrs. Davis is?" Miss Perkins thinks as she sits at the breakfast table covered with a lacy tablecloth, too fancy for her taste. But Mrs. Davis likes what she calls her "small luxuries." In Miss Perkins' own apartment, the table is covered in a cheerful but practical red and white cloth. In the center, she's arranged her salt and pepper shaker collection: Dalmatian dogs wearing sunglasses, alligators with holes in their long, green tails, Mary Poppins holding her umbrella...And of course, Winston Churchill. The salt pours out of his top hat. All the figures—many made out of porcelain—are breakable.

Miss Perkins started the fragile collection after the war to show that she had faith in peace. It was her way of proving that she would never again live in a country where bombs rained down on innocent people's heads. Where children could be playing one minute and trapped by wreckage the next.

She'll never forget the sights that she saw during the war, but there's one particular memory that haunts her. She was living with her parents and working as an aide at a hospital around the corner. Her parents had the deepest, darkest, blackest basement on their block, and when the air raid signal sounded, from two to five families usually hid there and listened for the vicious hiss of the aircraft flying low, then for the first bomb to fall, then for the last of the group. Finally, they waited for the hiss to start again. They had to drink cold water rather than hot tea. "What Hitler makes you put up with," they liked to grumble. To help the young ones with their jitters, the adults counted potatoes. Emily, their next-door neighbor, was only twelve years old. She was a lively girl with dark eyes who wanted to become a doctor. Sometimes, the group would count up to one thousand potatoes and still, the bombs kept falling.

The basement was cold and dark. Miss Perkins has never experienced darkness like that before or since. Her father claimed that hiding in their shelter was like being cooped up in a submarine. They were so crowded that she couldn't move without stepping on someone else. They squatted or sat, listening to the bombs and their own breathing until—after they had given up all hope—the All Clear sounded. How frightened they were on their hike up the stairs without any light. Had their house been hit? Where would they go then? How would they live?

She hated the basement, hated feeling trapped, and always considered pretending that she didn't hear the air raid signals until one day, the siren didn't go off. Without warning, she heard a bomb exploding. Home was only a few blocks away, and she began running.

Gray rubble was all that was left of her neighbor's house. At first, she couldn't make out the objects jumbled in with the mess. Onions and potatoes. They all had gardens, *Dig for victory.* The next memory is so vivid that Miss Perkins drops her head into her hands. Where once a sturdy brownstone had stood, only a crater and a mountain of debris remained. In the corner, Miss Perkins spotted Emily trapped in big hunks of concrete, her body twisted, her head hanging loose. Emily's eyes were open, and she was staring straight ahead at a future that was no longer hers.

Strangely on that terrible day, her parents' house was untouched. A gray brick miracle. When she walked up the back steps and opened the door, she found that someone had left the radio on, a bit of normalcy in the midst of the wreckage. As her family and neighbors gathered in the kitchen, bewildered and frightened, they heard Winston Churchill's voice: *We shall fight on the beaches, we shall fight on the landing grounds, we shall fight in the fields and in the streets, we shall fight in the hills; we shall never surrender.*[17] Miss Perkins has never told Sam about Emily; she's kept her secret all these years. Instead, she's poured all the ferocity of this memory into the love of Winston that she passes to Sam. *We shall never surrender.*[18]

When Miss Perkins takes her head out of her hands and looks up, she sees the frilly white tablecloth covering Mrs. Davis' table.

It's already been nine years since she answered Mrs. Davis' ad. When she walked into this room for the first time, Sam was facing her. His skin was pale, as if he never got out in the sun. His body was twisted in an uncomfortable angle and drool fell from his mouth.

Mrs. Davis was saying, "My son is very smart."

When Miss Perkins met the boy's gaze, he had smiled. All his features glowed, and she forgot his crooked body.

"Hello, Sam," she said.

"He doesn't like to talk to people who he doesn't know," Mrs. Davis said. "He's got cerebral palsy…."

The smile slid off the boy's face, and he stared off in the distance. Miss Perkins had remembered her last view of Emily, trapped in the concrete.

$$* \qquad * \qquad *$$

Sam hears the low murmur of voices in the entranceway. At last! His mother has returned. He waits anxiously for her to say goodnight to Miss Perkins. *What is taking you so long?* he wants to shout.

Finally, outside of Sam's room, the floor creaks. His mother's coming. She's nearer. He holds his smile ready, but something goes wrong.

Instead of stopping at his bedroom, her high heels pass his door and head straight for her own room. The spray of a shower, and then the slam of a drawer are the only sounds that Sam hears.

Distraught, Sam craves movement. He pretends to go outside to the rutted field. He lifts his right foot high and takes a step. Then, his left. After he's warmed up, he pushes himself to begin running. Finally, he wills his arms to pump at the same time. After so many fast laps that he can't count them all, he has to stop. He gasps for breath. Or maybe, he yawns.

Sam's pillow is soft. His blue blanket is warm and shimmers with moonlight. He yawns again.

He hears his mother's mattress groan.

"MMom! MMom!" he yells to greet her.

"Sam, hush," she shouts from the other side of the wall. "I can't stand another scene tonight."

This isn't a scene, he wants to explain. *I love you, Mom.* But he knows that he will have to shout for her to hear him, and he doubts whether she will understand.

Sam hears a jagged noise. Could his dainty mother be snoring? But in the next moment, he identifies the sound. His mother is crying.

He wants so much to be with her, but with the wall separating them, she might as well be sobbing on the moon. He inches his body close to the wall. But what to do with his thoughts? How to block out the crying? He holds his breath until Winnie's voice fills his mind, drowning out his mother's sobs, the hum of the refrigerator in the kitchen, everything.

In his escape from the Boers, Winnie had stumbled upon the only Englishman within twenty miles. His good luck had kept him from being hanged.

I felt like I had a purpose, so I never believed that I would go before my time, Winnie explains.

You've said this before, Winnie, but it doesn't help me because I don't have a purpose.

Oh, but you do, Winnie disagrees.

What?

Right now, you need to get Mickey Kotov on that basketball team,
Winnie reminds him.

Chapter Twenty

In the morning, Miss Perkins lets herself into Mrs. Davis' apartment.

Unusual for the hour, Mrs. Davis is awake and standing in the small kitchen. The blue and white speckled coffee pot is already on the stove.

Mrs. Davis turns toward Miss Perkins. Her eyes are red-rimmed. She has slept on her normally stylish hair, leaving it flat on one side and puffy on the other. Without makeup, her face is pale. At the sight of her employer so disheveled, Miss Perkins' heart rises up and flutters against her rib cage. "What's the matter? Is Sam all right?" she asks breathlessly.

"Sam," Mrs. Davis emphasizes her son's name, "is fine."

Even though she doesn't remember seeing Mrs. Davis shoeless before, Miss Perkins is not surprised that her employer's toes are neatly manicured with bright coral polish. "Well, what is it?" she pleads.

Mrs. Davis looks over Miss Perkins' shoulder. Her eyes seem to be searching a distant horizon. "I stayed up all night thinking. The way I see it, I don't have a choice." She begins talking faster. "I can stay with Celeste until I save enough money to rent another apartment. Of course, I can't take Sam."

"What do you mean?" Miss Perkins objects.

"Ever since he was born, everyone—my pediatrician, my husband, my neighbors, my coworkers— has advised me to send Sam away." Mrs. Davis' pale lips tremble as if she's about to cry.

"Send him away!" Miss Perkins exclaims.

"That's right," Mrs. Davis nods. "There are special places for handicapped children."

"What kind of places?" Miss Perkins asks, even though she knows that she will hate Mrs. Davis' answer.

Mrs. Davis takes a deep breath and seems to regain her composure. "My friend, Mr. Jordache, knows someone on the board of the Mannville Institution for Boys. He's offered to make arrangements for Sam to be admitted. I checked with the firm's insurance. They'll pay most of the cost."

"What!" Miss Perkins hears herself cry out.

Mrs. Davis puts a finger to her lips. "Hush. Or you'll wake him."

An institution! Miss Perkins can't take her eyes off this stranger with her white silk robe tied in a lopsided bow around her tiny waist.

"Mr. Crowe's eviction notice is the last straw for me. I can't afford to pay the deposit on a new apartment." Mrs. Davis' eyes are begging Miss Perkins now. Her fingers nervously tap the kitchen counter.

Miss Perkins can't help it. She feels her expression harden into one of steely disapproval.

"It will only be until I can get back on my feet." Mrs. Davis twists the cord on her robe. "I hate this as much as you do. But I don't see any other way."

"Let me take him, ma'am," Miss Perkins begs. "He can come to live with me. My apartment is poor, but we would be happy."

"And what would Mr. Jordache say if he found out that my son was living with my housekeeper?" Mrs. Davis shakes her head.

I could get a better job. I would have left a long time ago if it weren't for Sam, Miss Perkins wants to tell her. But she manages to stay silent.

"Mannville Institution is a reputable place. I'm going to ask Mr. Jordache to make the arrangements today," Mrs. Davis says.

"With due respect, I have to disagree, Mrs. Davis. A boy like Sam needs a home. Needs love. Why I..."

Mrs. Davis cuts her off. "I won't have you implying that I'm not a good mother!" Tears well up in her eyes. "I'm doing this for Sam. So that someday we may be able to have a home together again."

You, Sam and this Mr. Jordache—whoever he is? Miss Perkins thinks suspiciously. "When do you want the boy to leave?" she asks.

"As soon as possible," Mrs. Davis answers.

"When are you going to tell Sam?" Miss Perkins asks.

"I've thought about that," Mrs. Davis responds. "I don't want to talk to Sam until the morning he leaves." Her thin shoulders shudder.

Miss Perkins knows that Mrs. Davis is imagining the tantrum that Sam will throw when he learns about her plans. For once, she won't scold the poor boy. "Have you seen the place?"

"The Mannville Institution?" Mrs. Davis asks indignantly.

Miss Perkins nods. What else would she be talking about?

"Our pediatrician has told me all about it. Why he says..." Mrs. Davis' voice falters.

"You haven't seen Mannville?" Miss Perkins insists.

"You and I can go with Sam when he's admitted. I don't need to visit the place beforehand." She smooths back a lock of her hair. Then, she adds in a softer voice, "Miss Perkins, I told you. I stayed up all night thinking about this. I don't have any other choice. If all goes well, he will only have to stay there a few months. ..."

Miss Perkins works to keep her face calm.

"Now excuse me, but I can't be late." Mrs. Davis turns around and heads to her bedroom.

"What am I to do today?" Miss Perkins asks curtly.

"Go to school. Act normal," Mrs. Davis calls from behind the closed door.

"Act normal?" Miss Perkins shouts. She picks up the frying pan, and her grip doesn't slip; she purposefully bangs it down on the counter.

Mrs. Davis sticks her head out. "Stop your temper tantrum. You're going to wake Sam." She slams the door so hard that the windows rattle.

"PPerkins," Sam calls. "MMiss PPerkins."

It makes Miss Perkins angrier that she can't blame Mrs. Davis for waking the boy. Both of them are guilty. She opens his bedroom door and sticks her head in. "Just a minute, dear." She tries to control the trembles that she hears in her voice. "I'll be right back after I cook your oatmeal." But as she fills the pot with water, her mind is occupied with plans of rebellion. She'll have to find some way to visit this Mannville Institution for Boys. She'll tell Sam that her rheumatism has been acting up and that she has a doctor appointment. If she has to, she'll ask Mrs. Martin if she can leave Sam alone at school this morning. Ann will be happy to push his chair to recess.

She has her morning laid out, but if the Mannville Institution is the prison that she expects it to be, what will she do then?

Fifty-six-year-old Abigail Perkins, who has never even had a traffic ticket, will have to become a kidnapper.

Chapter Twenty-One

Sam watches the clock over the blackboard. Although the bell for recess rang a few minutes ago, Mrs. Martin still hasn't stopped talking.

"Finally, our school is participating in the League of Women Voters history contest."

Mrs. Martin continues. "Each student will submit an essay on 'My World War II Hero.' The winner gets a nice prize and a trip to Washington, D.C. Wouldn't it be great if someone in this class won?"

World War II. Sam sneaks a look around the classroom. Charlie has a bored expression on his face. He bets that he knows more than Charlie or anyone else in the entire classroom about World War II. He would love to enter the contest, but now that they are attending school, Miss Perkins is so busy. He knows that she won't have time to help him.

"Your essay will count as a test grade and will conclude our unit on World War II. Any questions?" Mrs. Martin says.

How long does the essay have to be? Sam wants to ask.

When no one raises a hand, Mrs. Martin sighs. "Dismissed."

The class stands and rushes out the door.

"Hey, Sam," Ann says. She is wearing a gray and blue sweater over a gray dress.

Sam smiles a big smile. "AAAnn," he answers.

"Ann, could you take good care of Sam during recess?" Miss

Perkins says. "I've got… to….go to the doctor's. I'll be back by…. lunch. Mrs. Martin…. has agreed to look after Sam."

"Yes, ma'am," Ann says. "Are you feeling O.K., Miss Perkins?"

"What?" Miss Perkins asks. Without waiting for an answer, she mutters, "My rheumatism…" In a bustle of activity, she slips on Sam's coat and checks his seat belt. She collects her purse and starts toward the door. "Thank you so much, dearie," she calls to Ann on her way out.

As Sam and Ann start for the playground, Mrs. Martin looks up. "Ann? I need to talk to Sam," Mrs. Martin says.

Ann pushes Sam over to Mrs. Martin's desk. The surface is clear except for her grade book and an empty rose vase.

"Sam, would you like me to help you submit an essay for the League of Women Voters Contest?" Mrs. Martin asks. She takes off her glasses and begins polishing the lenses.

"YYYes," Sam crows.

"All right," Mrs. Martin says.

Without the glasses, Mrs. Martin's face is more open, and Sam can see her brown eyes without the frame's black bars. He thinks that his teacher actually looks pretty.

"We'll start this afternoon," Mrs. Martin smiles.

As Ann pushes Sam to the basketball court, the autumn leaves gust around them. The October day is cold, and Ann's brown coat is buttoned to the top. But Sam doesn't want to bother Ann by asking her to get out his blanket. When they pass the empty tetherball court, Sam realizes that Mickey still hasn't shown up for class this morning.

Ann puts the chair in park and whispers, "I'll be back." He watches her run down the path towards Marigold.

"O.K. team. Let's go!" Charlie shouts. "We've got another game today. Another chance for an upset victory."

Charlie misses a rebound.

As the basketball rolls off the court, Sam thinks, *come towards me.* The ball zigzags for a bit but, just as he had hoped, it stops next to his chair. He stretches his foot out to touch it. As the tip of his shoe rests for a brief moment on the ball, Sam thinks, anything is possible.

Charlie reaches down to pick it up. To get Charlie's attention, Sam grunts. Holding the ball in his hand, Charlie's eyes meet Sam's for an instant. They match his reddish-brown freckles.

Sam is too cold to trust his tongue to talk, but the cards Ann made for him are laid out on his tray. With his finger, Sam taps, "Tomcats Score!"

Charlie wipes his dripping nose with his sleeve and smiles. When he says, "Thanks," his breath comes out in a puff. He starts to back away but stops. "You're our cheerleader, Sam."

Sam can't say, *Make me your coach.* The moment passes too fast.

Chapter Twenty-Two

After recess, Mrs. Martin starts writing the vocabulary words on the blackboard:

Interpretation.

Determination.

Character.

Sam is a whiz at vocabulary and memorizes their definitions even before she lifts the piece of chalk from the last word.

When the school secretary totters into the classroom with a note for Mrs. Martin, the class' attention turns towards the door. Today, both her high heels and her tight skirt complicate walking.

The secretary hands Mrs. Martin a note. "Principal Cullen would like to see one of your students," she says before leaving.

As Mrs. Martin reads the note, everyone's gaze automatically turns to Mickey. But his seat is empty. Sam senses the confusion in the room. If Mickey is gone, who does the principal want?

Mrs. Martin puts down her piece of chalk and reads the note. "Ann, will you take Sam to Principal Cullen's office?"

Me? Although Sam has seen Principal Cullen in the hallway, he has never met him. Why would the principal want him to come to his office? Even though he knows that he hasn't done anything wrong, he wishes that Miss Perkins were here.

"Sure," Ann says. She hurries to Sam and a few seconds later maneuvers him neatly through the doorway.

In the hallway, Ann points at one of the cards on Sam's tray.

"Hope you have a good day," it reads.

Sam points at the same card: "Hope you have a good day."

Ann must be happy today because she starts laughing.

Suddenly, Sam feels like laughing, too. But he stops himself. He's too embarrassed.

"You feel silly, too, don't you, Sam?" Ann says.

Sam's pent-up laughter bursts forth. He thinks that he sounds like a small dog barking or a kid whose hiccups have run away with him, but Ann doesn't seem to notice anything unusual. She joins in until finally she stops to try to catch her breath. "I'm so glad that you can laugh." She pauses. "Can you cry?" she says.

I'm not a rock, Sam thinks, but he doesn't believe it's manly to admit to crying. "No," he lies.

"Not even when something really bad happens to you?" When Ann bends down towards him, she looks so worried that Sam laughs again.

"I didn't know," Ann says.

Their carefree mood ends when they find themselves staring at the big wooden door to the principal's office. Ann opens it with one hand and awkwardly pushes Sam through.

The secretary is busy typing. A nameplate on her desk reads, "Miss Valerie Rawles."

"Principal Cullen is busy right now," Miss Rawles says. "Leave the boy there."

Ann parks his chair. "Don't worry. I'll be back for you," she promises.

Miss Rawles returns to her typing, and Sam examines the room. Spare and plain. It looks like a doctor's office, but with no hint that it has anything to do with kids.

Click. Click. Click. Sam likes the typewriter's rhythm. He is still wondering why the principal wants to see him when he becomes aware of some odd sounds coming from behind the closed door.

He hears thuds, then whimpers, and occasionally a cry. Before he has time to figure out how to communicate to Miss Rawles that something is wrong, the door bursts open, and Mickey Kotov barrels out. His face is blotched. His eyes are teary, and his shirt hangs over his pants.

Principal Cullen stands at the door, holding an enormous paddle. It's bigger than the Ping Pong paddles that Sam has seen on television, and one side is covered in worn sandpaper. "Tomorrow, if you're late, I'm going to double the number of swats again."

Mickey glares at Sam before running out of the room.

Why do you dislike me? Sam wants to call after him. *I haven't done anything to you.*

After Principal Cullen hangs the oversize paddle on a hook on the wall, he steps out of his office doorway and faces Sam. Sam can't help admiring Principal Cullen's soldierly posture and crew cut. Sam wonders whether he fought in World War II.

Principal Cullen nods. He is wearing slacks and a button-down cotton shirt with a navy blue tie. His black eyes examine Sam for so long that he begins to feel embarrassed.

"Hello, Mr. Davis," Principal Cullen says. "I've seen you a few times in the halls, but I haven't had a chance to introduce myself. I'm Principal Cullen. Come in."

Miss Rawles stops typing and looks up. "A girl pushed him here. I don't think that he can."

Of course, Sam could operate his wheelchair if Ann hadn't been diligent and engaged the brake, but he doesn't think that he should argue with the secretary.

"Miss Rawles, will you escort Mr. Davis into my office and take

notes while I interview him?" Principal Cullen says.

Miss Rawles pushes Sam into the principal's office, parks him across from his desk and closes the door. Principal Cullen's office is small, with a large desk and a bookcase. Its bareness causes the paddle, hanging next to a diploma on the wall, to stand out.

Miss Rawles sits down in a chair and immediately starts scribbling on her pad. *What are you writing?* Sam wonders.

"Your mother promised that your nurse would accompany you every day. Where is she?" Principal Cullen asks. Sam knows that he and Miss Perkins are in some kind of trouble.

That morning, Miss Perkins had surprised Sam by telling him that she had to go to the doctor's. Sam doubts whether he can make the principal understand his version of the word 'doctor.' Enunciating a "d" and a "t" in one small word is difficult. So he takes a deep breath.

"GGGone." It's a fair imitation, Sam thinks.

The principal frowns at Sam. "Hum." His fingers form a bridge as he stares at the ceiling for a moment. He looks around his office and grabs a dictionary from his bookshelf. He opens it, and walks over to Sam and presses it close to his face. The principal is a big man, and he has to bend over to press the book close to Sam's face. "Tell me, Mr. Davis. Can you read this?"

The print is too tiny—too small for Sam to see. "NNNo," he says. Since he misses Miss Perkins, he adds as she has taught him, "SSir." But he's not feeling respectful. He's feeling angry.

Principal Cullen shakes his head and looks at the secretary who is busy writing. "Did you get that, Miss Rawles?"

Miss Rawles looks up. "Yes."

Sam wants to tell Principal Cullen that he can read big type. To make his point, he tries to show the principal the cards that Ann designed for him, but in his excitement he loses control of his hand

and pounds his tray.

Principal Cullen shoots him an annoyed glance.

"I understand the parents' concerns, all right," Principal Cullen says to Miss Rawles.

Sam gives up on showing Principal Cullen the cards.

Principal Cullen smiles. "I think I have a simple solution to the problem." He turns to Sam. "Mr. Davis, I believe that you belong in a special school."

Special school?

Sam shudders. All of a sudden, Sam is certain that any school that Principal Cullen thinks is special, he is sure to find especially awful. "SSSchool good."

Principal Cullen gives a hearty laugh. "I think you'll like being with kids of your own ability even more."

Sam wants to tell Principal Cullen how much he respects Mrs. Martin. "LLLike tteacher," he says. But he can tell that the principal isn't listening.

"Miss Rawles," Principal Cullen says. "Go ahead and take Mr. Davis back to Mrs. Martin's class."

'Yes, sir," Miss Rawles says.

Principal Cullen sits down behind the large desk. "Good to meet you, young man, and good luck," he says.

Sam is used to people not understanding him. But Principal Cullen is an educator. Sam's not sure what he expected, but he feels a deep disappointment.

Miss Rawles drops her notebook on Sam's tray. She disengages his brake and begins pushing him back to class.

Sam can't help reading her childishly large handwriting: "EXIT INTERVIEW WITH S. DAVIS. WITNESS V. RAWLES. CAN'T TALK. CAN'T READ. NOT ON GRADE LEVEL."

Sam has been unfairly judged and has been found wanting.

Without even practicing his sentence in his head, he protests, "IIII...can...read."

Miss Rawles doesn't answer. Instead, she snatches her notebook from the tray and pockets it.

When they arrive at Classroom 114, Miss Rawles tries to force Sam's chair through the door. He has to pull his feet out of the way so that his toes won't hit the frame.

In her final maneuver, Miss Rawles slams her hand. "Darn you," she exclaims.

Sam doesn't know if she's angry with him or the door.

As they enter, the kids' eyes are trained on him. He has to use every ounce of self-control to keep himself from screaming, *Darn you, too.*

Chapter Twenty-Three

After class is dismissed for lunch, Mrs. Martin approaches Sam. When she leans down next to him, he notices dark circles under her eyes. "Sam, I've got to make a phone call to check on my twins. A horrible bug is going around, and my daughter caught it. Miss Perkins said she would be back for lunch. Are you O.K. if I leave you alone for just a minute?"

Ann has already gone. Sam looks doubtfully around at the empty classroom, but he finds the courage to say, "YYes."

"You need to practice talking more. You're really good," Mrs. Martin says.

"TTThanks," Sam says.

Mrs. Martin smiles at him. "Miss Perkins says that you can stand and walk a few steps. You ought to practice walking, also."

Sam doesn't like to walk. He's heard too often that he might fall and break his leg.

Mrs. Martin yawns. "I hate to leave you alone, but I'll check on you soon," she promises as she walks out the door.

Sam looks at the clock. It says 12:06.

Miss Perkins is never late to important stuff like lunches. Could she have gotten in an accident?

If something awful has happened, Sam wonders how long he will sit next to the potted plants before someone notices him. Will Mrs. Martin remember to come back? Who will take him to the restroom?

Since the class doesn't have an afternoon break, Ann won't be able to speak to him. Sam doesn't want to be alone. He might think about Principal Cullen's paddle. The pleased way the principal had said the words "special school."

Mickey Kotov walks by and glances into the classroom.

Miss Perkins always says, "Be careful what you wish for." As if he were on the basketball court, Mickey pivots and makes a fast break toward Sam.

Sam had wished for company, but he's attracted the wrong kind.

Mickey's T-shirt still hangs loose from his visit to the principal's office. Sam wants to sympathize. He longs to say, *Principal Cullen is a bully,* but Mickey doesn't give him a chance. As he strides over to Sam, Mickey starts talking so fast that spit shoots out of his mouth.

"I warned you, didn't I? Why do you keep spying on me, Vindow Boy?"

Vindow Boy? At first, Sam doesn't understand Mickey's funny accent. Then, it occurs to him that Mickey is saying, Window Boy. So Mickey has seen him at night.

"I know you want to play. You ever arm-vrestled?" Without waiting for an answer, Mickey says, "It's fun."

When Sam doesn't move, Mickey continues, "I bet your spazzy hand can grab mine." He puts his elbow down on Sam's tray and says, "O.K., now let's go over the rrrules."

Sam would rather have a broken leg than a broken right pointer finger. If Mickey breaks a bone, he worries that his finger will never work as well again. As he pulls it toward his chest, his heart begins fluttering. Who will he be without his finger? He uses it to write. It's his only way to communicate complicated thoughts.

Mickey leans towards Sam.

Sam wants to beg Mickey to spare his right hand, but he's breathing too hard to attempt speech.

"Hold out your hand," Mickey repeats his command.

When Sam really concentrates, sometimes, he can propel his legs into a flurry of activity, perhaps just confusing and chaotic enough to scare this boy away. Just as he starts to will his legs to kick, Sam hears someone enter the room. He prays that it's his dear sweet Miss Perkins.

Mickey turns toward the noise.

Charlie Simmons is standing in the doorway. He's much taller and stockier than Mickey. While Mickey's hair is shaggy, Charlie's is neatly brushed and oiled. "What rules?" he asks.

Mickey sneers. "Old Sam and I are arm wrestling. You want to try to beat me, too?"

Sam's heart thumps in his chest. What if Charlie doesn't understand? What if he thinks that Sam wants to play Mickey's game?

Charlie's gaze seeks out Sam. In response, Sam puts all his fear and frustration into a backward roll of his eyes.

Charlie steps inside the room. "You leave Sam alone," he orders Mickey.

"You think you're so great! You and that loser basketball team" Mickey shouts.

Charlie clenches his fists and rushes towards Mickey.

Mickey swings at him and misses.

Charlie rams Mickey into Mrs. Martin's desk. It shifts a few inches to the left, and her empty flower vase clangs on the desktop.

Mickey jumps forward. His hands are balled into fists, ready to fight.

Charlie charges again.

Sam thinks of Mickey's sweaty face when he was leaving the principal's office and his untucked shirt. He remembers Mickey's moans as he was getting beaten. Even though Mickey is mean, he can't bear to think that Mickey will get swatted again. In fact, both Charlie and

Mickey are going to get into trouble.

Sam takes a deep breath. "NNNo!" he thunders.

Mickey's fist freezes in midair. His mouth hangs open in surprise.

Sam remembers that Mickey hadn't been in class the day that he spoke out in history. Sam knows that Mickey never talks to the other kids. Maybe Mickey hasn't figured out that Sam can speak.

"Yeah." Charlie reacts to the astonishment written all over Mickey's face. "He can talk. He's a real person, not just a lump in a wheelchair."

It's then that Sam realizes that this is the moment that he's dreamed of for so long. He has the attention of both Mickey Kotov and Charlie Simmons.

He remembers Winnie's good advice: *Right now, your purpose is to get Mickey Kotov on that basketball team.*

Sam has never practiced the words "point guard." He doubts whether either of the boys will understand him, but he aims his finger at Mickey, anyway. He does his best to force his tongue to say the words, "ppynt gaaard."

Both of the boys stare at Sam as if he were a lunatic, but Charlie drops his hand from Mickey's collar.

Mickey's fists hang by his side.

Charlie wipes his nose on his sleeve. "Is he saying point guard?" he asks Mickey.

"That's my position at my old skool," Mickey says. "How did he know?"

Charlie shrugs. "Beats me."

"Ppynt gaaard," Sam insists as Miss Perkins bustles through the door. He has lots more advice: *Not only that, Charlie, you should be center. You should stay down low and get rebounds. You can't dribble.*

Miss Perkins' mouth forms an "O" as she takes in the sight of the boys' rumpled shirts and tousled hair.

Miss Perkins touches each boy lightly on the shoulders as she passes. She picks up the fallen vase and rights it on the desk. "You two need to go play in the cafeteria." She hurries over to Sam. "I'm so sorry. It's raining. The buses were late. But I'm here now. Not to worry."

Charlie casts a protective glance in Sam's direction.

Sam smiles at him. "T-Thanks."

Mickey rushes out the door. Perhaps he is afraid that Miss Perkins will report him to the principal.

Charlie follows at a slower pace. He seems to want to talk but all he says is, "See you on the court, Sam."

When Miss Perkins sits down next to Sam, she pulls his lunch sack from The Suitcase. She gets out a jar of mashed potatoes and digs for the spoon.

Sam waits patiently. He's glad that Miss Perkins hasn't been in an accident, but he can't help wishing that she had arrived just a few minutes later. He was on the verge of something. On the verge of fulfilling his purpose—the purpose that Winnie had talked to him about. And now his chance is ruined.

Chapter Twenty-Four

After school, Sam begins work with Mrs. Martin, Miss Perkins hovering anxiously over him. Although when Mickey had been about to break his hand and he had desperately wanted to see his caretaker, now he wishes that she would have another doctor's appointment.

"Your essay has to be about a wartime hero. I assume you want to write about Churchill," Mrs. Martin says. She takes a sip of hot coffee out of her Styrofoam cup.

"I'm sure that's right," Miss Perkins breaks in.

Sam knows that Miss Perkins is excited for him to get a chance to show Mrs. Martin all he knows. So why won't she let him do the talking?

"Sam?" Mrs. Martin repeats her question.

"YYess," Sam says eagerly.

"Let's start with a title," Mrs. Martin says.

"If you move the alphabet sheet closer, he can reach it easier," Miss Perkins points out.

After shooting a glance at Miss Perkins, Mrs. Martin moves the alphabet sheet closer to Sam.

"I can write down the letters for you," Miss Perkins offers.

Mrs. Martin turns and looks at her hard. Miss Perkins is just trying to be helpful, but Sam senses that Mrs. Martin wishes that Miss Perkins would be quiet, too.

"I've got an idea," Mrs. Martin says. "Doesn't Sam live close by?"

Miss Perkins nods. "Yes, ma'am."

"Let me have Sam for the afternoon." Mrs. Martin looks at her watch. "Would you mind coming back in an hour?"

Sam grins at Miss Perkins to show her that this plan is fine with him.

"That would be a real help," Miss Perkins says. "I could use the time on my chores. I'll be back at 4:30."

"Don't be late. My mother says my daughter is doing better, thank goodness. But I need to get home," Mrs. Martin says.

"I'll be right on time," Miss Perkins says.

Mrs. Martin mutters to herself, "Maybe starting with the title is too hard."

Miss Perkins picks up The Suitcase. "Sam has written essays for me. He knows all about titles."

Without glancing at Miss Perkins, Mrs. Martin says in a firm tone, "4:30." She turns to Sam. "Why don't you answer this question? What do you admire most about Winston Churchill?"

"His bravery," Miss Perkins calls from the doorway. As she exits, Sam feels ungrateful but he is glad that his shadow is gone. Not only his shadow but also his interpreter. And he reminds himself that it's not her fault that she cannot always express things just as he would say or mean them.

What does Sam admire most about Winnie? As usual, he has to admit that Miss Perkins is right. It's his bravery. After France surrendered to Germany in June, 1940, Britain, undermanned and underfunded, fought on alone. Winnie turned the terror of a possible defeat into a challenge. Sam remembers the speech Winnie gave after the surrender of France: *Hitler knows that he will have to break us in this island or lose the war. Let us therefore brace ourselves to our duties, and so bear ourselves that, if the British Empire and its Commonwealth*

last for a thousand years, men will still say, 'This was their finest hour.'[19]

Sam loves the knack that Winnie has of making danger and loneliness seem like opportunities. He also admires the way that during the war, Winnie never acted afraid.

Suddenly, Sam notices Mrs. Martin's hand hiding her yawn. She is nibbling on her fingernails in impatience. Her dark eyes dart to the clock, then back to the alphabet sheet, pencil and notepad.

He wonders how long he has been lost in thought. He starts writing.

He taps the *I*, then the *A...D...M...I...R...E* and she begins writing them down.

The thought of referring to the name 'WINSTON CHURCHILL' over and over again exhausts Sam. He decides to use *WC*.

When Sam selects these initials, Mrs. Martin nods as if she understands. He starts pointing as fast as he can. BECAUSE WC'S SENSE THAT HIS LIFE HAD A PURPOSE KEPT HIM FROM BEING AFRAID. Mrs. Martin is having a hard time keeping up, and he slows down. He loves talking to someone about the things that he thinks about all the time.

WHEN WC WAS FIGHTING IN WORLD WAR I, A GENERAL ASKED WC TO MEET WITH HIM AT A SITE THREE MILES AWAY. AS WC MARCHED TO THE MEETING, THE ROAR OF SHELLS WAS CONSTANT. WHEN WC ARRIVED, HE WAS ANNOYED TO LEARN THAT THE GENERAL NO LONGER WANTED TO SEE HIM.[20]

WHAT WAS THE POINT OF THE MEETING? WC ASKED AN OFFICER.

NOTHING IN PARTICULAR, THE OFFICER TOLD HIM.

WC WAS FURIOUS. HE BEGAN ANOTHER LONG, SLIDING, SLIPPERY, SPLASHING WADDLE BACK TO THE TRENCHES. WHEN HE ARRIVED AT HIS UNIT, ONE OF

THE MEN HE SERVED WITH SHOUTED TO HIM. YOU'RE IN LUCK TODAY.

HARDLY, WC REPLIED, THINKING OF HIS LONG POINTLESS TRIP.

YES, YOU ARE. FIVE MINUTES AFTER YOU LEFT, YOUR DUGOUT WAS BLOWN UP. WC'S ROOMMATE WAS DEAD, KILLED BY THE EXPLOSION.

WC SAID, THERE CAME THE STRONG SENSATION THAT A HAND HAD BEEN STRETCHED OUT TO MOVE ME IN THE NICK OF TIME FROM A FATAL SPOT.

I ADMIRE WC BECAUSE HE HAS ALWAYS FELT THAT HAND ON HIS SHOULDER.

DURING WORLD WAR I WITH THOUSANDS OF MEN DYING IN THE BATTLEFIELDS AROUND HIM, WC WROTE TO HIS WIFE, I BELIEVE THAT I AM TO BE PRESERVED FOR FUTURE THINGS.[21]

WHEN HE WAS FINALLY ELECTED PRIME MINISTER, WC SAID, I FELT AS IF I WERE WALKING WITH DESTINY, AND THAT ALL MY PAST LIFE HAD BEEN BUT A PREPARATION FOR THIS HOUR AND FOR THIS TRIAL. I WAS SURE I SHOULD NOT FAIL.[22]

Despite the dark circles under her eyes, Mrs. Martin is smiling eagerly at him now.

WC ALMOST GOT KILLED MANY TIMES. He pauses. His finger is aching, but he finds the strength to continue. HE LOST A LOT OF ELECTIONS. WHEN HE BECAME PRIME MINISTER DURING WORLD WAR II, MOST PEOPLE THOUGHT THAT GERMANY WOULD WIN THE WAR. AFTER WC LED ENGLAND THROUGH ITS MOST DANGEROUS PERIOD IN HISTORY AND THE WAR IN EUROPE WAS WON, THE VOTERS VOTED HIM OUT OF OFFICE.

BUT SOMEHOW, I THINK WC STILL FELT THAT HAND ON HIS SHOULDER.

Sam begins tapping out his final sentence: I ADMIRE WC SO MUCH BECAUSE HE FELT THE HAND HIS WHOLE LIFE, AND I'VE NEVER EVEN FELT IT ONCE.

When Sam finishes, his finger is shaking. He has never worked it so hard. He looks up to find Mrs. Martin staring intently at him as though she's never really seen him before. He appreciates the time she is spending with him, especially today when her daughter is ill, but he experiences that resentment that he always feels when someone is shocked by his abilities.

Even though I drool, I'm not stupid, he wants to say.

Just then, Miss Perkins walks through the door. "I'm sorry, Mrs. Martin, if I'm a bit late. You wouldn't believe how confusing my life has been lately."

"It's fine," Mrs. Martin says softly. "We're about finished, aren't we, Sam?"

His finger is so exhausted that it's almost limp, but he can't resist adding…

WC SAYS FREE WILL AND PREDESTINATION ARE IDENTICAL.[23†]I DON'T UNDERSTAND EXACTLY WHAT THESE WORDS MEAN, BUT AGAIN I WANT TO BELIEVE.

Mrs. Martin looks up at Miss Perkins. "He's written an incredible essay."

Sam feels proud. He also knows if it weren't for his shaky finger, he'd have a lot more to say. He's got twelve years worth of thoughts trapped inside.

"I'm not surprised," Miss Perkins says.

"So what's his complete diagnosis?" Mrs. Martin asks in a low voice as if this information were a secret, but Sam has heard Miss Perkins tell Sam's whole story to Mr. Crowe, the baker, the newspa-

per man and anybody else who is curious.

"You know he has cerebral palsy," Miss Perkins says.

Mrs. Martin nods.

"And on top of that, when he was born, the doctor did a bad job, and Sam's left hand was damaged. Mrs. Davis won a lawsuit against the hospital, but the money's all gone. The only things that we can do for him right now, like physical therapy, cost too much."

"Well, he's got a great mind," Mrs. Martin says.

"He's a genius," Miss Perkins says proudly.

Mrs. Martin turns back to Sam. "I'll type this up and submit it for you. I'll explain to the judges how you dictated it to me. There's a thousand-dollar prize for the winning essay." She smiles a big smile. "Don't tell anyone, but your essay is the best in our class."

"TTThanks," Sam croaks.

"I bet it's the best in the school," Mrs. Martin adds. She looks down at her watch. "Oh, I'm late! I really must go pick up my daughter." She squeezes Sam's hand. "I'll see you tomorrow. O.K.?"

"We've done it!" Miss Perkins whispers as they watch Mrs. Martin leave.

Chapter Twenty-Five

Miss Perkins pushes Sam home across the rutted field. In the distance, the trees are blazing red and orange.

Miss Perkins always claims that Sam is smart, but he has never really believed her. Now Mrs. Martin has said it. Two people think the same thing.

Me. Sam Davis. I'm smart.

Even while Sam is amazed, surprised, and even shocked by this thought, he knows that it is true. Although he often wishes that he could avoid the complicated process of speech by having his thoughts magically appear on a television screen attached to his head, for once he's glad that he alone has access to them. He's free to brag about himself, and no one can overhear him.

I'm smart, he shouts. Now, the cool air rushes over him and whistles in his ears, and he tries to believe that the wind feels just like it would if he were running.

"Well, Mrs. Martin's a sweet lady, after all," Miss Perkins chatters on.

The excitement stays with Sam until he arrives at the parking lot for the apartment. Mr. Crowe's dark Oldsmobile parked in its slot and a beat-up van with the sign, *Kotov Plumbers*, vie for his attention. As he looks at Mr. Crowe's dented black car, he tries to convince himself that he is having a nightmare. But he knows the difference between dream sobs and real ones. His mother had really been crying.

Miss Perkins turns Sam's wheelchair around to face the empty court. She raises it over the curb and backs it onto the concrete lot. Since the Tomcats have an away game, he won't be able to watch them play this afternoon. That's too bad. Because he has a lot of things that he wants to forget about this full day. Like Principal Cullen's threat.

He decides that no matter his promise to Miss Perkins, if his mother makes him go to Principal Cullen's special school, he'll stage the worst tantrum of his life.

But if Sam makes more noise, Mr. Crowe will be sure to kick them out.

That's when he has an idea. If he has to, he'll stage a quiet scene. He'll thrash around on the floor, drool a lot and act weird. He bets that his mother will go crazy over a mute performance. He applauds himself. *You are brilliant.*

As they approach the building, Sam hears someone yelling.

Mr. Crowe is standing in the front parking lot ten yards or so away from them. "I'm not going to pay you— foreign scumbag," he yells.

A short man holding a wrench in his hand is arguing with Sam's landlord. The man's overalls are stained and dirty. His face is lined with worry. "I feex problem. You pay!" the man shouts.

Immediately, Sam recognizes the voice from the basketball court—Mickey's dad.

"Don't listen, Sam," Miss Perkins says as she opens the door to the lobby. "No telling what those crude men will say."

*   *   *

She's on time for once, Miss Perkins thinks, as Mrs. Davis enters the apartment at 6 p.m. As always, she is beautifully dressed in a lacy blouse, but today she looks nervous. Her face is drawn and her smart hat is cockeyed on her head.

When Mrs. Davis sets a new blue suitcase down by the hat stand, Miss Perkins can't stop staring at it.

Mrs. Davis marches over to Sam, kisses him and says, hello. She is humming, "We can work it out. We can work it out…" When she returns, she leans over the counter. She reaches for the transistor radio and increases the volume until it's so loud that Miss Perkins can't even concentrate on stirring the crème of mushroom soup.

Mrs. Davis picks up the blue suitcase and catches Miss Perkins' eye. She nods in the direction of her bedroom; Miss Perkins follows her.

Mrs. Davis' bedspread is blue, and her one window is covered with green curtains. It would be a cheerful room but the clutter bothers Miss Perkins. Jewelry crowds her bureau. Mrs. Davis has so many shoes that she can't close her closet door. A waterfall of silk, wool and cotton dresses pours over her chair.

In front of her closet, Mrs. Davis turns and faces Miss Perkins. "Friday afternoon," she hisses.

"But that's two days from now!" Miss Perkins protests.

"Mr. Jordache is *very* persuasive. He managed to get Sam admitted quickly," Mrs. Davis brags.

Who is this Mr. Jordache? Miss Perkins thinks. What does he know about Sam? But before Miss Perkins can react, Mrs. Davis begins speaking, "You know what this means, right?"

Miss Perkins waits for Mrs. Davis to finish.

"I won't be needing your services anymore." When she looks away, Miss Perkins is surprised to spot tears in her gray eyes.

It's not you who need my services anyway, Miss Perkins wants to tell her. It's Sam. Still gazing into Mrs. Davis' wet eyes, Miss Perkins surprises herself. She has to fight the temptation to hug her. But her mood changes swiftly when Mrs. Davis says, "I can use a short break from taking care of Sam." She gives a little sigh as she slips off her high heels and begins to rub her calves. "I'm tired."

Miss Perkins has to bite her tongue. She wants to ask her—no, she really wants to scream—how do you think my poor boy feels stuck in his wheelchair all the time?

Mrs. Davis neatly stores her shoes in her closet before she stands and faces Miss Perkins again. "I really appreciate all you've done for Sam. I wish I could pay you a bonus."

"Don't worry about me," Miss Perkins says, cheerfully, falsely. She must be careful not to let any of the horror that she feels show. If Mrs. Davis were to guess her thoughts, how angry she is at this selfish woman, Mrs. Davis might fire her right now.

"Where will you work?" Mrs. Davis asks as she takes off her earrings and places them on her bureau counter.

"I have a little savings. I'll be all right," Miss Perkins wrings her hands. She can't stop a bit of her concern from leaking out. "But Sam...."

"Don't worry," Mrs. Davis interrupts. She smiles brightly at Miss Perkins. "I'm expecting good things to happen. Why, I might even marry and get a home of my own. One way or the other, I'll take Sam back in a few months....That is, unless he really likes it."

"This is too much!" Miss Perkins bursts out. "Sam cries when you stay out late. How can you convince yourself that he's going to like living in an institution?"

"Why can't you understand?" Mrs. Davis cries. "My family is hundreds of miles away. My husband left me. My son is all I have. I'm out of money." She picks up the shiny blue suitcase and thrusts it into Miss Perkins' hands.

Outside of necessities, Mrs. Davis rarely shops for Sam. As Miss Perkins grips the hard plastic handle, she understands: this decision is final.

*   *   *

From his spot by the window, Sam strains his ears, listening. Miss Perkins bustles into the kitchen and switches off the radio, throwing the apartment into abrupt silence. He hears a busy quiet, loaded with words not spoken, thoughts not expressed and feelings not shared.

Sam hates it when his mother and Miss Perkins turn up the radio so that he can't eavesdrop. He wonders if their secret conversation had to do with Principal Cullen's 'special place'? He prays that he doesn't have to go there. He doesn't want to lose his Tomcats, his basketball team.

I don't know why you like basketball so much, Winnie says to start a familiar argument. *Polo is the emperor of sports.*[24]

That's because you didn't grow up with basketball, Sam points out.

In sport, in courage and in the sight of Heaven, all men must meet on equal terms,[25] Winnie answers.

One of the problems with having a friend from a book is that, sometimes, Winnie's quotes don't fit into their conversation, but Sam decides to answer him anyway.

Nonsense, Winnie, Sam responds. *I can't meet anyone on equal terms in sports.*

You'd be a good coach, Winnie argues.

How can I be a coach when I've only touched a basketball with my shoe?

Well…maybe a good assistant coach, Winnie agrees, too quickly.

Sam still smarts from Principal Cullen's assessment of him. Now, his best friend, a creation of his own mind, is refusing to believe in him. Winnie's low expectations make him furious.

Winnie, Sam retorts, *you were a sickly youth with a bad stutter, and you became a champion polo player and a great orator.*

True, Winnie admits.

So I could become a basketball coach, Sam thinks.

146

When you leave off dreaming, the universe ceases to exist,[26] Winnie responds.

I'm not dreaming, Sam thinks. *Am I? Miss Perkins and Mrs. Martin both say I'm smart. I can be a coach.*

Our future is in our hands. Our lives are what we choose to make of them.[27]

I choose to be a coach, not an assistant coach, Sam insists.

First, before you make your decision, I beg you, please, watch a polo game.

Because he's at home, Sam laughs out loud. He, Sam Davis, a kid who can barely move, wants to be a basketball coach. At least, Sam has a basketball court in his backyard. As far as he knows, there are no polo fields in all of Stirling. *If I wanted to be a polo coach, I might as well wish to fly to Mars,* Sam thinks.

You would do well as an astronaut, because I suppose there would be long stretches in outer space where you have nothing to do, and you, my boy, have a rich inner life.

Sam laughs again. As usual, Winnie has found a way to sneak a compliment about himself into their conversation. Both he and Winnie know that Sam's inner life is Winnie. He tries but can't stifle a big yawn. Ever since he's been going to school, he's been so tired at night.

When you leave off dreaming, the universe ceases to exist[28]...Sam pictures his favorite sports team, the Tomcats. Charlie is playing at center, and Mickey is point guard. He tries to make out the small figure, watching from the sidelines.

It's a boy in a wheelchair: Coach Sam.

Sensing his mood, Miss Perkins appears next to him. "Ready for bed?" she asks.

Sam looks up. If he holds onto this image as he falls asleep, maybe, just maybe, his dream will come true.

Chapter Twenty-Six

Sitting in his regular place, Sam notices that the avocado seeds have sprouted tiny green shoots. A *Life* magazine photograph of the Pilgrims' first Thanksgiving has replaced the poster of Zeus.

The bell rings. It's time for recess.

Ann crams her books into her desk. But before she can head for Sam, Mickey Kotov taps her on the shoulder. Sam is surprised to see that they begin talking.

Sam strains to listen to their conversation, but he can't make it out, only fragments. Mickey is bending towards Ann confidentially, trying to convince her of something. Mickey's voice rises, and Sam hears, "I was in the principal's office...I heard Principal Cullen say..."

Ann backs away, doubting him. Until finally the expression on Ann's face changes, and she glances over at Sam. Her expression is soft, almost loving. Sam should be pleased, but he feels a stab of fear course through him.

"Now?" Ann says.

"Now!" Mickey exclaims.

"Are you sure?" Ann asks.

Mickey nods.

Ann shakes her head. "Thanks." She starts walking over to Sam.

Sam is still puzzling over what Mickey Kotov had to say to anyone in the class, much less Ann Riley, when another strange thing happens. Mrs. Martin meets Ann halfway. "Not today," she says.

"But…" Ann appears to be arguing with their teacher. Why won't Mrs. Martin let Ann talk to Sam?

"I feel terrible. My mother complained," Sam overhears Ann say.

"Several parents are upset. It wasn't just your mother, Ann," Mrs. Martin answers. "Now mind me and go outside for recess."

What's going on? Sam feels himself start to panic.

Ann stands with her hands at her side.

Mrs. Martin gives Ann a hug, before turning and walking purposely towards Sam and Miss Perkins. Even before she says a single word, Sam fears the worst. As he listens to Miss Perkins search her purse for Kleenex, he keeps his eyes fixed on Mrs. Martin's face.

"Principal Cullen told me the bad news," Mrs. Martin says quickly to Sam and Miss Perkins.

"Not more bad news. I don't think that I can take more bad news…. I'm almost at my wit's end. On top of everything, my rheumatism really is bothering me…" Miss Perkins rattles on.

"Miss Perkins," Mrs. Martin interrupts. "Don't make this conversation more difficult. I think you've guessed how fond I am of Sam."

"Why, yes. I think you like my boy. You know how smart and sweet he is, and…"

Sam wants to scream: *Be quiet. Let Mrs. Martin talk.*

"I was glad to learn that Mrs. Davis has found a suitable place for Sam," Mrs. Martin says.

Suitable place. The special school. The pain causes him to bend over.

"Oh, my goodness, Mrs. Martin," Miss Perkins cries. "Mrs. Davis has decided to send Sam to Mannville Institution. I don't know what to do."

Sam pounds his head on his tray to say, *This can't be true. An institution.*

Miss Perkins strokes Sam on the back. "Dearie me. I never intended to break the bad news to my boy this way."

How can you let this happen, Miss Perkins? Sam thinks.

"Some parents are upset that Stirling is overcrowded," Mrs. Martin says.

"But that's wrong, ma'am. You know that, don't you?" Miss Perkins breaks in.

"They think that Sam's needs are a burden to the system," Mrs. Martin continues as if she has not heard Miss Perkins. "When Principal Cullen called Sam's mother, he learned that Mrs. Davis had already decided to move Sam."

Sam knocks his head against his tray, hard.

Miss Perkins reaches out and strokes his hair. "Sam, don't! Remember your promise."

Sam remembers. But his promise applied to things like a burned dinner or a broken radio. He never meant that he wouldn't stage a tantrum if he couldn't go to school.

"I'm sorry. I share your concern about Mannville. If it were up to me, Sam could stay at Stirling." Mrs. Martin pauses. "But it's not."

Sam expects Miss Perkins to argue. But then he realizes, what's the point? The real problem is his mother, not the school. He guesses that Miss Perkins must agree with him because all she says is, "Thank you. We do appreciate all you've done for us. I guess we'll be leaving."

"You may certainly stay until the end of the day," Mrs. Martin offers.

End of the day. This is only his twentieth day of school, but it's the last day of his life. Without school, Sam will be reduced to watching from a window forever.

Miss Perkins studies Sam. "We better leave now."

"I'm sorry," Mrs. Martin repeats, listlessly.

Sam wants to speak, but out of all the hundreds of words spinning around in his head, he can't possibly catch the right ones, place them in correct order and then work his mouth around each slippery one. Instead, he drops his head again.

"Sam," Miss Perkins hisses. "Not here. Not now. You'll just prove Principal Cullen and those parents right." She puts her hand on his shoulder. "Mrs. Martin wants to say goodbye to you."

Although his head feels as if it weighs one thousand pounds, slowly Sam lifts his neck to look at his teacher.

Mrs. Martin leans close to Sam. Behind her thick lenses, her brown eyes appear huge and sad. "I'm ashamed that I didn't recognize your abilities from the beginning, but I promise you this: I'll never forget you. Thank you for teaching me about Winston Churchill and his bravery. Please remember you have friends here. Ann and I will miss you very much." She turns away from him. "Ann, I know you're there."

Ann pokes her head inside the door. Like always, she is wearing a dress. This one is brown with a black belt. Sam takes no pleasure in the fact that her lower lip is trembling like she's going to cry.

"You can come in and tell Sam goodbye," Mrs. Martin calls to her.

Ann runs to Sam. "Bye, Sam." She squeezes his hand hard.

The word that Sam needs to say is the hardest word that he's ever pronounced, harder even than the first few words that he worked on: 'Mother, window'. Harder than the longest word that he unsuccessfully tried but was never able to master: 'Mississippi.' Sam finally manages to croak it out. "GGGoodbye."

Chapter Twenty-Seven

Ann runs ahead of Sam to the basketball court. Despite her blue coat, she has goose pimples on her legs, and he feels sorry for her. Marigold and the rest of her dance group have stayed inside today. He doesn't know Ann's plan, but he senses that her presence outside on such a cold day has something to do with him. Mickey is playing tether ball alone. Miss Perkins pushes Sam past him. On the court, the team is huddled around Charlie Simmons, who watches Ann with mild curiosity as she waves at him. Although none of the boys have zipped their jackets, a few are stamping their feet to keep warm.

"Charlie," Ann calls from the sidelines. "Come here."

Charlie turns toward Ann, frowning. "Can't you see we're practicing?" he yells.

"Sam's leaving," Ann shouts bravely.

"What do you mean?" Charlie walks over to Ann, who is standing on the sidelines.

Ann points at Sam. They have a hurried conversation. Sam guesses that she is telling Charlie that he is going to live in an institution, and for an instant, he feels vaguely ashamed.

"Oh, my goodness. What are we going to do?" Miss Perkins fusses to herself.

"Sstop!" Sam snaps.

Miss Perkins stops his chair a few yards from the basketball court. "Of course, you want to say goodbye to your friends. Oh, Sam…"

Sam had meant that he wanted Miss Perkins to stop talking, but when she quits pushing his wheelchair, Sam realizes that she's right. He has one last chance to help his Tomcats. After all, no one in the whole school knows that Mickey's a great basketball player, except for Sam. "CCharlie."

Charlie and Ann are still talking.

"CCharlie," Sam repeats.

Charlie runs over. He bends down and stares into Sam's eyes.

When Sam points at the card, "Tomcats Score!" he experiences a familiar frustration. He has managed to communicate only a tiny fraction of what he needs to say. He shifts his tongue into position so he can speak clearly and carefully. "MMickey." By turning slightly, he is able to point at Mickey. "Ppynt gaaard."

Charlie nods his head slowly. "I understand. It's just that the other kids don't want to play with Mickey."

This is Sam's last chance. He tries to put all of Winnie's conviction and determination into his words. "Ppynt gaaard," he insists.

Charlie looks off into the distance, hesitating.

Sam needs to find one word that will help Charlie understand Sam's vision for the team. What is it? "WWWin," Sam bursts out.

Charlie scratches his head. "What?"

"WWin," Sam repeats.

"You're probably right." Charlie agrees slowly. "The other kids don't like losing all the time, either."

Relieved, Sam nods.

"O.K. Thanks." Charlie turns away from Sam.

You did it, Sam, Winnie says.

Although the tip of his nose and his fingers are freezing, Sam feels his accomplishment warm his body.

Charlie stands in the middle of the court with the basketball in his hands. "Mickey," he shouts.

Mickey's hands drop to his sides, but he doesn't turn to look at Charlie.

"Come here," Charlie orders.

Mickey takes a few steps away.

"Me?" he says.

Charlie throws Mickey the ball, and Mickey leaps sideways and catches it.

"We don't want to play with him," Bobby Sur and A.J. jeer.

"Shut up," Charlie shouts at them. "I saw him the other night. He's good."

When Mickey's feet touch the court, he begins dribbling.

He moves the ball so fast that it's a blur. The boys all part to let Mickey through. He stops in front of Charlie.

Charlie points at Mickey. "I need to talk to Mr. Fitzpatrick. But I want Mickey to be our point guard," he says. "Now, play."

Bobby and the rest of the team are staring at Charlie. They all ignore Mickey, who is standing on the court in torn jeans, looking lost.

"What are you doing, Charlie?" Bobby says.

"Sam's right. Mickey's our only hope to win the tournament," Charlie says.

Bobby scratches his head. "Sam Davis?" he asks. "The kid in the wheelchair?"

"What does he know about basketball?" A.J. says.

"I can't explain what's happened. Just play," Charlie shouts. He turns to Mickey. "Come on."

Mickey continues to look doubtfully at him.

"Come on," Charlie encourages him. "We don't have all day."

Mickey begins dribbling the ball toward the basket. He goes for an easy layup. The ball slices cleanly through the hoop.

Can't you see? Sam wants to shout to Bobby, A.J. and the others.

Mickey's great!

"Bobby, guard Mickey," Charlie demands.

Sam grins. Bobby's too slow to stop Mickey.

As Bobby glares at Charlie, he blows a gum bubble as big as a baby's head.

"Afraid you can't do it?" Charlie goads him.

Bobby's bubble pops as he darts forward to block Mickey.

Sure enough, Mickey feints, turns and drives to the basket. He is a small boy, but so quick. Popping in and out of the stronger, taller boys on the court effortlessly, he makes Bobby Sur and the others look as if they are moving in slow motion. Mickey shoots and scores.

"Stick closer to him, Bobby," Charlie orders.

Bobby is furiously chomping on his gum. His blemished face has turned bright red. He raises his hands and jumps in an effort to block Mickey.

Mickey bounce-passes the ball past Bobby into A.J.'s out-stretched hands.

With Bobby chasing him, Mickey races underneath the basket. He holds out his hands, and A.J. throws the ball to him. Just as Sam knew he would, Mickey makes the layup.

"Mickey's not bad," Larry shouts.

"You won't get past me this time," Bobby threatens.

As if Mickey hadn't heard the taunt, he dribbles right past Bobby.

Yeah, Mickey, Sam thinks. Despite the fact that Mickey has a foreign accent and a funny last name. Mickey scores again.

Miss Perkins jiggles the handles of his wheelchair. "It's cold. We need to go."

Sam wants to stay courtside forever, but when she starts pushing him away, he's too tired to object. His eyes feel swollen, as if he had already been crying for hours. His head aches.

"Sam," Charlie shouts. "Goodbye."

We could have been friends, Sam thinks sadly as Miss Perkins turns towards the apartment.

Chapter Twenty-Eight

Miss Perkins stands behind Sam and rubs his shoulders. He faces the window.

"It's been a rotten day, and I hate to make it even more rotten, but I've got to leave you again, Sammy," Miss Perkins tells him.

Yesterday, she was unable to figure out a bus route to Mannville. After wasting a lot of time, she ended up going to the bank and withdrawing the money for a cab. Today, she intends to visit the place. "I have to go back... to the doctor... this afternoon. I was going to ask Mrs. Martin if you could stay with her, but now I can't. You know I don't like to leave you alone."

"I'll be...back in plenty of time for dinner. Then, we can.....talk." She pauses. "I promise. I know you've got lots of questions. I do, too. I'm working on the answers. I really am. Tonight... I'll have some."

She hopes.

*   *   *

The door slams, signaling Miss Perkins' departure.

Sam faces the window. Almost immediately, Sam's seat belt catches as his chair begins to drift backward toward a dip in the floor.

Before Miss Perkins bustled out in such a hurry, Sam had detected the hitches in her voice that told him that she was nervous. She must be as worried as he is and had forgotten to set the brake. Why couldn't she have picked any other afternoon to go to the doctor's?

And then the wheelchair starts to slowly roll. When it reaches the dip, the chair slowly rotates. Now Sam faces the couch and the back of the television. He considers wheeling himself back over to the window, but what's the point? Since he can't set the brake, he'll just end up in the dip again.

On top of everything, Miss Perkins has forgotten to give him water. Or maybe she didn't forget. Sam honestly can't remember. All he knows is that he's thirsty.

Usually, his mouth is a spit factory. It manufactures extra spit twenty-four hours a day, more than he can use, sometimes so much it's a nuisance. Now his tongue and mouth are dry.

Drip. Drip. Drip. A leak in the kitchen faucet? As if the sight of water would quench his thirst, he tries to turn his head toward the sink.

But his neck won't carry his eyes that far.

Although it's freezing outside, the sun streams through the window and warms his shoulders and his face. He hasn't been home for a while during midday, and he's forgotten how hot it gets in the apartment even in late October. He touches his head. It feels hot, too. He wonders if it's better or worse that Miss Perkins forgot to turn on the television. Sometimes, he enjoys his own thoughts more than the constant stream of programs and commercials. But today the loss of school is a dull ache all over his body, and entertainment might help. Why did Miss Perkins have to go to the doctor today of all days?

Sam has had to visit the doctor too often. So often, that he does his best not to think about Dr. Adams in between appointments. Dr. Adam's office—even with its huge goldfish—is not Sam's favorite place. He's had too many shots and X-rays there. His body has been twisted and turned into too many awkward positions. Too many experts have stared at him naked with frowns on their serious faces.

There's one memory of the doctor's office that Sam works harder not to think about than any other. He was about five or six, lying on the examining table. Dr. Adams and his mother were outside the door, talking. He heard Dr. Adams say as casually as if he were prescribing an aspirin, "This boy may need to be institutionalized one day."

For all these years, that word has haunted him. What kind of place is an institution? Will an institution have other kids?

If Sam goes to live in an institution, he might never see Ann Riley or Charlie Simmons again. He might never be able to tell Mrs. Martin all that he knows about Winnie. With Mickey as their point guard, Sam is sure that the Tomcats will start winning. He longs to see his team play. To cheer for Mickey. To see him score points.

Why, he'll even miss the eleven potted plants.

Institoooshen. No matter how much he practices, he will never be able to say the word, but when Miss Perkins gets back, he promises himself that he will try.

From his Churchill books, Sam's heard the phrase, "the institution of government." He thinks that the word means a government building. But why would he, a boy with CP, be housed in a building with the government?

He checks the clock on the wall again to be sure. It's only 12:19. For him it's rare, but this afternoon, he's living in slow time.

For one thing, his brain feels incapable of a story. He is staring stupidly at the blank television when out of the corner of his eye, he becomes aware of something. A gray object darts across the floor.

A cat? One hot summer, Miss Perkins had left the door open, and a stray had slipped inside. He can't twist his neck far enough to be

159

sure. Then, the confusion that has filled his mind like a gray fog lifts, and he remembers that it's not summer, but fall, almost winter. Besides, the blur of fur was too slick to be a cat's.

The gray animal scurries out from the couch's shadows. A rat. As if sizing him up, the rat stares at him. Then, it disappears.

Luckily for me, I have no horror of rats,[29†] Winnie brags.

When Winnie was twenty-five, he was taken prisoner in South Africa. Eventually, he escaped. He knocked on a random door, and the Englishman who answered helped Winnie by hiding him in a mine for three days. The mine was infested with rats.

Once I awoke from a doze by one actually galloping across me, Winnie reminds Sam. *They seemed rather nice little beasts.*

But you were a grown man and strong, and I just have my pointer finger, Sam tells Winnie.

That's not exactly true, Winnie says. *What about your legs?*

Sam starts to concentrate on his legs, on making them kick.

But wait a minute. Why is he considering this unreliable weapon? Surely Sam is dreaming. There's no large rat in this empty apartment craving him for its delicious dinner.

Just as Sam feels himself start to accept this conclusion as the only logical one, he spots the creature again. This time, he is sure. It's a rat that he sees.

From beneath the couch, a pair of beady eyes are fixed on Sam. The rat appears to be the same size as Sam's foot.

After three days in the mine, Winnie's new friends decided to smuggle him out of South Africa. They packed wool tightly in a train car and hid him in a small space in the center of the bales.

The rat has crept out from underneath the couch and continues to watch him, curiously. *You were in great danger, weren't you, Winnie?* Sam asks.

I had a revolver with me, two roast chickens, some slices of meat, a

---

loaf of bread, a melon and three bottles of cold tea. The journey was going to take sixteen hours. To check the progress of the journey, I had learnt by heart beforehand the names of all the stations on the route. I can remember many of them today. Witbank…

Sam can't recall the rest of Winnie's train stops, but he knows the bus stops on the way to Miss Perkins' doctor. He's never been there, but she's told him: Evergreen, 34th, Harvard Street, and Glade Avenue.

He looks again at the clock. The hands have actually moved surprisingly fast, all the way to 1:30.

He pictures Miss Perkins. Right now, she's talking to the receptionist. Any minute, she will look at her watch and say, "Oops. I've got to go. I can't be late. I have to get back to my Sam." Still talking, she'll head for the door. The bus will start back with her on it. Soon, he'll hear her footsteps in the hallway and her key in the front door.

Not soon enough. But Miss Perkins never runs. She always moves at the same steady pace. *Run, Miss Perkins. Run.*

The rat scurries across the field of carpet and stops only a few paces in front of Sam.

But what would I do with the pistol, if I were caught? Winnie is still talking about the train trip that he took hidden in the wool car. *Shoot the whole Boer army?* Winnie asks. *I was at the mercy of events, and I knew it.*

Hush, Sam orders Winnie. *I don't care about your adventures.*

Except for the rat's breathing, the apartment is completely quiet.

Is Sam losing his mind? The loud exhalations are not the rat's but his own. Because of the heat and his thirst, Sam's breathing is raspy, like an animal's. When he meets the rat's serious gaze, he understands the reason the rat is completely silent. The rat is getting ready to jump him.

Sam remembers the rat's body that he saw twisted by the steel bar. Now, in revenge, this rat has trapped Sam. The hair rises on the back of his neck, and he tenses, readying for battle. He focuses all his energy into his legs, hoping to produce the wildest and jerkiest of his kicks. Of course, his legs have minds of their own. When they respond with little more than twitches, Sam despairs.

Winnie continues to drone on about events that took place over fifty years ago. *I squinted through my peephole…*

Be quiet, Sam shouts. *I'm in a real-life predicament.*

Winnie ignores him: *I saw that we had reached safety, I was so carried away by thankfulness and delight that I fired my revolver two or three times…*[30†]

Wait a minute! Sam has been trying to shut Winnie out, and now Winnie has given him a great idea.

The rat lopes towards him. Sam braces for the animal to attack.

No time to lose. ACT, Winnie orders.

Sam cocks his finger. He takes a deep breath. "BBBBAMMM," he shouts. The blast is so loud that it hurts his ears.

Even as his arm drops, he understands too well that his gun is fake, ineffective. Just a finger, after all.

He shuts his eyes and waits to feel the creature's claws tear through the cloth of his pants leg.

Nothing happens.

He opens his eyes. How long have they been closed he wonders. He searches the carpet and finds the rat is gone. His head droops. He can't feel glad about the fact that his gun has worked.

After all, his whole body aches; he's so thirsty; and it's only 1:48 p.m.

Chapter Twenty-Nine

Sam hears footsteps in the entranceway.

In a very remote corner of his brain Sam realizes, at last, she's home.

"What are you doing in the middle of the room?" Miss Perkins asks. "Hello," she calls out. "Are you here, Mrs. Davis?"

The ticktock of the clock in the kitchen and the hum of the refrigerator are her only replies.

"I must have forgotten to set your brake," Miss Perkins decides.

"YYes," Sam squeaks. His mouth is so dry.

"What's the matter?" Miss Perkins peers down at him. "How can you look so hot? It's chilly in here." She leans closer and presses her freezing hand against his forehead.

"Why, you're burning up with fever! Mrs. Martin told me that a bad virus is going around the school. You must have caught something from one of the kids.

"Oh, my poor Sam. I was gone, and you needed me. What good is someone you love if they're not there when you really need them? I'm so sorry that I stayed away so long. I'll explain everything someday, darling. I had to go. I'll wash you down with a cool cloth and get you to bed. You're probably thirsty, too."

Sam listens to the soft pat of nurse's shoes heading to the kitchen. With Miss Perkins here, the rat won't bother him. Finally, he can relax.

Miss Perkins feels sorry for her poor boy, but she can't help but be happy. Surely, since Sam has a high fever, Mrs. Davis won't send him away tomorrow.

His illness will buy her a few more days to think and plan.

Mannville Institution. A three-storied gray building in the country surrounded by farmland. Cleaner than a public institution but not a loving, caring place by any means. Better than she had feared. But still impossible. The staff seems kind, but few attendants watch over many boys whose parents don't want them. Some residents have been institutionalized since birth and have no visitors. Not all of them are small, sweet boys; many have large muscles and small IQ's. Miss Perkins is sure that the attendants will have no time for a smart but quiet boy like Sam.

From the next room, Sam cries out in delirium, "Rat. Get the rat."

Miss Perkins hurries to bring Sam a glass of water. Frantically, she thinks, what else can I do to make my poor boy more comfortable?

A few minutes later in the kitchen, Miss Perkins opens cans of tuna and cream of mushroom soup. Mannville doesn't even offer a school for its charges. She pours the tuna and soup over the noodles and tosses the mixture together. Only informal tutoring.

Sam will never achieve her dream for him and attend college if he's parked at Mannville.

She crunches a handful of potato chips and sprinkles the pieces on the top of the casserole. The image of Emily returns to her. The girl's poor body twisted by the concrete. Mannville would be Sam's death. A slow death. She opens the oven and sticks the casserole inside. She wipes her hands on her apron.

She did come home with one tiny bit of good news. Mannville has heavy staff turnover, and the director is looking for a nurse's aide. The application is in her purse.

The key turns in the lock. Mrs. Davis has returned.

Although Miss Perkins had to leave the kitchen many times to take care of Sam, she is proud that the casserole is in the oven. Mrs. Davis will have no chance to complain about dinner.

Mrs. Davis starts to take off her wool coat.

Miss Perkins knows that she ought to wait, that Mrs. Davis can't stand it when Miss Perkins pours out her problems immediately. "Mrs. Davis." Too late, she notices that Mrs. Davis has barely begun removing her second arm from the coat sleeve. "Sam is sick. With due respect, he cannot go to that place tomorrow. I visited it today. It is a fine place for some, but not a boy of Sam's intelligence, and…"

"Miss Perkins," Mrs. Davis interrupts coolly. She draws herself up to her full height. "I am Sam's parent. Not you."

Miss Perkins wants to ask, if you're his parent, why are you acting like a spoiled child? But she tells herself, think of Sam. Think of the poor little boy. Think of how he kept his temper today when Mrs. Martin told him that he had to leave school.

"And I made my decision about Sam's future based on what's best for us," Mrs. Davis adds. "Neither Sam nor I want to be living on the street. Why can't you understand?"

Perhaps Mrs. Davis hadn't understood her. "Sam is sick," Miss Perkins explains again.

"That's one of the wonderful things about this institution. They have a full medical staff," Mrs. Davis says.

Sick or not, Sam must go tomorrow, Miss Perkins thinks bitterly.

"Have you taken Sam's temperature?" Mrs. Davis asks casually.

"It's 103," Miss Perkins says.

"Have you tried aspirin?" Mrs. Davis asks.

The two of them have lived for years with the anxiety of caring for Sam, and they have both learned not to overreact. But at this particular moment, Miss Perkins finds her employer's casualness infuriating.

"Yes. But his fever hasn't come down. I've tried to reach Dr. Adams, but I got his answering service…" Miss Perkins tries once more.

"I'll call Mr. Jordache," Mrs. Davis interrupts. Her voice sounds tired. "If the institution is still willing to pick him up, we'll both leave in the van with him as planned."

"Surely, we can wait a few days, ma'am?" Miss Perkins says.

"Now that Sam is taken care of, Mr. Jordache has invited me on a business trip with him to Europe. When we come back, I may be," she pauses, trying to swallow her grin which is growing unusually wide "his wife."

So that's what's going on, Miss Perkins realizes. But she can't help feeling suspicious: if Mr. Jordache plans to marry Mrs. Davis, why hasn't Mr. Jordache even bothered to meet Sam?

"Our tickets are for this weekend," Mrs. Davis continues, and the excitement in her voice is unmistakable. "I have a lot to do before then." She pauses. "Stop staring at me like that. Besides, I spoke with the principal of that school you like so much. Principal Cullen agrees with me that Mannville Institution is a great place for a boy like Sam."

"Has Principal Cullen visited Mannville lately?" Miss Perkins baits her.

Mrs. Davis refuses to meet Miss Perkins' eyes. "I didn't ask him. Now, I'd like my dinner," she says.

Miss Perkins resists the impulse to dump the hot tuna casserole on Mrs. Davis' clean floor.

One potato. Two potato. She tries but can't hold back a harsh reply. "Ma'am, you're going to need to get your dinner yourself," Miss Perkins says firmly.

"Fine. Be that way." Mrs. Davis heads to her bedroom.

Miss Perkins pulls off her apron. "I'll check on Sam and be back in the morning. Mark my words, you're making a mistake."

Instead of answering, Mrs. Davis slams the bedroom door.

Chapter Thirty

It's dark, and Sam hears voices. He feels movement. He's in a car. He doesn't have a chance to feel worried because a rough worn hand squeezes his.

It grows darker. He grips the hand.

When Sam wakes up, he's lying on a narrow bed. Too narrow, he thinks. The mattress is both softer and lumpier in places than his own. Sensing that he is not home, he has to force himself to open his eyes. He's not staring up at his bedroom ceiling. This one is higher. The sheets that he is resting on are scratchier.

Someone lies next to him. Whoever it is coughs a lot. Sam wants to turn and face him, but he's too weak to move his body.

The next time Sam awakes, the bed closest to him is quiet.

A woman wearing a white nurse's uniform flits in and out. Her hand is soft when she touches his forehead. Her steps are light when she approaches his bed. But mucus blurs his vision and seems to cover the stranger's face with a white gauze. Right after he opens his eyes, he feels himself overcome by sleep again. Glad to leave this strange place, he doesn't fight the tiredness, just gives in.

He dreams fitfully. In one dream, Mickey Kotov crumbles Sam into tiny seeds and scatters them by a basketball court. A tiny Sam-seed grows into a huge apple tree. Its tangled branches overhang the court. In another, Sam's mother stands by his bedside. She is mur-

muring to him words that he can't hear.

One morning, Sam's eyes open wide. He's still sleeping on the same lumpy, soft bed and staring up at the same high ceiling. But he realizes that he's been asleep for a long time, and he's doesn't know where he is.

In panic, his head flops about. Thank goodness, his gaze lands on Miss Perkins. She is wearing a white dress, sort of like a nurse's uniform, sitting in the metal chair next to him.

Miss Perkins answers one of his questions before he can form even a word to ask them.

"Hello, dearie. I bet you're wondering what I'm doing all dressed up in my aide's uniform, with this little hat on my head." She points to a white hat that he hadn't noticed. "I had to get a job here. Actually, it's a decent place to work."

But Miss Perkins fails to answer his most urgent question.

Then Sam realizes: he hasn't forgotten the answer to this question. He's never known it.

"That way I can be here all the time."

Miss Perkins says the word 'here,' so casually.

Where is here?

"I'm on duty in the ward, so I can't stay with you for long." In a gesture that Sam has witnessed thousands of times, Miss Perkins pulls a Kleenex out of her pocket and blows her nose. Only Sam is not reassured.

Ward? He must be at a hospital, but why would Miss Perkins get a job at a hospital? If Sam's in a hospital, he ought to be able to leave some day soon. No one lives in a hospital. But what if he's at Principal Cullen's special school?

One of the many problems with not liking to talk is that people—even Miss Perkins—assume so much. He'll never get used to it.

"But at least you're better, dear." Miss Perkins smiles. "I'll bring you some broth. You've lost so much weight. I can carry you easily now. I have to go help with lunch, but I'll be back." Her lips graze his forehead before she disappears.

Sam stares again at the strange gray ceiling.

Having spent much of his life lying on his back and looking up, Sam is an expert on ceilings. He has identified three circus animals in the gray discolorations—an elephant, a monkey and a skinny crocodile—when he hears a cough and realizes that he's not alone.

He struggles to flip over and to stretch his head. A gray woolen lump lies in the bed next to him. He guesses that the blanket hides a kid.

On the side of the blanket facing him, he reads: 'Mannville Institution."

He flips onto his back again and gazes upwards. The circus ceiling is less worrisome.

Sam must have fallen asleep again, because when he opens his eyes, a lady with golden hair smiles down at him.

"I'm Nurse Beck."

He recognizes her green eyes from his dreams.

"You must be a very special boy to have Miss Perkins so devoted to you," Nurse Beck says.

After any illness, even a cold, Sam's voice box feels far away. Following this long illness, it has sunk to his toes. All he can do is stare at her dimpled mouth.

"I'm told that we need to fatten you up. When your mother comes again, we want her to be able to recognize you," Nurse Beck says cheerfully.

Sam notices that she uses the word 'again.' Perhaps, Sam's vision of his mother wasn't a dream.

"So try to stay awake long enough for me to get you some food," Nurse Beck says.

Sam nods.

"Now I want to turn you." Nurse Beck helps him turn ever so gently onto his side. He should be able to do this by himself, but he is so weak. He faces the bedside table.

My Early Life, by Winston Churchill, lies there, alongside an open card.

He can't read the front, but the inside bears his mother's handwriting. She won the penmanship award in third grade, and every word is perfectly formed:

Get Well For Me. I've Gone to Europe but Will Have Some Exciting News Soon,

Love,

Mom

Tears begin to dampen Sam's cheeks. He longs for Ann. *Yes, I can cry,* he wants to tell her.

Chapter Thirty-One

While Dr. Brandon examines Sam, Miss Perkins waits in the clinic.

Will Sam be released tomorrow? Or the day after? Miss Perkins knows that it will be soon. She blows her nose and tries to get her mind off the prospect of Sam in the ward.

Now that Miss Perkins has worked at Mannville for a week, she's learned a lot more about the residents. Although a few have cerebral palsy, polio or other problems moving around, most of the kids are simply retarded. The institution is understaffed, and many of the kids are quite active. With Sam so weak, she's afraid that one or two of the bigger boys will be a danger to him. Particularly, she's worried about a boy named Ralph.

No sane parent…But she won't allow herself to think about Mrs. Davis either. She'll just get angry. Before Mrs. Davis left for Europe, she spent an afternoon at the clinic. The poor boy was so sick that Miss Perkins doubts that he even remembers her visit, but Miss Perkins will never forget it.

On her way out, Mrs. Davis had cooed, "I'm so relieved that you're here, Miss Perkins. I know we had our disagreements, but I'm not sure that I could leave the country while Sam was sick if you weren't with him." She smiled. "Thank you."

"Are you ready to tour the ward, Mrs. Davis?" Miss Perkins snapped.

"I'll do it when I get back. I know Sam is in good hands." Then, Mrs. Davis had batted her eyes at Miss Perkins as though she was trying to charm a boyfriend.

"I'll call you both often. Tell Sam that I'm sorry to leave him for this long."

The sound of approaching footsteps interrupts Miss Perkins' musings.

Dr. Brandon is a tall man. His white coat is crumpled. Often, Miss Perkins has overheard him complain to Nurse Beck about his hundreds of patients. With his ashen complexion, he indeed looks overworked. He sits down in the chair opposite her.

"Sam's lungs are clear," the doctor assures Miss Perkins, but his smile doesn't reach his eyes.

"I know he's over the illness," Miss Perkins argues, "but he hasn't eaten much, and he's so weak. I worry about him in the ward."

The doctor shrugs. "I think Sam should do just fine."

Miss Perkins says slowly, "When?"

"Tomorrow morning," Dr. Brandon answers. "Good luck."

Miss Perkins nods and exits.

"Abigail, you're wanted on the phone," Nurse Beck calls to her.

In the clinic office, Miss Perkins goes to Nurse Beck's desk and picks up the receiver. It is Mrs. Davis. Her voice is faint. Miss Perkins presses the phone more tightly to her ear.

"I can't talk long," Mrs. Davis says. A crackle sounds on the line. "Long distance is too expensive. I'm in Paris. France! How's Sam?" she asks.

"The doctor says he's well. He's moving into the ward tomorrow."

"Can I talk to him….?" Mrs. Davis asks eagerly.

Miss Perkins puts her hand over the receiver. "Nurse Beck, would you do me a favor and bring Sam in here to talk to his mother?"

"Sure," Nurse Beck answers. She rushes off.

"When are you coming back?" Miss Perkins says into the phone. She works to keep her tone polite.

"I'll be there in ten days," Mrs. Davis pauses. "With big news."

"I see," Miss Perkins says.

"I don't know if you can understand this, but I've never gotten to travel before. I've seen palaces. Museums. We're going to London next week. I'm having the best time," Mrs. Davis says.

Miss Perkins feels herself losing her patience.

"Now, can I say hello to Sam?" Mrs. Davis asks. "I've bought him a football. It's the French sport."

Nurse Beck pushes Sam into the office. He has a big grin on his face.

"Sam will like your gift," Miss Perkins lies. His mother's return, she knows, is the only thing Sam wants.

Chapter Thirty-Two

The instant Miss Perkins pushes Sam through the door of the infirmary, the smell changes. He no longer breathes in Nurse Beck's flowery perfume but fried food with a hint of pee.

Sam understands why when he sees the inmates. Inmates? Is that what he and the other prisoners are called?

The room where he finds himself has three separate seating areas and several blue flowered rugs. In the background, more than one radio is playing.

A few of the boys are teenagers. Some are in wheelchairs. One of the boys is perhaps nine or ten. He is wearing only a T-shirt and a huge diaper.

A boy about his age walks up to him. Even though his hair is combed and his face is clean, the way his eyes are sunk into his pudgy face makes him look lost.

"Daddy?" the boy asks.

Sam resents his stiff neck which won't allow him to turn away.

A few boys in wheelchairs are scattered around the room. Miss Perkins pushes Sam past a group of boys who are piecing together puzzles on a circular rug. A big burly attendant, wearing a hairnet which covers her ears, is helping them.

Sam can't take his eyes off the large, bright puzzle pieces. The bears, cakes and houses look like they're designed for three-year-olds.

Miss Perkins stops in front of some purple drapes. "Your new window." She pulls back the curtains, and sunlight floods the room.

At first, all Sam notices is the dust cloud glittering in the light.

Miss Perkins pushes him closer.

Sam gazes out on a circular drive, green grass, stone benches and a big oak tree. Without a basketball court, it isn't as interesting as his old view. But he knows instinctively that he will be able to stare at that oak tree for years and still find a new twist in its branches or a new stain on its bark.

He might have to. He has gotten used to his body holding him prisoner. For the first time, he feels like the place where he lives is a prison, too.

I certainly hated every minute of my imprisonment more than I have ever hated any other period of my life,[31†] Winnie breaks in. He's talking about when he was captured by the Boers.

I'm glad that you agree with me, Sam answers. But Winnie's confession isn't exactly comforting. Sam realizes it makes him uncomfortable to realize that being a prisoner was hard even for Winnie, who makes everything seem easy.

"Past that fence," Miss Perkins is saying, "you can spot a horse."

Sam is searching the horizon when an adult voice screams, "Ralph, no!"

Behind him, Sam listens to the footsteps. The thumps sound broad as if made by large tennis shoes.

"Ralph, put that puzzle down," Miss Perkins scolds.

Miss Perkins probably has the kid under control, but Sam slumps anyway to protect himself.

"That's a good boy, Ralph," Miss Perkins says. "Let me introduce you to Sam."

Miss Perkins pulls the big boy over to him.

Ralph cocks his head and grins. His front tooth is half gone. He wears a short-sleeved T-shirt and baggy pants without a belt. His biceps are huge, as if he lifts weights.

Sam drools, so he shouldn't criticize, but Ralph's mouth is like a water fountain.

Except for a few thank-yous in the clinic, Sam has not spoken to anyone for over a week. "HHHii!" he croaks.

Ralph cocks his head one way, then the other, all the while studying Sam curiously.

"Ralph is like a big, strong, four-year-old," Miss Perkins says. "It's going to be really…important that you make…friends with Ralph, Sam."

Miss Perkins' nervousness is a warning. Sam tries to smile at Ralph.

Ralph reaches over and pats his cheek.

Sam smiles harder.

Ralph pinches his cheek.

"Ralph, no," Miss Perkins says firmly.

"Ralph, come here," the attendant calls from the floor.

Ralph's gaze lingers on Sam and then he turns. Sam hears the thud of his tennis shoes as he walks away.

"He's not a bad kid," Miss Perkins whispers. "He just doesn't know his own strength. Now, I'll be right back."

Miss Perkins walks away.

Sam stares at the tree and listens. He can't follow the background conversation. It's a din of voices, footsteps, and radio songs.

Although he usually doesn't have to call to him, Sam finally asks, *Winnie, are you there?*

No answer.

Panicked, Sam cries, *Winnie? Where are you?*

Chapter Thirty-Three

Out the new window, Sam stares at the morning rain streaming down. Since it's chilly, Miss Perkins has draped a blanket over his legs. The day is so gray that he can barely make out the horse. The horse's mottled coat is dingy, and it never kicks up its heels or acts happy like horses are supposed to do. He's named the horse after his mother's pony, Peter.

Until she went to college, his mother took care of Peter. After she got married, his mother visited California only a few times, but she still keeps a photograph of Peter in her bathroom.

"Won't you *please* eat some macaroni and cheese?" Miss Perkins begs him for the fourth or fifth time.

Sam looks down again, orange noodles pooled in melted margarine, the color of urine.

"Oh, Sam, what am I going to do with you?" She removes the cold food.

Sam knows that he's growing smaller. After almost two weeks at the institution, his wheelchair feels too big for him now.

His mother and Winnie don't like this place, either. Winnie hardly ever talks anymore. His mother is traveling in Europe with a friend. No one has mentioned the friend's name, but Sam suspects that Mr. Jordache, the man with the diamond rings, is in Europe with her. When his mother called, she said that she wasn't coming back from Europe for another week.

Sam's starting to believe that, unlike Winnie whose purpose was to save the free world, his purpose was really small. He changed a basketball team. Now, his purpose is over.

Sam hopes that, at least, Mickey is still playing with the Tomcats.

I'm still here, Winnie says.

Where have you been? Sam answers.

I came to tell you that famous men are usually the product of an unhappy childhood.[32]

Is that supposed to make me feel better? I'm not famous, Sam reminds him.

You will be one day, Winnie answers.

That he, Sam Davis, will some day be famous is such a crazy idea that Sam chuckles. *Famous for what? For sitting in a wheelchair?*

In the distance, Peter paws the ground. Although Sam doesn't even like the horse, he reaches for the window anyway. The pane is freezing cold. As if his finger were a warm blanket, he covers the image of Peter with his thumb.

Sam's wheelchair is facing the window. It is mid-day, but he struggles to wake up. He remembers his old self as a kind of fond dream about a boy who used to have the energy to have tantrums, to go to school, to and to care about a basketball team.

Through half-closed eyes, he sees a Channel 2 News truck parked on the circular drive.

Draped in blankets, his wheelchair feels so cozy that when Sam hears people yelling, his eyes are already closed again.

"You can't come in here with that camera," a man bellows. Sam recognizes the voice of Director Bentsen, the head of Mannville.

"Wait a minute, Director Bentsen," a male voice answers.

"I'm a reporter," the unknown voice continues. "But we're not going to do a story on your place. We're just trying to talk to one of

179

your residents."

"Who is it that you want to speak to?" Miss Perkins takes charge in her calm, determined way.

"Sam Davis," the stranger answers.

Sam's eyes open wide for the first time that day. *Sam Davis?*

"Why do you want to talk to my Sam?" Miss Perkins asks.

"His essay about Winston Churchill won a national contest," the reporter answers.

Maybe Winnie was right. I am going to be famous, Sam thinks.

"We want to congratulate him," the reporter continues. "And ask him what he intends to do with his prize."

"Oh my goodness! That's great news." Miss Perkins says. "It's all right, Director Bentsen, don't you see? They just want to talk to Sam."

Then, before Sam can even try to straighten his head, he's surrounded.

Both men are wearing khaki pants and rumpled shirts. The one who holds a notepad has a double chin which matches his stomach, a round mound above his belt. A camera nearly the size of a phone book hangs around the other man's neck. A lit cigarette sticks out of one side of his mouth.

Miss Perkins introduces Sam.

"Can he talk?" the cameraman asks doubtfully, as an ash from his cigarette falls onto the floor.

"He hasn't said much lately." Sam hears the sadness in Miss Perkins' voice. "But he can." She puts a hand on his shoulder. "Sam, where's your alphabet?"

Ralph had stolen it….Sam can't remember how many days ago. "GGGone."

"Let me see if I can find it." Miss Perkins turns her back to them.

"Are you sure there's not some mistake?" the cameraman murmurs to the reporter.

As the man looks down at his notepad, his chins ripple. "The winner is Sam Davis at Mannville Institution. Did you read the kid's essay?"

The cameraman blows out a ring of smoke. "The first paragraph," he says.

"It was good," the reporter remarks.

"So it's impossible…." the cameraman says.

Miss Perkins returns and interrupts the men's rude conversation. *I'm not a stick of furniture,* Sam wants to tell them.

"Here it is." Miss Perkins opens Sam's alphabet and lays it out on his tray. "Sam, you're going to be in the newspaper."

Like the rest of him, Sam's finger is weak, but the men's treatment of him has made him angry. He feels a little bit of his old determination returning.

The reporter holds his pencil ready. "Did you write the essay on Winston Churchill and fate?" the reporter asks.

Sam looks up.

"That means 'yes,'" Miss Perkins explains. "If he looks down, that means 'no'."

The reporter jots down a note. "So you really like Winston Churchill?" the newsman asks.

"YYes," Sam croaks, tired of Miss Perkins' constantly answering for him.

The cameraman whispers something to the reporter. Sam overhears the word 'test.' As he readies himself, he remembers Ann's questions about the number of potted plants, and he misses school so much that he shudders. The reporter looks at Sam out of the corner of his eye. "What was Winston Churchill's wife's name?"

Sam spells out 'Clementine.' The reporter says each letter out loud.

When Sam finishes, the men look surprised. The cameraman nods at the reporter.

The reporter throws up his hands. The cameraman shrugs.

"One thousand dollars is a lot of money for a boy like you," the reporter says. "What are you going to do with it?"

On the alphabet sheet, Sam spells the sentence: "Give it to Perkins."

"Who's that?" the reporter asks.

Miss Perkins doesn't tell them right away. When she does, Sam can see that her lips are trembling as if she is about to cry.

"Doesn't the boy have parents?" the reporter says.

"His father and mother are divorced. He lives with his mother. I mean," Miss Perkins corrects herself, "he used to live with his mother."

Used to? What's the point in having a beautiful mother when Sam can't see her? When she is going to stay in Europe for three whole weeks? At this last thought, he feels so discouraged that he slumps further into his chair.

The reporter is scribbling furiously. "Your name and address?"

Miss Perkins gives the man the information.

The cameraman returns from stubbing out his cigarette. "Well, let me get a photo of you and the kid," the cameraman says. He motions for Miss Perkins to stand close to Sam.

Miss Perkins wipes Sam's face with a tissue and straightens his robe. She angles his wheelchair towards the ward so that he faces the kids.

Ralph and the rest of the kids are staring blankly at him. After the flash goes off, the men hurry out, muttering their goodbyes. As suddenly as the news crew had arrived, they're gone.

Miss Perkins beams at him. "My prizewinner!"

With his mother in Europe, Sam has a hard time caring.

Chapter Thirty-Four

In her apartment, Miss Perkins leans over the rotary phone. She sticks her fingers in the holes and pushes around the metal frame to dial the number of the London hotel. Mrs. Davis gave her the number in case of an emergency. Mrs. Davis picks up on the second ring. "Oh, it's you." From her sleepy voice, Miss Perkins guesses that Mrs. Davis is in bed. The connection is better than usual. She doesn't sound so far away.

"I have some lovely news, ma'am," Miss Perkins says.

"I could use some."

Miss Perkins tells her about the national prize. Oddly, Mrs. Davis remains quiet.

"Are you all right?" Miss Perkins asks her.

"That's a lot of money," Mrs. Davis says.

Ever since she's heard about the prize money, Miss Perkins has only been able to think about one thing. "Enough for a deposit and the first month's rent on a new apartment."

"Here you are lecturing me on what to do again," Mrs. Davis says irritably.

"Sam is still weak, ma'am," Miss Perkins pleads. "I have many duties and can't be with him all the time. If only you'd return. You'd understand that Mannville is not a good place for a small quiet boy like Sam."

"Thousands of kids live happily in institutions," Mrs. Davis interrupts. "I don't know anyone else who has as many problems as I do."

"Sam has more problems than you do."

"What do you know about my problems?" Mrs. Davis asks, her voice trailing off.

Miss Perkins sucks in her breath. The next few words are hard for her, but she thinks of her sweet boy, Sam, and how small he's gotten. No good can come from angering Mrs. Davis. "I apologize, ma'am. I was just…"

"Miss Perkins," Mrs. Davis interrupts. "Mr. Jordache was a fraud. A fraud. He stole about a hundred thousand dollars from my law firm. We were having dinner when he got word that Scotland Yard was after him, and he disappeared. He left me sitting alone in a pub. I don't even have the money to buy a ticket home.

For once, Miss Perkins is speechless.

Mrs. Davis sobs. "It's been awful."

She sucks in her breath jaggedly. "Sam….I deserted my son. I quit my job. Because of that jerk."

All of a sudden, Mrs. Davis' long absence makes sense. "Whenever you return, Sam will be very glad to see you," Miss Perkins says.

"I found out that Mr. Jordache is married, with five children." Mrs. Davis breaks down in sobs again. "He was too good to be true," she says. "Everyone at my law firm knows that I've made a fool of myself."

After a few more attempts to comfort her, Miss Perkins remembers that this call is long distance. "I've got to go, when can I tell Sam that you're coming?"

Mrs. Davis sniffs. "The lawyer that I used to work for is wiring me money for a ticket. I'll be home soon. Name a day."

"I'm so thankful," Miss Perkins says. "How about next weekend?"

"I'll be there." Mrs. Davis sighs.

"Now are you sure, ma'am? Because I'm going to tell Sam."

"You can count on me," Mrs. Davis says.

Miss Perkins hopes that she can count on Mrs. Davis.

Chapter Thirty-Five

A plate of mashed potatoes and ground chicken sits untouched on Sam's plastic tray.

Beverly, the attendant, who loops the silver hairnet underneath her ears, is standing over Sam. Mr. Bentsen, Mannville's director, has forbidden Miss Perkins to feed Sam all the time. It's not fair to the other patients for Sam to have his own personal attendant. That's why Beverly is holding the spoon.

Sam is too excited to eat. His mother was supposed to come Saturday, but she called and changed her visit to Sunday, this very afternoon. Sam's been expecting her for several hours. Miss Perkins has explained the reason for her delayed return from Europe. His mother lost her plane ticket. As far as he's concerned, it's not a good excuse. When he sees her for the first time he plans to shout at her. He wants to yell, *You're a bad mother*.

"I'm not leaving until you take a bite," Beverly says. She holds a spoon loaded with mashed potatoes.

Sam opens his mouth but closes it when he hears footsteps. Sure enough, what he dreads is true. The feet belong to Ralph.

For the first few days that Sam lived in the ward, if Ralph found him alone by the window, he just touched his arm. But lately, Ralph has seemed to select Sam as a favorite friend. He likes to peer inquiringly into Sam's face. Once, he even stuck a finger up Sam's nose.

"Where is Arnetta, Ralph?" Beverly asks.

Arnetta is one of the other caretakers. Ralph is never supposed to be left unattended. But the ward is big. Sometimes Ralph wanders off.

Ralph just cocks his head and looks at her.

"Arnetta!" Beverly calls.

As the big woman lumbers over, a tattoo of a heart jiggles on her arm. "Sue Ann is sick today," Arnetta tells Beverly. "So I've got the whole ward to take care of. I could use some help here." Her tone is sharp and unfriendly. She takes Ralph's hand and starts leading him away.

Beverly sighs. "I understand," she says. "Let's go, Sam," she jabs the overloaded spoon at his teeth. "I don't have all day."

Grasping anything is hard for him, but Sam holds out his right hand.

Beverly leans over him. She smells like Jergen's Lotion. "That's good. I told Miss Perkins that she does too much for you. A big boy like you can feed himself." She places the spoon in his outstretched hand.

Sam is barely able to curl his fingers around the spoon, but his aim is swift and sure. He drops the spoon inside his mouth and clamps his lips down on it. Feeding himself is so much work that he decides to be efficient. He lassoes the whole glob of potato with his tongue.

He spits the clean spoon onto the tray.

"Beverly," Arnetta shouts, startling Sam. "I need help now!"

Sam is feeling relieved that Beverly has disappeared until he hears footsteps behind him. They are sloppy and heavy—not sharp and light like his mother's, nor slow like Beverly's.

Sam is still trying to nudge the potato glob—a whale beached on his tongue—towards his teeth, when Ralph bends over Sam and smiles curiously at him. The lower part of his face is wet with drool.

Ralph draws closer until his face is just a few inches from Sam's.

Your smile is crooked just like mine, Sam thinks. Then, he coughs. The potato glob slides down his throat. Like he did the time he nearly drowned in the bathtub, he struggles to breathe. He feels as if someone is clutching his throat, squeezing it. His brain fills with panic, and Winnie's words start racing through his mind: *I now saw death as near as I believe I have ever seen him. He was swimming in the water at our side, whispering from time to time.*[33†]

One minute. Two minutes before he passes out? Death whispers into his ear.

No! Not yet. With all his strength, he shakes his fist in Ralph's face.

Effortlessly, Ralph pushes Sam's hand aside.

Sam butts at Ralph with his head. Ralph lets out a low growl. Now his dark eyes are flashing with anger. His large hand pulls back and slaps Sam's cheek.

Sam bends over his tray and drops his face into the leftover mashed potatoes. Squishy. Ralph pounds the only available part of Sam—his back—so hard that he feels tears come to his eyes.

Sam coughs a great cough. Ralph hits him hard again, just as a noise sounds near the door—a familiar sharp tapping.

The glob of potato loosens and shoots out of his mouth onto the tray.

"Sam!" His mother screams. "That's my son! Stop beating him, you bully!"

Sam hears Ralph run away.

"Nurse! Nurse! Help!" His mother yells. "Oh, my God!" his mother cries. "That kid could have killed you!"

Sam lifts his face from the tray and stares into her eyes. "Noooo," he says. He wants to tell her, *Ralph helped me.*

"Are you O.K.?" She picks up his napkin and cleans the bits of potato off his face.

Sam nods. Maybe he has died, because his mother looks like an angel. In her green dress and hat, she is so beautiful that he can't bring himself to be mean to her. And like an angel, she floats away. As he listens to the familiar patter of his mother's shoes, he sucks in great gulps of air. He promises himself that he'll never take air for granted again. It's wonderful, delicious stuff, better than ice cream or popsicles.

This time, two pairs of footsteps approach.

His mother is yelling, "A huge boy was hitting my son. If I hadn't arrived when I did, I don't know what would have happened. This is the kind of supervision that I pay you for?"

"I was feeding him just a minute ago, ma'am," Beverly says.

His mother leans closer and stares into Sam's eyes. "Tell me the truth. Are you all right?"

Sam looks up. "MMOOTHER!"

"Sam," she grabs his hand. "Where is Miss Perkins?"

He shrugs.

His mother hauls herself up to her full height. Dramatically, she points in the direction that Ralph has gone. "Why was my son left unattended…."

"We got lots of kids. Not just your son," Beverly says.

"So your standard practice is to leave my son alone!" his mother is screaming. "To be bullied and picked on." She stamps her foot. "I want to talk to the director."

Sam laughs inside. His mother is having a temper tantrum. About him. She has a lot to make up for, but he is feeling a little bit loved.

"Yes, ma'am," Beverly says. "If you can find him, you can talk to him. He's not here much."

"Where is he then?" his mother demands.

Beverly rolls her eyes. "He's one of those golfers, ma'am."

His mother looks as angry as Sam has ever seen her. "I'll be back in a minute, Sam," she says.

Forget about the director, Sam wants to tell her. *Come back and talk to me.* But her high heels patter rapidly down the hallway until they fade away.

Chapter Thirty-Six

"Miss Perkins," Beverly says.

Miss Perkins looks up and sees the aide standing in the doorway to the small library. Miss Perkins is teaching a boy named Calvin his letters. As a baby, Calvin had polio but he is very bright.

"What's wrong? Is Sam all right?" Miss Perkins asks.

"Yes," Beverly says. "But Sam's mother is here. She's pretty upset." She explains that Sam and Ralph were left alone together. "But only for a minute, Miss Perkins. I swear it."

"Can you watch Calvin for me, Beverly?" Miss Perkins asks.

Miss Perkins can hear Mrs. Davis' angry voice from the front room. As she gets closer, she can smell her sweet perfume. Through the open door of the director's office, she catches a glimpse of Mrs. Davis' bright green wool dress.

Miss Perkins is surprised to see Director Bentsen at work on a Sunday. Then, she notices the golf bag on his shoulder. The aging director is wearing white pants and an orange golf sweater. Mrs. Davis blocks the door. It looks as if her former employer has ambushed the director on what he had hoped would be a quick stop to pick up his golf bag.

"I may not have much money," Mrs. Davis is wagging her finger in his face. "But I used to work for a major law firm. When I tell lawyers how my son is being treated, they will be very upset."

"We are so sorry, Mrs. Davis," Director Bentsen tries to reassure her. Mrs. Davis is half the director's size, but he seems to be cowering. "However, we can't give any resident special treatment."

"Special treatment," Mrs. Davis scoffs. "Sam had no supervision."

"We do the best that we can with our limited resources," Director Bentsen answers calmly, but his beefy face is growing red.

"Sam was left alone with a bully. The aide told me that you are frequently absent." Mrs. Davis says.

Director Bentsen sucks in his flabby stomach. "Madam, I'm here on a Sunday."

"To collect your golf clubs," Mrs. Davis responds.

Director Bentsen drops the golf bag. "I resent that."

"I want to know if you are going to take care of my son!" Mrs. Davis shouts.

"Mannville Institution is a fine place," Director Bentsen says. "If you don't like it, I suggest that you look elsewhere for care."

"That's just what I'll do," Mrs. Davis says before she sweeps out the door.

If Miss Perkins were the type, she would faint from happiness.

"When will your son be leaving?" the director calls after her.

"As soon as I can rent a new apartment," Mrs. Davis answers. "Until then, I demand that you take care of Sam."

"We'll do our best for your son, Mrs. Davis," Director Bentsen says.

Mrs. Davis shoots the director a steely look, but he is hoisting his bag of clubs onto his shoulder.

"Director Bentsen, *no* child deserves to be mistreated," Mrs. Davis calls over her shoulder.

Miss Perkins follows her into the dark hallway. "I'm so happy, Mrs. Davis. This is a great idea that you have to take Sam home," she says. "I can't wait to tell the dear boy the good news."

"I feel terrible. Since you were with him, Miss Perkins, I thought that he was safe," Mrs. Davis says.

"I tried to tell you, ma'am." Miss Perkins says.

"I know. You're always right," Mrs. Davis snaps. "You think that I'm a rotten person for going to Europe. You just can't seem to understand that I used to be full of such hope."

"I didn't mean that. Why I..." A terrible thought stops Miss Perkins mid-sentence. What if Mrs. Davis doesn't rehire her? What will she do then?

"I am so angry at that fat director." Mrs. Davis mutters.

"I'm glad that we're leaving," Miss Perkins says. "But where will Sam go to school?"

"Oh, I never told you. Before I left, the new principal of Sam's school called." Mrs. Davis says.

"New principal?" Miss Perkins says.

"It seems Principal Cullen was fired for paddling too hard. He paddled some boy and broke his rib," Mrs. Davis says.

"I'm not surprised," Miss Perkins says. Then she realizes that once again she has acted the part of the know-it-all.

"Mrs. Ellsworth—that's the new principal," Mrs. Davis says. "She wants Sam to return to Stirling."

"This is wonderful news," Miss Perkins says, pushing down her frustration that Mrs. Davis didn't tell her this before. "Why, we can start when he gets back." She waits, but Mrs. Davis doesn't say anything. In the silence between them, Miss Perkins thinks about all the times that she's lectured Mrs. Davis and tried to make her feel guilty. Why would an employer choose to rehire a caretaker who is an almost constant reminder of her faults as a person and as a mother?

Together, they enter the front room and see Sam at the window. He's asleep again. Ever since his illness, he sleeps a lot.

"Sam." Mrs. Davis kisses him.

His eyelids barely flutter.

"We're going home," Mrs. Davis says.

"Did you hear your mother, Sam?" Miss Perkins says. "Home."

Sam keeps his eyes squeezed shut.

Miss Perkins crosses her fingers and makes a wish. Let the sweet word 'home' include me.

Chapter Thirty-Seven

Sam is waiting in the dingy hallway inside Mannville Institution. It took his mother only nine days to rent and move into a new apartment. In a few minutes, she'll arrive in a taxi-van to pick him up.

The only bench is next to a furnace and waves of heat roll over him.

Miss Perkins leans closer and fans Sam. "I know you're feeling discouraged, but your mother ought to be here soon."

For once, Miss Perkins can't read his mind. Sam's not worried about the wait.

"Sam," his mother is hurrying down the hall towards him. She is wearing a blue raincoat and carrying an umbrella.

Since Sam's lost the habit, speaking is hard. As a warm-up, he touches the roof of his mouth and swings his tongue around, touching his teeth. To get rid of any extra spit, he swallows. "MMom," he answers.

"Off we go," Miss Perkins says as she steps behind his wheelchair. "Home!"

But Sam knows that they're not going home. They're going to a new apartment. Sam's place by the window is gone. Who will he be without his view from the window? Most important, he wonders, how long will he be able to stay with his mother this time? In the new apartment, he'll try his best to act better, but he's not perfect. He might have one or two scenes. What if his new landlord objects to the noise? If his mother decides to travel to Europe with Mr. Jordache again, will she send him away? One night will he go to bed and the next morning wake up in some new institution?

Now he knows what an institution is.

When the taxi-van halts in front of Colonial Apartments on Elm Street, it's stopped raining. The sun is shining on a red brick building. Unlike his old apartments, these windows are covered with blue awnings. Bright red Santa Clauses, leaping reindeer, shiny Menorahs and other holiday decorations grace many of the balconies. The sight of so much holiday cheer makes Sam hope that his mother will be able to afford a tree this year.

"The apartments are almost brand-new," Sam's mother is saying.

While his mother pays the driver, Miss Perkins helps Sam out of the car and into his wheelchair. Miss Perkins begins to push him.

"I want to take him, Miss Perkins," his mother breaks in. She grips the handles of the chair. "I got an apartment on the first floor so we don't need an elevator...." Uncharacteristically, his mother chatters away.

Sam thinks of how lonely he feels when she doesn't share his excitement. He longs to share hers.

His mother guides him through the parking lot and down a hallway. She stops in front of a strange brown door. After unlocking it, she flings it open. Together, they go inside. He smells soap, fruit and coffee.

Sam's old furniture has been rearranged to fit a smaller apartment. The familiar blue and green couch takes up one wall. The television sits across the room. There's no carpet, but the tile shines, and the appliances in the kitchen sparkle. A large bowl on the counter is filled with apples and bananas.

The biggest surprise is the large picture window that spans one whole wall.

The view is of Elm Street, but not the part of the street that he knows. On their errands, he and Miss Perkins rarely travel this far south. Throngs of people—wearing jackets and coats, mittens and gloves, and hats of all colors and sizes—pass by carrying packages and briefcases. Across the street is the Elm Street Bowling Alley. Despite his sour mood, the sight of the bowling alley interests him. Who bowls? When do they bowl? Is bowling a sport, he can't help wondering?

His mother is beaming at him. "What do you think about our new home."

Sam feels too sad to smile. *A home is a place you can count on. Not a place that you might have to leave.*

"What's wrong with you, child?" Miss Perkins scolds him.

"LLLLike it," Sam answers quickly.

"I'm so glad," his mother answers. She steps behind the wheel-chair. "Now let me show you your room."

After Miss Perkins has gone home, his mother sits on the end of Sam's bed. On his bedside table, the cactus hides behind a glass of water. The walls and ceiling of his new room are light blue and blend with the gray carpet.

His mother is wearing her silk robe, and her dark hair is tied back in a green ribbon. *Why do people who can easily talk, refuse to?* Sam wants to ask her.

Sam has many questions. Yet he knows that if he asks for his alphabet sheet, she won't be able to find it, and he will waste his opportunity for a conversation to talk to her in a fruitless search. He's also certain that if he fails to ask his most important question tonight, he may not have the courage to ask it at all. He draws on all his strength. "MMMister JJordache gggone?"

His mother's blue eyes widen. She starts as if Sam had slapped her. Her beautiful dark eyes grow wide. Sam senses that she has understood all the questions that he hasn't asked. Why did you send me away? Why do you want me back? Will you ever send me away again?

"Yes." His mother says firmly. "He's gone. Now, goodnight." She leans over and kisses him.

Chapter Thirty-Eight

Miss Perkins lets herself into the new apartment.

Wearing her white silk robe and slippers, Mrs. Davis is already drinking a cup of coffee at the breakfast table. Miss Perkins has never understood why a person would wear a garment to bed that needs ironing, but she has to admit that Mrs. Davis looks lovely.

As they exchange greetings, Miss Perkins relaxes. The morning feels like old times, she thinks. She pours herself a cup of coffee from the pot on the stove. She prefers tea, but over the years she's drifted into this American morning habit. She's settled at the kitchen counter, when Mrs. Davis surprises her by picking up her cup and saucer and walking across the room. She sits down on the stool next to Miss Perkins.

In all the years of Miss Perkins' employment, Mrs. Davis has never once joined her for coffee. If she can change, I can change, Miss Perkins promises herself. I will try to keep my opinions more to myself. I won't say anything when she buys a new dress. I…

Mrs. Davis trains her clear eyes on Miss Perkins. "We've had our differences."

Expecting the worst, Miss Perkins sets down her coffee cup. What will she do if she can't be with Sam?

"But I want you to promise me that you'll help me raise Sam."

Miss Perkins lets out a sigh of relief. "Gladly." This is the most wonderful request that Mrs. Davis could have made. Miss Perkins feels honored and included. Why, it's almost as if Mrs. Davis has decided not to resent her anymore. "I think Sam'll go to college and..."

"It's not going to be easy," Mrs. Davis cuts her off.

Miss Perkins reminds herself that *for once* she needs to listen.

"Last night, Sam asked me a funny question." She looks sharply at Miss Perkins. "What did you tell him about Mr. Jordache?"

"Why, nothing," Miss Perkins protests.

Mrs. Davis continues to train her gray eyes suspiciously on Miss Perkins.

"You have my word," Miss Perkins says.

Mrs. Davis sighs. "Sam always knows more about my business than I think he does."

"You're right about that, ma'am," Miss Perkins says.

Tears collect in Mrs. Davis' eyes. "Mr. Jordache promised that when we got married, Sam could have all the tutors that we wanted. That he could go to college. I wish Sam could forget Mannville ever happened." She pauses. "That awful director and his golf."

Mrs. Davis made a mistake, all right. She underestimated Sam, her own son. Shut him up in a place that she refused to visit. She put her own life ahead of Sam's. And now Mrs. Davis needs to apologize. But if Miss Perkins tells her this, she'll just make Mrs. Davis angry.

"I need to talk to him," Mrs. Davis finally says. "I should tell him that I'm sorry."

Miss Perkins studies her coffee to hide her smile.

Mrs. Davis takes one last sip, dabs at her lips with her napkin, and sighs heavily. "Even when I was going to expensive restaurants in London, I missed Sam. I wished he were there. He's all the family I have."

*　　　　*　　　　*

200

Sam has caught only snatches of the conversation between his mother and Miss Perkins. But one thing he did hear—his mother missed him!

His heart is so full that it feels like it's going to burst. His mother missed him. As far as he knows, no one has ever missed him before.

His mother is standing in the doorway in her white robe.

As beautiful as an evening star,[34†] Winnie says.

"MMom," he calls.

Her house shoes shuffle towards his bed. "Someday, you'll understand that even adults can make big mistakes."

Sam nods.

"But right now," his mother continues, "I just want to tell you that when I saw that big bully hurting you, I realized that if anything happened to you, I would die." She leans over the bed and stares into his eyes. "From now on, I promise that I am going to protect you. You can stay with me always." His mother clears her throat. "Now, do you have any questions?"

Sam, who is an expert on how much words cost, knows that she has paid dearly for this question. It's the first that she's asked in months and months. "No, MMom," he says.

Chapter Thirty-Nine

In Mrs. Ellsworth's office, Principal Cullen's paddle is gone. Two diplomas and a photo of six grandchildren hang on the wall in its place. The grandchildren, who are dressed in matching red vests, are all trying to touch a Great Dane.

"Mrs. Davis said that Sam would be at school tomorrow," Mrs. Ellsworth says.

"Sam is so excited," Miss Perkins says. "He wanted to start today, but his mum convinced him to let her take him shopping."

"Was there anything in particular you wanted to discuss? Because, if not…" Mrs. Ellsworth's gaze fixes on the clock on her desk.

10 a.m. My goodness, Miss Perkins thinks. I have been here for a while, haven't I?

"I just wanted to make sure. You see, Sam's been through so much. I know that Mrs. Riley, the P.T.A. president …"

Sometimes, despite all her words, Miss Perkins thinks, she has as much trouble communicating as Sam.

Mrs. Ellsworth nods. "The P.T.A. was upset about Sam. Luckily, we have an enlightened superintendent. When the newspaper story broke about Sam's prize, Superintendent Dewitt called and demanded an explanation as to why Sam was no longer at Stirling."

Miss Perkins catches a hint of steel behind Mrs. Ellsworth's smile. "If any parents are upset about Sam, they'll need to talk to Superintendent Dewitt," Mrs. Ellsworth says.

Miss Perkins lets out a sigh of relief. "I'm so grateful. I can't…"

"If you arrive by 8:15," Mrs. Ellsworth interrupts, "we'll still be in assembly, and I'll welcome Sam."

"Thank you so much," Miss Perkins says.

"Times are changing, Miss Perkins. Soon, I believe that even crippled kids will be entitled to a public education," Mrs. Ellsworth says.

As Miss Perkins gathers her purse to leave, she does feel hopeful. More hopeful than she's felt in a long time.

The next morning, Sam rolls across the parking lot in back of Stirling Junior High. The trees are bare now, and the wheelchair crunches dead leaves. Due to the cold, Sam sees the puffs of Miss Perkins' breath, small clouds. He hears the band playing *The Star-Spangled Banner.* The school must be having an assembly. He's never been to one before, and he's excited. Along with his coat, he is wearing a new pair of blue jeans and tennis shoes. He's refused a haircut. All to get ready for school.

He stares at the double green doors. He's really returned to Stirling. He's escaped from the bad food, the smell of pee and the noisy front room. He's heard of people who stay in school for their whole lives, and at that moment, he wants to be one. He'll gladly memorize thousands of prepositions now.

When he and Miss Perkins arrive at Mrs. Martin's room, the classroom is empty. As they pass by the open door, he eagerly soaks up the sight of the potted plants and the dusty blackboard.

"Mrs. Ellsworth tells me that not only was Principal Cullen fired, but he can't ever teach school again. He hit Bobby Sur so hard that he broke the boy's rib. All because Bobby was blowing a gum bubble." Miss Perkins pushes Sam past the classroom doors down the long hallway. The other classrooms are empty, too.

Inside the auditorium, Sam sees a petite woman with white hair standing on the stage. She is holding a microphone.

Sam takes it all in. The kids wiggling in their seats. The band on the stage. The flagpole. The box marked *lost and found*. The red and white banner—Stirling Tomcats, Tournament Champs. Unlike the noise at Mannville, this din sounds happy.

"Those who want to go on the field trip need to turn in their permission slips," the woman says into the microphone. Sam decides that the speaker must be Mrs. Ellsworth, the new principal. "I repeat. No one can attend who has not returned their form."

"Our final announcement." Mrs. Ellsworth gestures towards the back of the auditorium. Sam doesn't even have time to straighten in his chair. "Sam Davis, our League of Women Voters award winner, has returned to school today."

The kids start clapping.

"T-Thank You," Sam murmurs.

If you can't have the world's applause, a whole school's is pretty good, Winnie says.

For once, Sam is tongue-tied inside and out. He can't think of anything else that he even wants to say to the auditorium of cheering kids.

Sometimes, short speeches are best, Winnie says.

Chapter Forty

After the special assembly is over, Miss Perkins pushes Sam down the hallway. Kids throng on either side of him. A boy pretending to play a guitar walks behind him. Two kids are arguing over a locker.

Marigold hurries past, her arms swinging at her sides. He hears another set of footsteps, and Ann joins him. She has on the same red and white dress that she wore the first day Sam met her.

"I'm excited that you're back," Ann says.

"NNot hher." Sam raises his finger and points at Ann's dance partner and friend.

"Marigold will be fine. I just have to remind her that I can have two best friends," Ann says.

As a question, Sam points at himself.

Ann nods. "You and I are best friends." She grabs his hand and squeezes it.

Sam grins. He's never had a best friend before.

What about me? Winnie asks.

Ann's a real best friend, Sam thinks.

Can you talk to a "real" best friend anytime that you want? Winnie asks. *Can a real best friend read your thoughts? No. The advantages of a "real" best friend are limited,* he points out.

Sam realizes that Winnie's pride is hurt. *If Ann can have two best friends, I can too,* Sam tells Winnie. But as Ann grips his hand and Sam stares into her blue eyes, he's not sure that he means it.

Charlie rushes up. He stares at Sam for a minute before punching him playfully on the arm.

Sam points outdoors. "YYes," he says.

A few minutes later, Ann parks Sam right in his spot next to the court. She is wearing her blue coat. It's a cold but sunny day.

"Marigold and I are going inside. It's too cold out here," Ann says.

"TTThanks, Ann Riley," Sam calls.

"Brrr," Ann says. "You're welcome, Sam Davis."

"You shouldn't be out here either, Sam," Miss Perkins scolds.

"PPlease," Sam says.

Their eyes meet, and Miss Perkins' face melts into a smile. Sam knows she is remembering Mannville Institution, Ralph and the bad food. She buttons Sam's coat. She unlocks his seat belt and removes a blanket that Sam has been sitting on and drapes it over his legs.

Before she drapes it over him, Sam catches a quick view of his legs. He is amazed at how skinny they've become.

"We won the championship game." The day is so cold that Charlie Simmons rubs his hands together as he tells Sam this amazing fact.

Charlie motions toward Mickey. "All because of our new point guard."

Mickey dribbles the ball up to Sam. He stops and stares at him. "Thiinks, Sam."

Did Sam hear Mickey right? Did Mickey just thank him? Mickey's taunt is still fresh in his memory. *Window Boy.* Luckily, Mickey doesn't wait for a response but passes the ball to A.J. Watching Mickey run back onto the court, it occurs to Sam that people change. Losers become winners. Like the Tomcats. Like Mickey. Like himself. Now, Sam is an award winner. A Window Boy no more.

Do people change, Sam wonders, or is it just the way we think about them that changes? After all, Mickey was always a good basketball player, and Sam was always smart.

Charlie leans closer to Sam. "At first, I thought you were our cheerleader, but now I know better. Got any other tips, Coach?"

Sam smiles.

Is that it? Winnie asks. *Is that all you're going to say or do? You have no sense of the dramatic.*

What should I do? Sam asks.

Why, old chap, surprise all of them, Winnie orders him. *Stand up and say something big!*

Why not? Sam thinks as he grips the arms of the wheelchair. His legs feel shaky, but they'll bear his weight for a few seconds. Then, he remembers his seat belt.

I can't stand after all, he tells Winnie.

You have no excuse. Winnie reminds him. *Miss Perkins removed your seat belt when she got out the blanket.*

Sam grasps the handles of the chair and shifts his weight onto both legs.

"What are you doing?" Miss Perkins asks, but he ignores her.

"Be careful," she cautions him.

Charlie and the other kids gawk at Sam. They are probably noticing his trembling legs.

Sam lifts his pointer finger. "PPPlay Ball," he bursts out.

Afterword

I. The Man

After that day in the playground, I never heard Winnie's voice again. At least, not in the strong personal way that I did during my days of watching from the window—before I went to school and had friends. Once I lost my imaginary friend, I asked myself many times: who was the voice who talked to me? The voice that gave me hope? The voice that I trusted?

For many years, I was confused by the fact that Winnie's voice was a man's. It couldn't be my father's. I had never known him. A boy's idea of God? Then, the night of my graduation from high school, Miss Perkins had a bad cold. When she hugged me, she rasped into my ear,

"You made it, old chap."

And I did.

With the help of physical therapy, I have regained the use of all my fingers on my right hand. I can:

Operate an electric wheelchair—I no longer have to wait to be pushed.

Type—I can now communicate even complicated thoughts quickly and easily.

Feed myself—I love not having to eat peas when I don't want to.

And I can perform simple chores, like pulling on my pants by myself.

Although I read many books, both fiction and non-fiction, I still want to learn as much as I can about Winston Churchill. I remain fascinated by him, partly because I believe that my life was shaped by his.

Just to mention one example: without him, I wouldn't have become a sportswriter for the *Boston Tribune*.

First, let me say, it wasn't easy getting out of junior high, but with

Mrs. Martin's help in Math, I graduated. I went on to high school with Charlie, Ann, and Mickey. Ann and Charlie showed me how to use my electric wheelchair. After I got my typewriter, I used to type papers for friends, including Mickey.

I don't remember Mickey's grade on his paper—*A Startling Moment*—but this is still true: nothing gives me more pleasure than helping a friend. In 1979, I received a full scholarship to University of Massachusetts, and graduated *cum laude* with a degree in journalism.

Even though our lives are very different, I've stayed close to my friends from high school. I've been in all three of Mickey's weddings. I rejoiced with Ann when she was admitted to medical school at age thirty-nine. I'm the godfather to Ann's oldest daughter. Charlie is a sports car salesman living in Rhode Island, but every year or so, we meet in Boston and go to a Celtics game. As for Mrs. Martin, a few years ago, she was diagnosed with throat cancer. In a major reversal of our fortunes, I am the one who is able to speak to her now. We remain good friends.

Back to my point. The first time that I applied for a job with the newspaper, I was turned down.

In a last-ditch attempt to secure employment, I asked for an interview with the managing editor, Mr. Tom Rains.

Tom Rains had a reputation as a tough manager. I was just out of college, very scared, and I had no idea what arguments I was going to use to convince him to hire me. As I wheeled into his room, I happened to glance at his bookshelves and spotted two volumes of works by Winston Churchill.

I tapped on the old-fashioned screen that I used back then to communicate and wrote one of my favorite Winnie quotes: "We're all worms, but I do believe that I am a glowworm."[35]

Tom Rains leaned over my shoulder and looked at my screen.

"What? What are you talking about?" he growled.

"I'm quoting Churchill," I answered him.

"Oh, are you a Churchill fan?" Mr. Rains asked me.

We stopped talking two hours later.

I got the job and have worked for the *Boston Tribune* ever since. I live with my mother and with Miss Perkins. I'm proud to say that I support our whole family. My mother retired a few years ago when her arthritis got so bad.

I'm most comfortable with batting averages, NFL statistics and turnover statistics, but I believe that because I'm disabled I think about abstract ideas like fate more often than the average sportswriter.

If Miss Perkins had not read to me about Churchill, I doubt that I would have had the courage to go to Stirling Junior High.

If I hadn't gone to school, I wouldn't have written the award-winning essay.

If I hadn't written the essay, I might have lived long enough for my mother to rescue me from the Mannville Institution, but then again… Who knows?

Although I don't pretend to understand this, I take comfort in the fact that what Miss Perkins always told me was right.

I was meant to live and to live exactly as I am.

Diary entry 9/17/1986
Sam Davis

II. The Caretaker

To the editor of the *Stirling Banner*:

For most of us Englishmen and women who suffered through the war with Winston Churchill, he was the greatest man in the world. And we'll never forget him or change our opinion.

Therefore, I was shocked when your paper carried news of Winston Churchill's death at 79 on your second page and reduced his remarkable life to only TWO paragraphs. I hope that you will print my letter and allow me to remind your readers of his long full life.

Winston Churchill was born on November 30, 1874, in a palace. He talked with a stutter and was a poor student. As a boy, his parents never paid much attention to him. But he had a wonderful nanny named Mrs. Everest. Her love and support made him the great man that he was.

Your article spoke of Churchill's role during World War II. However, even before he became prime minister, he led a fascinating life. When the Boer War in South Africa broke out in October 1899, a London newspaper hired Churchill as a reporter. He hadn't been in South Africa long before the Boers ambushed an armored train that he was riding in and imprisoned him. He made a daring escape. Overnight, he became famous, a hero to the English people, and he was only twenty-five.

In 1901, Churchill took his seat in the House of Commons—his first political success. In 1911, Churchill was appointed First Lord of the Admiralty and began working to strengthen England's navy. In August of 1914, due to his efforts, England entered World War I, better prepared.

In your article, you mentioned that Churchill made a terrible mistake in World War I and resigned in disgrace from the Admiralty.

It is true that as a way to break the World War I stalemate, Churchill urged an attack on the Dardanelles and the Gallipoli Peninsula, both controlled by Turkey. He was hoping to open up a route to the Black Sea. However, I do not believe that Churchill should have been blamed for the disaster. The plan of attack that was followed by England was very different from the plan that Churchill had approved. In any case, his exile from mainstream politics just makes his comeback all the more remarkable.

During the years between World War I and II, unlike the rest of the world's leaders, Churchill paid attention to the Brownshirts marching through Berlin. He listened to Hitler's speeches urging all Germans to revere the Fatherland. Even though few people paid attention, Churchill gave talks and wrote articles about the need to stand up to Nazis. While Great Britain's own prime minister, Neville Chamberlain, urged appeasement, Churchill was a lonely voice warning of the dangers posed by Hitler.

Unfortunately, as we all know, Churchill's predictions were right. On September 1, 1939, German troops marched into Poland. On September 3, England and France declared war on Germany. In April 1940, when Germany attacked Denmark and Norway, Neville Chamberlain lost his job. The whole country breathed a sigh of relief when Churchill took Chamberlain's place. Churchill was sixty-five. He wrote: "I felt as if I were walking with destiny and that all my past life had been but a preparation for this hour and for this trial."[36]

It was a terrible time. Great Britain was underequipped, not ready to fight the war. We all were secretly afraid we were going to lose. Churchill perfectly captured our country's plight when he said, "I have nothing to offer but blood, toil, tears and sweat."[37] Soon Belgium surrendered to Germany, and we were certain that France was going to be defeated. Churchill made us all feel brave when he told the House of Commons that even though all of Europe might fall, "....we shall not flag or fail. We shall fight in the seas and oceans...we shall fight on the beaches..."[38] On June 22, France surrendered to Germany.

We all expected the Germans to cross the English Channel. But first they had to defeat the Royal Air Force. In July, the German Luftwaffe began to bomb British shipping and ports—the Battle of Britain. In September, the Luftwaffe began nightly air raids on London. I myself am one of the lucky ones; I lived through those raids. My next-door neighbors were not so fortunate.

While the Battle of Britain raged, Churchill traveled everywhere. He went into the streets as the bombs fell, holding up two fingers in a V-for-Victory salute. I actually knew people who saw him with their own eyes. By ignoring the danger, he gave us all courage. Although the Royal Air Force was outnumbered, our pilots fought bravely and finally defeated the Luftwaffe. Churchill praised the Air Force for all of us when he said, "Never in the field of human conflict was so much owed by so many to so few."[39]

During these years, Churchill developed a close relationship with President Franklin Roosevelt. After Japan attacked Pearl Harbor on Dec. 7, 1941, the United States finally entered the war. Germany surrendered on May 7, 1945. There were parties in the street, parades, strangers kissing strangers on that joyful day, almost five years after Churchill became prime minister.

Soon, an election was held in Britain. It was a terrible thing the British people did to him. We voted him out of office. Churchill lost his post as prime minister.

Churchill came back to power though, six years later. He became prime minister again when he was almost 77 years old.

I am now a proud American citizen, but at heart, I will always be a Londoner. As you can see, Winston Churchill was much more than England's prime minister during World War II. He was our strength, our spirit, our bravery. I deeply mourn his death. Please print this letter and pay proper respect to this great man.

Respectfully yours,

Abigail Perkins

III. The Teacher

I didn't understand how backwards our schools were in educating kids with disabilities until I met Sam. He was in a wheelchair, and I mistakenly thought that he couldn't talk. I was a new teacher with thirty kids in my class. I felt panicked. I didn't think that I could teach him anything. Of course, once I got to know Sam, I found out how bright he was. He was like a sponge, soaking up information. I was so moved by Sam's situation that I did some research and found that he was not alone. In 1968, only one out of five children with disabilities went to school. Three and one-half million children were warehoused in places like Mannville Institution. Many states even had laws that prohibited children with certain types of disabilities from attending public school.

That's why I worked to pass the Education for All Handicapped Children Act. Although by then Sam was about to graduate from high school, I wrote letters to my congressmen and senator and spoke a few times to teacher groups. Thankfully, the law was enacted in 1975.

I was watching the television when I heard the news. I called Miss Perkins and told her.

"It's about time," Miss Perkins said.

Since the passage of the 1975 law, the tide has turned and the American educational system has come closer to the ideal of providing opportunities for all children. As of 2006, more than six million children in the United States receive special education through current laws.

I know that teachers are supposed to teach students and not vice versa, but Sam Davis taught me more than I taught him. He taught me about determination and about courage. I have been very ill for the last few years, and not a day goes by that I don't think of Sam's example. When I want to whine or complain, I think of Sam stuck in a wheelchair, without the ability to communicate. When I want to give up, I remember that Sam never did. And when I feel pessimistic, I pick up the newspaper and read one of Sam's sports columns.

Sometimes people do beat the odds.

Sam Davis—the boy who I thought was hopeless the first time I saw him—is now my most successful former student.

Mrs. Judith Martin

IV. The Friend

A Startling Moment
by Mikhail Kotov

I was in the sixth grade with a boy named Sam Davis. He was in a wheelchair, and I didn't know that he could talk. I'm ashamed to say that one day I was taunting him, egging him on to arm-wrestle or something obnoxious like that. The captain of the basketball team, Charlie Simmons, came in, and Charlie and I started fighting. In the middle of throwing each other around, Sam shouted two words at us. "Point guard." It was the most miraculous moment of my life. I thought anything might happen. Like Sam might fly around the room in his wheelchair. Like my father might not make me do chores every morning, and like I might manage to be on time for school. At my old school, I had been the star of the basketball team. A point guard. Until that moment, I didn't even know that Sam Davis could speak. Not only was Sam talking, but he was the one kid in the whole school who knew me, who I really was. Sam and I are good friends now, but I will never forget that startling moment—the most surprising in my life.

V. The Author

A few years ago, I was reading a biography of Winston Churchill. One sentence in the book that caught my attention said that Churchill had no problem standing up to Hitler, because he had already done the hardest thing of all: he had overcome the despair of being a child whose parents didn't love him.

I decided to write a book for young adults about Churchill. But I didn't have a character or a plot. Then, one Sunday afternoon, I picked up a *New York Times Magazine*. On the cover was a photo of a boy in a wheelchair with sparkling, interested eyes and a droopy wet smile. When I read the moving article by Lisa Belkin about Thomas Ellenson, I had found my character.

Our son, Stephen, is a dedicated basketball player. For Stephen to be interested in my book, I thought, it should be about basketball. But if my main character was in a wheelchair, how was he going to participate in this sport? As I answered this question, I discovered my plot.

I could never have written this book alone. Thank you first and foremost to Lisa Belkin for her inspiring story. Although Sam is fictional, Lisa's article illustrates that there are many kids like Sam.

If you lift the rock of so many good deeds in Houston over the past thirty years, you find the imprint of Dr. Maconda O'Connor. Her life of service has been a great example to me.

Sis Johnson got a phone call, and the next day began teaching advanced high school English after a hiatus of over ten years. She has a remarkable intelligence and diligence besides being a true friend.

Franci Crane has read many drafts of this book, and each time she has offered valuable and insightful suggestions. My life has been blessed by her generosity in too many ways to detail here.

Michael Zilkha is the most discerning reader of cultural trends whom I have ever known. He is also among the most supportive and generous of friends.

The amazingly competent Elena Marks wrote me a note after I sent her the first draft. She said, "If your agent doesn't like this, get a new agent." I keep it pinned over my desk.

Justin Cronin is a brilliant writer but an even better human being. The House of Fiction has changed my life. Thank you to all my fellow writers: Lucie Smith, Shirley Redwine, Brenda Liebling-Goldberg, Angelique Jamail, Kahla Dunn, Gabrielle Hale, Mimi Swartz, Sarah Warburton, Kat Hunter, Georgina Nelson, Charles Alcorn, and Steve Gullion.

Rue Judd is the classiest publisher that I have ever met. She is a pro, and a wonderful person to work with. Lucy Chambers is diligent, skilled, and so talented as an editor. Sally Doherty has been a good friend to the book.

Thanks to Mina Gerall for the information about Pittsburgh and for believing in my books. To Paula Douglass for the amazing marketing campaign. To Bill White for encouraging me to write. To Allen Gee for his many thoughtful comments. To Bobbi Samuels, Donna Vallone, and Kathryn Kase for crying over several drafts. To Gene and Susan Vaughn and Dick and Diane Trabulsi, Dr. Mark Leifeste, Ellen Susman and Dr. Gail Gross for their interest and enthusiasm. Buddy Haas, Mayor Bob Lanier, Helen Chang, Eric Pulaski, Denton Cooley, Bud Frick, Jonathan Day, James T. White, Kitty Rabinow, Lynn Crowley, Becky and Doug Ferguson, Kathryn and Craig Smyser, Robin Morse, Rusty Hardin, Mike and Marcia Nichols, Shafik Rifaat and Steve Susman—it meant so much to me that you were so supportive of my first book. To Rich Kinder, I am waiting for your book about Churchill. Thank you to Sharon Haley, Hazel Mitchell, Louise Van Vleck, Pam Rosenauer, Bette John, Suzanne Crowley and Ann Todd for their support and encouragement. To Ben Stein, Charles Simmons, Ryan Friedman, Daniel Leebron, Katie Kellner, Alice Johnson, Alexander Bennett, Iris Cronin, Alexander Jefferson, Hannah Smati, Emily Lahourcade, Stephanie Mallard, Brittney Prause, Ford Hubbard, Salima and Shamsa Mangalji, Hannah Phils, and Francie Williams for reading my books. To Chas, Jackson and Lauren Jhin, and Will, Elena, and Stephen White for being the best teenage friends a children's book author could have. To Gary and Andrea Lynn for befriending me and helping me with my DVD. To Dr. Larry Jefferson, Dr. Michelle Lyn and Cynthia Petrello for their technical help with cerebral palsy. To Nora Shire for fact-checking and obtaining all the permissions. Nora was endlessly patient with the many drafts. To my elementary school friends whose names I borrowed for this book. You know who you are. To Erin Kline and to Katie Moses for all their helpful research. To Judy Baldwin and Maribel Castro. One of the gifts of my life has been that I've gotten to meet librarians who are fellow readers and wonderful people. Thank you all for the gift of your time.

Not only have these great friends helped me, but I've also been inspired by Winston Churchill and Sam Davis. Since they never gave up, I decided not to.

VI. The Inspiration

The Lessons of Classroom 506

September 12, 2004
By Lisa Belkin

I. First Impressions

It was the first day of school last year, Sept. 8, 2003. The kindergartners were arriving in batches at Classroom 506 at the Manhattan School for Children, on 93rd Street between Amsterdam and Columbus Avenues. The parents of these 5-year-olds said they felt lucky to be taking their children to M.S.C. that morning, lucky to have won the scramble for admission to this sought-after institution – a public school with particular cachet among artistic, educated Upper West Side families who can't or won't pay for private education.

Only half the class was there that morning; the other students would come later in the day, the better to ease the transition to "big-kid school." Taylor, an African-American girl, was coloring a picture. Evan, one of two blond-haired boys, was playing with blocks. Thomas, one of two motor-impaired, nonverbal children, was in a custom-built wheelchair, his blue eyes wide, his gentle face animated, watching from on high as the others drew and chattered and explored.

Richard Ellenson, Thomas's father, was also there, surveying the room. It was Ellenson who devised this experiment, this attempt to reconfigure a classroom – and, in some sense, the system around it – so that his son, who has cerebral palsy, could find a way to fit into a world that often seems to resist him. Ellenson, a wiry man dressed all in black against a room awash in primary colors, was watchful, and what he was noticing was how much more work there was to be done.

"The way the space is set up, there are only four possible places to fit his wheelchair," he said to his wife, Lora, who stood with him. The other children had 16 places to sit, he explained, sweeping his hand past four brand-new tables, each with four child-size chairs. He pointed to a threesome of students sitting at a table, not interacting but at eye level with one another, unlike his son. "They are in a moment when they can become friends," he said. "Thomas is not."

There were other parents watching too. They glanced first at Thomas, then at the little girl next to him, who, though seated in a standard chair, had very little head control and was slumped over her Play-Doh. They noticed that while the class list, posted by the cubbies, had barely a dozen names, a small army of teachers – including an occupational therapist, a speech therapist, an "augmentative communication" expert and several other aides – had greeted them at the door. Even those who were arriving as kindergarten parents for the first time could sense that this class was different.

"Inclusion," said Suzanne Blank, the head teacher in Classroom 506. There was a small circle of parents around her, and everyone seemed to be smiling just a bit too broadly as she explained what was going on.

"Inclusion" is the latest in a series of evolving strategies for special-needs education. Though the definition of the word varies, inclusion, as used by educators, generally means making a child with a disability a full part of the class. Instead of merely placing that child in a standard classroom for part or even most of the day and expecting him to keep up (a strategy often known as "mainstreaming"), inclusion involves rearranging the class – both the physical space and the curriculum – to include him. Ideally, once an inclusive classroom is rethought and reconfigured, it will serve clusters of children with

224

special needs, not just one, so that impaired and nonimpaired children can come to see one another as peers. Proponents of inclusion say that it is the best way to prepare all children for the real world; skeptics contend that it too often gives teachers responsibility for impaired students without giving them sufficient training and resources, resulting in children with special needs getting improper attention and children without special needs not getting enough attention – a poor-quality education for everyone in the class.

When Thomas Ellenson began kindergarten last fall, the New York City school system had more than 1,000 classes that met the definition of inclusion to some degree. But the impaired children in those classes struggled with more manageable problems like learning disabilities and speech impairments. Thomas fell at the serious end of the disability spectrum – he could not speak or walk or sit unassisted or feed himself. By that distinction alone, Thomas's disabilities made his classroom a first. "There is nothing else like this in the city," Linda Wernikoff, the deputy superintendent for special-education initiatives, who helped create the program, told me. "This is a step beyond for us."

To chronicle a year, as I did, in and around Classroom 506, was to observe the most ambitious step toward inclusion by the largest school system in the country. But the story of Classroom 506 is also something more. It is an extended look at just what it means to be the parent of a special-needs child in the United States right now – a time when it effectively falls to the most vocal and persistent parents to shape policy and practice. These parents attend workshops, then take what they have learned and educate their children's teachers. They hire experts to write reports and document exactly what their children need. Many quit their jobs so they can have the time to choreograph their children's care. Some go even further and change careers, turning their hard-won expertise into a full-time profession.

And at least one set of parents, Thomas's, have gone the distance – persuading the City of New York to design a classroom and a curriculum to their specifications.

If their experiment were to work, Richard Ellenson said at the outset, it would "provide a template for how to teach children like Thomas so we don't have to recreate the wheel for every child who comes along." And if it were to fail, he said, he and his wife would have no idea how to educate their son.

A mere four months earlier, Classroom 506 was not a possibility for Thomas. In May 2003, he was finishing preschool at a private program called Standing Tall, which served children with severe motor impairments but a wide range of cognitive abilities. The Ellensons, like the parents of preschoolers throughout the city, were determined to find the perfect elementary school for their child. To them, education was everything. Richard is a graduate of Cornell and a founder of the advertising company where he works. Lora, a physician and a scientist, runs a research lab at New York-Presbyterian Hospital. (By way of full disclosure: Richard's mother was my kindergarten teacher, though Richard and I met only when I started to write about him.)

But the longer the Ellensons searched, they said, the more they came to believe that what they wanted for their son did not exist. Thomas did not belong in District 75, the city's classification for programs serving students who are severely disabled, because, they reasoned, he might get lost in a system that included so many children who were cognitively as well as physically impaired. Thomas might be a better fit in a school designed just for children with an array of physical problems, but they feared that that experience would not prepare him to interact in the real world. And while they could mainstream him into a standard public- or private-school classroom, that would present the opposite problem: he would not interact with anyone else like him.

A solution to the Ellensons' dilemma began to take shape one evening in May of last year when they were the hosts of an end-of-term thank-you dinner for the teachers and therapists who had helped Thomas through preschool. The group gathered at Zoe, a SoHo restaurant, and talked about there being no appropriate place they knew of for the boy to go next. At one point in the evening, all heads turned as Mayor Michael Bloomberg arrived for a dinner of his own. Richard, who has never been described as shy, excused himself and, moments later, returned with the mayor. Bloomberg promised the table that he would help and provided a telephone number. Within the month, Richard was meeting with Dennis Walcott, the deputy mayor for policy, and, with Wernikoff, sketching plans for a kindergarten class that would include three or four children like Thomas.

Such a classroom would not be cheap. The law requires that a district pay for needed services for special-education students wherever they are schooled; during his last year in private preschool, for instance, Thomas cost the city $40,000 in supplemental services. Therefore, many of the costs – for physical, occupational and speech therapy – would be accrued by the district whether it created this class or not. And the argument could even be made – and the Ellensons certainly made it – that the long-term cost would be lowered because so many children at one site would centralize the work of the therapists. That said, it would still be more expensive to educate the 18 children who would be in this class than it would the 25 students in the school's largest kindergarten class. It would cost $35,000 more, Wernikoff said.

Because they were involved in the planning, the Ellensons knew exactly what awaited their child on the first day of school, while the other parents in the room were taken by surprise. There had been no announcement, no meeting, no letter home. Susan Rappaport, the crisp and polished principal of the Manhattan School for Children, had insisted on that. "We wouldn't warn parents that there would be African-American children in the class or children who need glasses," she told me before the program began. "If they believe their child should not be in this class, then I believe their child is not a good fit for this school."

No parent objected that first morning. They smiled. And they watched. Kate's mother beamed when her daughter showed off a star she had drawn. Daniel's parents gave him a hug after he put his toys away. Thomas's parents grinned nervously when they met Thomas Parham – who immediately became known as Big Thomas – the muscular, impeccably dressed "para" (classroom-speak for paraprofessional) who would be their son's aide every day of the school year. Big Thomas wheeled his

The morning ended with circle time. Big Thomas wheeled his new charge to a spot on the rug. At one point, as the teachers read a story, Thomas looked back at his mother, then down at his wheelchair tray, then toward the door and then back toward his mother again. His para didn't know how to read his message, but Lora did. "He has to use the bathroom," she said, and sped over to take him there.

When the story was finished, and Thomas had returned, the teachers taught the children a getting-to-know-you kind of song. At the end of each stanza there came a pause designed for a child to say his name, which was then sung by the entire class. "Annaliese," Annaliese said shyly. "Evan," Evan trilled. "Taylor," Taylor sang, bouncing.

Richard saw the awkward moment looming and raced over to Thomas's wheelchair to dig out an electronic device from the storage pouch in the back. He was frantically trying to turn it on and show Thomas the button that would cause the machine to speak his name when the teacher pointed their way. She could see that they were not ready, but she had no choice – she had saved Thomas for last, and the song was about to end. Thomas tried to do his part, and pushed the button, but his attempt resulted in silence.

Flailing a little, he tried again. A deep, mechanical male voice, completely out of rhythm, said: "Hel-lo. My. Name. Is. Tho-mas." Thomas grinned in victory. Richard tightened his jaw in defeat.

II. Learning to Advocate

The Ellensons' sleek three-bedroom apartment on the Upper East Side has no hallways and few interior walls. Every space is wide enough for a wheelchair to maneuver in easily, and if you stand in the living room, the kitchen, the dining area or the TV room, you can see into nearly every other room in the loftlike home. This way, Thomas, who cannot motor on his own, is never left behind. The Ellensons gutted the space and redesigned it five years ago. Becoming the parent of any child means figuratively reconstructing a life with the child at the center. Becoming the parent of a handicapped child means literally doing so, too.

Thomas was the Ellensons' firstborn. (Their daughter, Taite, who is "typically developing" – a phrase that parents and educators in this language-sensitive world prefer to "normal" – is 2.) Until Thomas's birth, in September 1997, they knew virtually nothing about educational theory and practice for the disabled or about recent changes in the law and society that offer equal parts opportunity and frustration for the parents of children with special needs. Those changes began nearly 30 years ago, with the passage, in 1975, of federal legislation that has come to be called the Individuals With Disabilities Education Act, or I.D.E.A. Echoing the language of civil rights law, it required public schools to provide free education that met the spe-cial needs of students with disabilities. In practice, this resulted in the creation of separate classes, programs and even school wings for chil-dren with disabilities, who were then "mainstreamed" with their able-bodied peers at lunch or for music and occasionally for some academic lessons.

In the '90s, the legal backdrop changed again. Further amend-ments and court interpretations of I.D.E.A. required that disabled children be guaranteed the "least restrictive environment" in which they can learn. This has been taken to mean that a child will be placed in a general classroom unless the school district can document that educating that child would be impossible in that classroom even with "supplementary aids and services," which the courts have defined broadly.

Notably absent over the years from these laws and interpretations has been financing. The states receive some federal funds but must provide the rest of the resources themselves, sharing that responsibil-ity with individual school districts according to complex formulas that vary in detail from place to place. Few districts have gone knock-ing on the doors of disabled children to offer a long list of expensive educational options. The effective outcome has been to place the onus largely on the shoulders of the parents. Across the country, the more vocal the parent, the more accommodating the school.

In the years since Thomas was deprived of oxygen at birth, result-ing in cerebral palsy, the Ellensons have learned how to advocate. They have come to understand that "the law says we have to be heard," as Richard explained when we met at the opening of school. More important, though, the Ellensons have learned that the provi-sions of I.D.E.A. have to be reauthorized every five years and that Congress has yet to agree on the latest reauthorization. In other words, their protections are not guaranteed.

From his first meeting with Wernikoff, Richard Ellenson stressed that his crusade was not merely about his child in this school in this year. He and Lora are aware that they have been heard not only because they are articulate and untiring but also because they have resources and connections. And they said they feel a responsibility to children whose parents do not have those things. "We are not here just to build a good classroom," he said. "We are here to build a program that can be recreated."

In June 2003, Wernikoff and Ellenson set out to find a school that could be home to Thomas's new classroom. Ellenson, who never met anyone whose contact information he didn't keep, spread the word and received a suggestion from a lawyer named Tucker McCrady, whose daughter, Valente, was a fragile but spunky girl a year older than Thomas. Like Thomas, she was nonverbal and barely mobile but bright. Unlike Thomas, she suffered from a seizure disorder, which came on often and without warning.

Valente had just completed kindergarten at the Manhattan School for Children. M.S.C. was founded in 1992 as part of the "small schools" movement, which brought about the subdivision of many large city public-school buildings into more manageable spaces. As a kindergartner, Valente was the only disabled child in her grade and up to that point, according to Susan Rappaport, the principal, "the most challenging student we had worked with." Rappaport said that the school had not given Valente all she needed during her kindergarten year because though "we had people who were very good and worked very hard, we didn't have the support system." And it was not only Valente who needed more – more time with outside therapists, more classroom equipment adapted to her needs. The little girl's teachers needed more as well. "They needed training and also moral support," Rappaport said. "They needed to be part of a team instead of out there on their own."

When Rappaport met with Ellenson, she told him she was eager to help. Together with Wernikoff, they decided that there should be two classrooms. Each class would be team-taught by two teachers – one with experience in kindergarten, the other with training in special ed. Having two classes would not only give the teachers an empathetic sounding board across the hall but also prevent the inclusive classroom from being stigmatized as the "special ed" classroom. The McCradys said they felt that this arrangement would benefit Valente and decided, for this and other reasons, to have her repeat kindergarten in one of those classes. Before long, two classrooms at M.S.C. were reserved for the program that Ellenson, ever the adman, branded "MotorVation." They would be standard classrooms filled with adaptive furniture and wide aisles. A third, a small activity room, was also set aside for the children in the MotorVation program. It was called the Blue Sky Room, so two parents painted its walls a shimmery blue with puffy white clouds. Rather than pull the disabled children out of lessons to have physical therapy by themselves, the entire class could have organized exercises together in this room – treatment masquerading as fun.

The teachers were chosen by mid-July of last year. Alysa Essenfeld and Tracy Chiou would teach in Classroom 503, which would be Valente's class. Across the hall, in Classroom 506, would be Suzanne Blank, whose calm yet energetic manner had led M.S.C. kindergartners to fall in love with her for the five years she had been there, and Brooke Barr, who was new to M.S.C. but jumped at the chance to help initiate the program. Barr became a special-education teacher because her son, Matthew, who is now 12, was found to have severe autism. Classroom 506 is the kind of environment, she told me, that she wished her own child could be in.

There were two other disabled children signed up in Valente's class – one who was moderately motor- and speech-impaired and another who had a degenerative bone disease and was learning to use headgear attached to a special stick to write, paint and draw. Initially, there was just one other disabled child in Thomas's class, but on the second day her mother decided it was not a good fit and chose not to enroll her. That left only Thomas. His father spent a few days feverishly working the phones, and Thomas was soon joined by a boy named Fredy, afflicted with moderate cerebral palsy, and Danielle, who could drive her own motorized wheelchair and move on her own if she walked on her knees.

When the first day of school began and Ellenson looked at what he had started, he saw the seeds of permanent change in special education. But Wernikoff had simpler goals. "We want these kids, all of them, to get high-quality instruction and be truly included," she said. "You can be in the class. It's another thing to be truly part of the class."

III. Story Time

It was story time in Classroom 506. Suzanne Blank gathered the students on the rug and placed the storybook on an easel up front. This book was not like any she used to teach kindergarten in the same classroom the year before. It was oversize – each page was two feet wide and two feet high. And the pages were laminated, with two Velcro strips along the bottom. On the top row of Velcro, words were attached forming the text of the story: "Who will help me plant this wheat?" asked the little red hen. "Not I!" said the duck. "Not I!" said the cat. "Not I!" said the dog. On the lower row was a series of pictures that corresponded to the words above. The word "duck" was represented by an image of a duck; the verb "plant" was represented by a hand putting a small plant into the ground.

Children who cannot hear learn sign language. Children who cannot see learn Braille. Children who can hear but not speak, like Thomas, learn their own language too. The symbols used in

Classroom 506 are known as Mayer-Johnson symbols – thousands of little pictures that represent words and actions and thoughts. Long before nonverbal children can write or read, they can recognize symbols that mean "I want" and "milk" and point to them to make themselves understood. Thomas had been immersed in these symbols since he was 1 year old. His wheelchair tray was filled with dozens of them – ways of saying yes, no, happy, mad, wash, play, eat, drink. His teachers were now using that foundation to teach him to read.

A few days before each storyboarded book was read to the class, it was previewed for Thomas and Danielle, so they could learn the symbols for new words like wheat and hen. Those symbols were added to their Tech/Talk devices – Tech/Talk being one of a variety of brands of speech technology that let nonverbal children be heard. The Tech/Talk device is a box with a series of squares in which plastic strips with symbols are inserted. For each new book, a teacher would record the spoken word for each symbol into a digital recorder inside the box. So when the class chanted, in unison with the little red hen, "Then I will do it myself," Thomas could press the appropriate button and join in.

Producing these adapted texts was the never-ending job of Carol Goossens, an expert in "augmentative communication" – the art of providing means of expression to those who cannot speak. She had ambitious plans for helping Thomas when she first began, but as autumn turned to winter last year, it was all Goossens could do to keep up with adapting the books. "Everything about this was more complicated than we'd thought," she said in November. "Even the experts are learning as we go."

One unexpected complication that first term was that Thomas resisted using his personal communication device at school. Long before he started kindergarten, his parents had experimented with a variety of augmentative-communication devices and settled on a Fujitsu Tablet PC as the one he could most effectively use. By the time Thomas arrived at M.S.C., Richard had programmed countless words and phrases into the device. It was the Fujitsu that the family had scrambled to set up on the first day so that Thomas could "sing" along. By the second day, Ellenson had scanned digital photos of every child in the class into the Fujitsu, and he called them over as they arrived at school to show them that his son could "speak" their name. Once he had their attention, Thomas flipped to another folder in the machine and told his classmate a couple of jokes: What do you call a fairy that doesn't take a bath? Stinkerbell.

Why did the cow cross the road? To get to the mooovies.

After a few days in Classroom 506, however, Thomas started insisting that the device be kept out of sight. He wasn't much happier with the Tech/Talk that his teachers had prepared for story time, which meant that he could not really participate in class. His father could not understand Thomas's resistance, but Goossens said she thought the reason was clear. "The device came with the risk that he would hit the wrong button and say something wrong," she told me. While he was willing to take that risk in front of his parents, she speculated, "he didn't want to do it in front of the other kids."

Another early obstacle was deciding where and how Thomas should sit. Seating and positioning children with resistant or spastic muscles is something of an art. "If he could sit cross-legged on the floor and use his hands, it would change his life," Lora said. But he can't, and deciding where he should sit always involved a tradeoff. His custom-built wheelchair provided the support he needed, and gave him his best hand control, but left him several feet above his peers. On the other hand, a series of low-to-the-floor chairs that the school's physical therapists provided for use at story time and for tablework brought him eye level with his peers but caused him to slouch and slump and made it all but impossible for him to use his hands. Thomas made it clear as the year went on that he wanted to be like the other children. He wanted to sit near the floor, whether he slumped or not, and when his classmates were writing with crayons and pencils, he wanted to use those things, too, even if he could produce only scattered scrawl. In other words, he wanted to sit in the least-supportive place and use the least-efficient tools. Yet becoming more like the other kids in the long term, learning to read and write and communicate, often meant not being like those kids in the short term – sitting high up so he could write, using letter stamps instead of crayons.

Where Thomas should sit became a constant source of tension between Rappaport, who wanted Thomas to be close to the floor whenever possible, and Ellenson, who thought he belonged in his custom-made wheelchair until a better close-to-the-floor option could be found. Such friction is common between a parent and a principal when the parent becomes a constant, vocal presence in a school, but no less frustrating. "A parent has to be willing to let the school explore," Rappaport said. "That's why the parents partner with schools."

The teachers navigated these clashes as best they could, tending to sit Thomas on the floor for circle time but in his chair for most other activities. Barr, for one, said that she believed that Thomas needed fewer choices and began to act on that belief. "It's what I call my British-nanny persona," she said. "It's not, 'Would you like to go to the park?' It's, 'Off we go to the park!'" Slowly the approach worked. Thomas took what was offered and even started warming to his communication devices again.

Barr began helping Thomas write stories on the classroom computer. Using special software and a track ball, he could click on the Mayer-Johnson symbols for "my" and "sister." But the computer, while liberating, was also frustrating. By necessity, Barr limited what Thomas could write about, because she had to enter the available symbols in advance. And his use of the track ball was spotty, so the results were sometimes less than perfect.

One November morning, Thomas, working one-on-one with Barr, had painstakingly entered "My sister Taite" on the computer screen. Asked to choose his next word, he clicked on "a lot."

"What does she do a lot?" Barr asked, not at all sure if the word was purposeful or random.

"Runs talks falls falls hugs," Thomas typed by clicking the matching symbols. As each word appeared on the screen, the computerized voice spoke it aloud.

Barr had certainly seen children write stories that made little sense, but she suspected that Thomas was actually trying to say something succinct. The whole exercise was like working a Ouija board – was she helping him write what he meant or what she thought he meant? "Um, let's try that again," she said. "What does Taite do a lot? Does she run a lot? Hug a lot?"

"Falls hugs falls talks runs," Thomas wrote.

"O.K.," Barr said when it became clear that Thomas's energy for this task was spent. "Let's print this out and read it together."

Children in kindergarten at M.S.C. turned their stories into "books" by adding "covers." So a short while later Thomas was in his wheelchair with a piece of construction paper taped to his tray and the alphabet arrayed in front of him in the form of 26 small rubber stamps.

"What's the first sound of 'By'?" Barr asked. "Buh. Do you see it?" Thomas's hands moved everywhere but to the B. He put his face nose-distance from the tray, searching for the answer. As he did, his flailing hand landed in the inky stamp pad.

Sensing his frustration, Barr handed him the letter B, and he pushed the stamp onto the paper. "Great job," Barr said. "Now how about the next sound. 'By-ayyyyye.'" Thomas glanced back over his shoulder. At first it looked like a random motion, but when he did it a second time, Barr followed his gaze. He was looking toward the basket of books that students had already finished. "Oh, you want to look at what you've already written – good strategy," she said. She brought over a previous effort, done just as painstakingly on another day. Seeing that the letter he wanted was Y, he pointed right to it on his tray.

The teacher's smile was nearly as wide as the student's. "Now, who's this story by?" she asked. "Who wrote this story?" The boy's hand went shakily, but deliberately, over to the T. Then the O. Then the M. Barr handed him each stamp, and he made a blurry impression. "BY TOM."

IV. Making Friends

One morning near the start of the school year, Blank took Ellenson aside when he brought Thomas to class. The other children were asking questions about Thomas, she told him, and they stared at the boy more often than they talked to him. Blank knew that Ellenson had spent a lot of time explaining his son to other children, and that he had volunteered to do the same for his son's class, if necessary. She said she thought it might be necessary.

Ellenson agreed, but said he did not want to be the only parent to talk about his child. "If the message is that every child is an individual, then we have to talk about another child or we're singling Thomas out," he said. The following Friday, Ellenson arrived for morning circle time to "share" about Thomas, and another father, Stephen Lee Anderson, came to "share" about his son Evan.

At the center of the Ellensons' dreams for Thomas is the hope that he will make friends. It is one of the few pieces they can envision with any clarity in the puzzle that will shape itself into his life. They think he is smart, but they understand that a parent's lens can be cloudy on that subject, and they also know that it is hard to test a child who cannot speak. If he is smart, they are sustained by visions of Stephen Hawking, who has changed the world of physics despite being trapped in a body that is little more than a container for his brain.

And they think Thomas may have other gifts too. His favorite television channel is the Food Network. One of the handful of words he can physically speak with relative clarity is "Emeril," the name of his favorite chef. He loves to help his parents in the kitchen. A chef can direct without doing, his father says, and a sophisticated palate is within the realm of the possible for Thomas. If he does harbor talent, then the Ellensons' hopes are buoyed by their friend Dan Keplinger, known to the art world as King Gimp, the subject of an Academy Award-winning documentary about how he paints, using a paintbrush on a headstick, despite his cerebral palsy.

But even if Thomas's future doesn't hold such creative or intellectual promise, he will need friends. He lights up when other children are around. He craves interaction, thrives among other people. Equipping him for this part of his life was one reason – as important as teaching him to read and write – that his parents fought for this class. They know that socialization gets only harder as disabled children get older.

Starting down that road was Richard Ellenson's goal when he stood at the front of the class, alongside Thomas, on the second Friday of school. I was not there that morning, but Ellenson, Anderson, Barr and Blank were all moved by the visit and described it to me in the same way.

"We want to talk about something that's very important in our family," Ellenson began. "Thomas has cerebral palsy. Does anyone know what that is?"

The children shook their heads.

"Thomas's brain got hurt when he was born," Ellenson continued. "Because of that, Tom can't actually speak, and he has to be in a wheelchair. But other than that, he understands everything we say. Right, Tom?"

Thomas smiled and looked up toward the ceiling.

"Thomas speaks in his own way," Ellenson went on. "Isn't that right, Tom?"

Again the boy raised his eyes.

"When Thomas wants to say yes, he looks up," Ellenson explained. "Does everybody else want to try that?"

The children looked up. Then Thomas and his father taught them how to say no – by putting their heads down.

"Everything we're doing, he's doing," Ellenson said. "It's just that he does it all inside his head." He paused. "Any questions?"

Connor raised his hand. "Can Thomas swim?" he asked.

Ellenson said he could, then showed the children how. He lifted the boy out of his chair, and Thomas put his arms around his father's shoulders. Then Ellenson got on his knees and walked around, the way he and Thomas do in the shallow end of a pool.

The children giggled. Connor raised his hand again. "What color bathing suit does he wear?" he asked. "Does he wear water wings? I wear water wings." Soon afterward, Anderson talked about how he and Evan do puzzles together on Sunday mornings. That, Ellenson told me, was when he thought, It's going to be O.K.

And in many ways, it was O.K. A few days after the fathers came to share, Thomas's classmate Taylor broke the ice. She wanted to sit next to Thomas in circle time and push his wheelchair to the table at lunch. "If I ever need a wheelchair, I want one just like Thomas's," she told the class, and soon everyone wanted to try out his chair and be pushed around the room.

Evan also developed protective feelings toward Thomas, and within a few weeks he was giving voice to what Thomas wanted to say. The others recognized the depth of their friendship. One day, Ellenson watched as his son tried to make himself understood to another classmate, a little boy who was never completely comfortable around Thomas. "Evan will be here in a minute," the boy said. "Evan always knows what Thomas wants."

Richard and Lora tried to help by making new friends of their own. The more they could include Thomas's classmates' parents in his world, they argued, the better life would be for Thomas. The surprise expressed by the other parents on the first day of school had turned into varying degrees of warmth. Some, particularly Evan's parents and Taylor's, developed real affection for Thomas and brought their children over to play at his house. Others never really got to know the boy but made their peace with this experiment when they realized that the small size of the class meant that their own children got more attention from the teachers than they would in a regular classroom.

Each time he visited Classroom 506, Ellenson scanned the class for social moments for Thomas. When he couldn't find any, he created some. One day, he arrived at the playground during recess and saw Thomas sitting alone in his chair while the other children ran and played. So Ellenson became the Pied Piper and created an obstacle course, with Thomas stationed as one of the hands to be high-fived as each runner reached the finish line. His message seemed to have taken. A few days later, Thomas could be found beneath the slide, next to the play steering wheel. He was the bus driver. Big Thomas took out a MetroCard, and the other children took turns getting on the bus and telling their driver where they wanted to go.

Birthday parties, too, looked different to the Ellensons. "The minute we walk into a party," Lora said, "we're thinking, How can we make Thomas part of this world?"

When Kate had a soccer party at the Chelsea Piers sports-and-entertainment complex, Richard tried to hint to the athletic 20-something in charge that maybe Thomas could be "official score-keeper." But the suggestion was ignored, and Thomas sat on the side-lines, his father crouched alongside. When a ball came their way, Ellenson scooped it up and placed it in Thomas's lap, then helped roll it down his legs and onto the field. "I'm not sure it kills him," Ellenson said of his son, "but it really kills me."

A week later, at a party for Taylor, the bowling alley supplied an adaptive device for wheelchairs: an orange metal contraption that looked like a walker but with a ramp attached, sloping down from the top of the device to the floor. Thomas could push the ball down the ramp and watch it roll toward the pins. Evan, who was Thomas's teammate, thought this was a nifty way to bowl, and soon he was using the apparatus too. By the end of the party, children all over the bowling alley, even those who happened to be there for other birth-days, were pushing their bowling balls down the slide.

V. Frustrations and Breakthroughs

By early spring, Ellenson was frustrated. On the one hand, he was grateful to Rappaport, and Wernikoff, and the mayor, and to everyone else who had made the program possible. On the other hand, nothing was as fast or as complete or as ambitious as he knew it could be. Lora, who worked in the incremental world of science, accepted that progress was often slow. But Richard was in advertis-ing, and to him, if something was slow, it wasn't progress.

"Where I come from, you have a deadline, and you stay up all night, and you meet it," he told me on one of his frustrated days. "I thought everyone would be working nights and weekends on this."

He was grateful for the Blue Sky Room, which was designed and equipped in just a few weeks. But he was disappointed that it was used as much for an ordinary therapy room as for whimsical activities for the entire class. "Have yoga every day," he said. "From a marketing point of view, that would make parents choose this over Dalton."

He liked that Thomas's teachers had started preserving tidbits of each day's class into a digital recorder so that when Thomas came home he could answer the question "What did you do at school today?" But Richard was also frustrated that so many good ideas that had been used before, by other parents in other schools, hadn't been widely shared. He learned at a conference that another family had thought of using a recorder in the same way for their child a year earlier: how many more days of conversation could he have had with Thomas had he known?

Ellenson was still baffled that an effective low-to-the-ground seating option could not be found for Thomas. And he said that he felt similarly stymied that while Goossens, the augmentative-communication expert, was hired to devise an array of opportunities so Thomas could communicate – like programming a Tech/Talk with vocabulary versatile enough to discuss everything from cookies and milk to the relative merits of building Lego airplanes and trucks – much of her time was being spent adapting books. He worried that Thomas's own "voice" was rarely being heard.

What seemed to trouble Ellenson most of all was that, as he saw it, others didn't share his urgency to create a reproducible template for future classes. To his mind, the entire effort was wasted if it did not result in a program that was a model not only for schools in the district but also for others throughout the country. "At the end of all this," he said, "we should have a packet we can hand to the next team and say: 'This is what works; this is what doesn't. You don't have to start from scratch.'"

The teachers and administrators were not so sure. "Children are too different," a therapist told him during one of many conversations that bordered on arguments. "You can't write a recipe book for a classroom."

"If you had to build a new bridge every time you reached the East River," Ellenson replied, "no one would ever get to Brooklyn."

Lora gently prodded her husband to focus on the progress amid the obstacles, and when he looked, it was certainly there to see. Thomas was thriving, Richard knew, and it was because of steps he and his wife had taken. Several months into the year, for instance, Richard had introduced the M.S.C. team to Pati King-DeBaun, an expert in teaching reading and writing to nonverbal children. Her energy was infectious, and Ellenson wanted her aboard, but Wernikoff worried that it might take months for her to be paid through city channels. So Ellenson paid her consulting fee himself, hoping that he would be reimbursed eventually. In all, he laid out about $15,000 last year filling what he saw as gaps in the program. He did this not only for Thomas, he said, but also because he felt a responsibility to the other students enrolled in the program he started. "Had Lora and I not been willing to spend the money," he said, "then I would be asking six other children to come along with Thomas on a ride to nowhere."

King-DeBaun flew in from her home in Utah about once a month. During her visits, she held workshops on specific issues of literacy training but imparted more sweeping lessons as well, like how to view learning through Thomas's eyes. "She changed everything," Barr said. "I had a lot of tools. She taught me how to use them."

One of King-DeBaun's insights was that children typically learn to write before they really learn to read. And one way they learn to write is by speaking. They feel sounds in their mouths, trying them out, rolling them around, and then they come to picture those sounds as letters and words. Children who cannot speak must be helped to hear their own voices in their heads, she said, because that voice, though silent to onlookers, was definitely there. This lesson proved to be the key to more than just teaching Thomas to read. It transformed the way Thomas was seen, not only by his teachers, but also by his parents.

This change did not occur in a single moment, but in tiny increments over many months. It was most evident in the sign-in books the children used every morning. The books were the idea of King-DeBaun, who said that each child should start the day by expressing himself in whatever way he chose. There was no right or wrong way to fill the day's page in the individual books, and while the other children drew pictures or wrote stories, Thomas used stamps at first, then started asking for a crayon. Slowly his scattered scrawls became loose interpretations of letters. By spring he was determined to write his name.

To his parents, Thomas's sign-in book was a window onto his inner life. "He's thinking what the other kids are thinking – he just doesn't have a way to express it," King-DeBaun assured them, and while they hoped that was true, it was not always easy to believe. One day, for instance, Thomas was in his bedroom, and his father pointed to the bookcase and asked how many books were on the shelf. "Eleven," Thomas answered, correctly and without hesitation, by pointing to the numbers on his tray. Richard found himself thinking, Does he really know that, or was that just luck? A short time later, Richard asked, "How many children are in your class?" Again, without hesitation, Thomas answered, "Seventeen." Again Richard wondered if that was an accident.

"Of course a 6-year-old can count to 17," he said later. "But every age-appropriate accomplishment that Thomas has comes as a surprise. That's a shame."

If Richard could not see the whole of Thomas, how could his teachers be expected to? Following King-DeBaun's lead, Ellenson prodded Thomas one evening. The boy had just pointed to the symbols for "Thomas," "Natalie," "wash." Ellenson understood that he wanted Natalie, his home health aide, to give him a bath.

"When you point to 'Tom,' 'Natalie' and 'wash,'" Ellenson asked, "what do you hear in your head?" Ellenson held out one palm toward his son as he said, "Does your head hear 'Tom. Natalie. Wash'?" Then Ellenson held out the other palm. "Or does your head hear something like, 'I want Natalie to give me a bath'?" Thomas pointed toward the second palm.

Ellenson tried again. "When you said, 'Taylor ball pink' this afternoon, did you hear: 'Taylor. Ball. Pink'? Or something like, 'I want Taylor to bring me the pink ball'?" Again Thomas chose the full sentence.

Over and over, Ellenson asked, and over and over his son gave the same answer. In his head, he was letting his father know, he spoke just as fully and completely as anyone else did.

VI. 'Do You Know About Valente?'

Across the hall from Thomas, in Classroom 503, Valente McCrady was falling behind. The year before, when she was in kindergarten for the first time, "she was a sponge," her father said, "learning her letters and solidifying her colors." Her goal for this repeat year, she had told her teachers, was to learn numbers. But as winter turned to spring, she seemed to be losing ground.

Her parents were in the unique position of seeing firsthand how MotorVation changed the way the same child was taught in the same grade, and they knew that Valente was stalled not for want of effort from her teachers. During her first year in kindergarten, her father said, the staff always seemed to be "playing catch up – preparing a lesson and then scrambling at the last minute to adapt it for Valente." During the second year, by contrast, he saw them "beginning to plan the activity itself around Valente."

Her lethargy was not a result of unhappiness, either. She loved being with other children, particularly "typical" children, her father said, and that was why the McCradys had placed her in the Manhattan School in the first place. The reason she was failing was physical. Her seizures were coming more often, leaving her limp and exhausted. Her motor skills declined. "At the start of the year she was a demon with technology," Goossens said. But as the months went by "we were picking up her arm, putting her hand on the button and saying, 'C'mon, honey, can you just press it?'"

Her doctors tried new medications. Her parents consented to brain surgery. Then, in February, just before the operation was scheduled, the McCradys heard about a diet designed to bathe the brain in fat. For every gram of carbohydrate or protein Valente ate, she would eat four times as much fat. Her food was slathered in butter, margarine, olive oil, mayonnaise and heavy cream.

Her teachers and paras learned a lot about fats and proteins. They knew that a small misstep could throw the girl into seizures. "We weren't worried about them messing up because they were as scared as we were," McCrady said.

For several weeks she became bubbly and attentive. She had a growth spurt. She began learning. As quickly as the improvement started, however, some worrisome signs reappeared. Valente started having seizures again. One morning she suffered four of them before 11 o'clock. "That poor little body, how much can it take?" Rappaport wondered.

The answer was not much more. On Thursday, April 22, Valente died at home, in her sleep.

Rappaport learned of Valente's death the next morning and called the kindergarten and first-grade teachers in, a few at a time, to tell them. "That little girl was a very, very important part of the foundation of this school," she told me. "Last year we had nothing to offer her but love and support, and that grew into what you see now."

Soon afterward, Rappaport went from one classroom to the next to be there as the teachers broke the news to their students. As she walked toward Classroom 506, she found Chan Mohammed, Thomas's baby-sitter, frantically pushing Thomas out the door, so he would not hear about what happened. Mohammed called Ellenson to ask if Thomas should stay to listen. "Yes, absolutely, bring him back in there," Ellenson said, though he later confessed that he was not certain it was the right answer.

Soon the children were gathered on the rug with their teachers. Thomas was on one side of the group, Danielle on the other. Both were high in their wheelchairs, Rappaport noticed, when they should have been down on the floor, but she didn't say anything about it. The other adults were standing behind the children, separated from them by a bookcase. That message was wrong, too, Rappaport noted later, but she didn't say anything about that, either.

Blank, the head teacher in Classroom 506, sat on a low chair at the front of the group. "Valente was sick," she said, explaining in simple language what a seizure disorder was and that Valente had died. "Some of you are going to feel different kinds of feelings," she continued. "Whatever you are feeling is O.K."

Taylor crawled into Blank's lap and began to cry.

Rappaport patrolled her building all day, burdened by new knowledge. "This is one thing I had never thought of," she said. "That you bring in this new group and medically they are much more fragile. I thought about this program in terms of the mechanics: where do you seat the child, how do you toilet the child, how do

248

you feed them? But I never thought about losing them."

That night, when they were alone at bedtime, Lora talked to Thomas. "Do you know about Valente?" Thomas looked up to say yes. "Where is she?" Thomas looked way up, past yes, toward heaven, a concept he learned a year earlier, back when Richard lost both parents within three weeks.

"'Valente had a sickness called seizures, and you don't," Lora said. "Are you scared?" she asked. Thomas said yes.

VII. Making Plans

Each year, the kindergarten teachers at the Manhattan School for Children choose a theme and build the curriculum around it. When Thomas was in kindergarten, the theme was bread. From late fall through early summer the students read stories about baking it, did math lessons about buying it, visited a local bakery on a field trip and even performed an adaptation of "The Little Red Hen," who bakes a loaf herself when none of her fellow farm animals will help. Thomas played a duck. His Tech/Talk was programmed to say "Quack, quack, quack."

At the end of the school year, all four kindergarten classes at M.S.C., those with children in wheelchairs and those without, created a bakery of their own. For two weeks beforehand, they baked – banana bread, pumpkin bread, chocolate-chip cookies, chocolate cake, cupcakes, cinnamon rolls – then stored their goods in a freezer. They drew a big sign that said "Madison Square Bakery" and smaller ones that priced the items at multiples of 10 cents each. They spent arts-and-crafts time making placemats and baker's hats and vases with paper flowers.

As the "customers" – the parents – arrived, Thomas was positioned right at the classroom door, near the muffins. His love-hate relationship with his Tech/Talk was pure love that day, and he grinned at anyone close enough to hear him. If you were just out of range, he gestured wildly until you came near.

"Can I help you?" he said. "We made that fresh. It costs 10 cents. Thanks for coming." Barr, his special-ed teacher, had programmed the device, and it was two of his classmates whose voices actually spoke the words, but from the expression of joy on his face, the words seemed to come from deep inside Thomas.

By the time the Ellensons arrived, there was already a crowd. "Can I help you?" Thomas asked them. Richard began to cry.

The end of the year was the usual blur. Richard Ellenson was elected president of M.S.C.'s parents association. Thomas, who was eager to get to his sign-in book every morning, could now write his name legibly and boldly in crayon. He also gained new mastery of the computer. One of his last projects was an alphabet book filled with animals, and he made it clear that he wanted to sound out the spellings of the words, just like the other children, rather than choose words from a prefabricated list. "Q IS FOR QUJAXL" he typed under a photograph of a quail. "R IS FOR RA!EBBIT." "S IS FOR SKUFNK." Barr was gleeful. "That's the way a kindergartener should be writing," she said.

At an end-of-year meeting, Ellenson and the M.S.C. staff members found themselves talking about the same things they were talking about at the beginning of the year. But now they spoke like veterans, not first-timers. Ellenson expressed his frustration that there still was nothing tangible – no booklet, no instructions – to hand down to others who might want to start a similar program. Wernikoff offered more support – more money, more staff development – for the coming year and told Ellenson that the school district would in fact reimburse him for the $15,000 he spent from his own pocket. Rappaport said she was determined to find a low-to-the-ground chair that would facilitate Thomas's use of his hands.

For the coming school year, they agreed, there would again be two MotorVation classes in kindergarten, each with four disabled students. Rappaport knew she could fill those eight slots, because word was out and parents were inquiring. In the first grade, Thomas's grade, there would be only one MotorVation class, taught by Barr and Blank. It would include the motor-impaired children who attended the first year, along with 14 nonimpaired children. All summer the parents of Thomas's kindergarten classmates waited to learn which of their children would be allowed to move up with him into what was now considered a very desirable class. Thomas Ellenson will start first grade tomorrow morning, in Classroom 406, down on the first-grade floor. He is excited because his best friend, Evan, will be there too.

Notes

The author and publisher gratefully acknowledge the following for permission to reprint pieces from the copyrighted material listed below. Quotations are cited using the abbreviations listed before each work.

BD: *The Blitz, The Story of December 29, 1940,* Margaret Gaskin (New York: Harcourt, Inc., 2005)

FW: *Forty Ways to Look at Winston Churchill,* Gretchen Craft Rubin (New York: The Random House Ballantine Publishing Group, 2003)

MEL: *My Early Life* 1874 – 1904, Winston Churchill (New York: Simon & Schuster Inc., 1996) Copyright Winston S. Churchill, 1930 & 1958
Reproduced with permission of Curtis Brown Ltd., London, on behalf of The Estate of Winston Churchill.
Also, reprinted with permission of Scribner, imprint of Simon & Schuster Adult Publishing Group, from *My Early Life: A Roving Commission,* 1930.

NGI: *Never Give In: The Extraordinary Character of Winston Churchill,* Stephen Mansfield (Nashville, TN: Cumberland House Publishing, Inc., 1996)

WC: *Winston Churchill,* John Keegan (New York: The Penguin Group Inc., 2002)

GB: *Winston Churchill: The Greatest Briton,* Dominique Enright (London: Michael O'Mara Books Limited, 2003
Reproduced with permission of Curtis Brown Ltd., London, on behalf of The Estate of Winston Churchill

SC: *Winston Churchill: Statesman of the Century,* Robin H. Neillands (Cold Spring Harbor, NY: Cold Spring Press, 2003)

LLA: *Winston Spencer Churchill - The Last Lion Alone, 1932 – 1940,* William Manchester (New York: Little, Brown & Company, 1989)

LLV: *Winston Spencer Churchill - The Last Lion, Visions of Glory, 1874 – 1931,* William Manchester (New York: Little, Brown & Company, 1989)

WW: *The Wit & Wisdom of Winston Churchill - A Treasury of More Than 1,000 Quotations and Anecdotes,* James C. Humes (New York: HarperCollins Publishers, 1994)

WBE: *World Book Encyclopedia,* Vol. 3 C-Ch (Chicago: World Book Inc., 2001)

Notes

1. GB, p.10
2. MEL, p.3
3. LLV, p.127
4. MEL, p.5
5. GB, p.187
6. GB, p.57
7. MEL, p.37
8. MEL, p.37
9. MEL, p.37
10. LLA, p.677
11. MEL, p.11
12. MEL, p.13
13. GB, p.62
14. NGI, p.142
15. GB, p.184
16. MEL, p.272
17. GB, p.184
18. GB, p.184
19. WW, p.121
20. LLV, p.581
21. NGI, p.107
22. NGI, p.108
23. MEL, p.28
24. LLV, p.286
25. WW, p.91
26. WW, p.45
27. WW, p.29
28. WW, p.45
29. MEL, p.292
30. MEL, p.295
31. MEL, p.259
32. FW, p.232
33. MEL, p.37
34. MEL, p.5
35. GB, p.62
36. FW, p.181
37. LLA, p.677
38. GB, p.184
39. GB, p.187

About the Author

Andrea White was born in Baton Rouge, Louisiana, but has spent most of her life in Houston, Texas. She received her undergraduate and law degrees from the University of Texas. Her first book, *Surviving Antarctica*, was listed on the reading lists of several states, including the Bluebonnet list. In 2006, she won the Golden Spur award given by the Texas State Reading Association for the best book by a Texas author.

In addition to writing, Ms. White serves as an active community volunteer. Partnering with the Houston Independent School District Board, she and her husband, Houston's Mayor Bill White, have started the program Expectation Graduation to try to keep more kids in school. The Whites have three children: Will, Elena and Stephen. Stephen, the youngest, is a basketball player.

When his mother started *Window Boy*, Stephen had never heard of Winston Churchill, the prime minister of Britain during World War II. He also had no idea that a boy in a wheelchair could be a basketball genius. Ms. White wrote *Window Boy* with the hope that it will help middle schoolers everywhere to understand that sports heroes come in many packages, and, more importantly, that it will inspire them to learn more about Winston Churchill–an unloved son, a poor student and a mischief maker who, despite what many people said about him, became one of the greatest men in the world.

The text of *Window Boy* is set in Garamond, a typeface attributed to Claude Garamond, who is considered the first independent typefounder. Although he did not invent movable type, he was the first to make type available to printers at an affordable price. In 1541 Garamond was commissioned by François I to cut a sequence of Greek fonts known as the *grecs du roi*. Modern typefaces bearing the Garamond name are not always based on these designs, but they share certain characteristics of timeless beauty and readability.